PERFECT SPIRAL

PLAYING DIRTY
BOOK TWO

LANE HART

COPYRIGHT

This book is a work of fiction. The characters, incidents, and dialogue were created from the author's imagination and are not to be construed as real. Any resemblance to actual people or events is coincidental.

The author acknowledges the copyrighted and trademarked status of various products within this work of fiction.

© 2017 Editor's Choice Publishing

All Rights Reserved. This book or any portion thereof may not be reproduced or used in any manner whatsoever without the express written permission of the publisher except for the use of brief quotations in a book review.

Editor's Choice Publishing

P.O. Box 10024

Greensboro, NC 27404

Edited by Angela Snyder
Cover by
Cover by Vanilla Lily Designs
https://www.vanillalilydesigns.com/

WARNING: THIS BOOK IS INTENDED FOR MATURE AUDIENCES 18+ ONLY. THE STORY CONTAINS ADULT LANGUAGE AND EXPLICIT SEX SCENES.

PROLOGUE

Callie Clarke

Six months ago...

As soon as I make the final turn onto Saint Andrews Drive, I see my sister's flashy red car parked at the curb of my now lonely cottage home. The anger that had started to sizzle out over the last few months comes roaring back to life like a scorching inferno. Her presence here is the equivalent of pressing play on the live-action horror show of her betrayal, one that I've tried desperately to forget but haven't quite managed. Maybe I never will.

Climbing out of my much more conservative, metallic blue Corolla, I slam the door at the same time she rises from hers. The first word out of my mouth to her is "Leave!"

"Callie, wait. Just hear me out. Please?" she comes across the yard and begs, her normally sunny blonde hair dyed a depressing black.

"I don't care if you're starving or homeless or whatever other sad sob story you have. I will *never* give you another penny for you to spend on heroin," I tell her before scurrying up the three steps of the front porch.

"I'm pregnant."

Just two words, but they manage to steal my breath and weaken my knees. I have to reach for the stair rail to keep myself standing.

"I've been clean...since I found out. I swear," my little sister sobs from behind me.

For a moment, I even feel a hint of sympathy starting to swirl in the pit of my stomach for her, despite my hate. Until the realization hits me.

"It's his, isn't it?" I spin around to ask her, tears burning my eyes, my emotions putting a stranglehold around my throat.

"No, Callie. It's not John's –"

I slap my hands over my ears because I can't bear to hear another word following the name of the man who vowed to love me through sickness and in health and all the other bullshit. After eight years of marriage and seven years of trying to conceive, he couldn't give me the one thing I've ever wanted. No, but he obviously had no problem knocking up my sister.

"Leave and don't *ever* think of coming back here!" I scream at her through my sobs. "I'm done with you and your lies! I took you in more times than I can count when you had no other place to go. I spent *thousands* of dollars on rehab and attorneys to get you out of your self-destructive messes, and how did you repay me? By fucking my husband for a hit like the worthless drug whore you are!"

"John *knew* I was weak, that I couldn't resist! This is all his fault. Please, Callie!" she pleads.

Turning back around, I climb the last step, unlock the front door and slam it closed for the final time on my sister begging in my front yard.

CHAPTER ONE

Quinton Dunn

I'm a pretty lucky son of a bitch.

Some people spend their entire lives searching for that one unique thing that they're completely and utterly passionate about, their God-given purpose, if you will, and never actually succeed in finding it.

Me? Well, I found my calling when I was only seven years old.

Tall and lanky for my age even then thanks to my father's giant German ancestors, I was assigned to the Roanoke Bulldog's quarterback position. I didn't understand the importance of this role on our pee wee team until our first game. We were down fourteen to nothing in the first seconds of the fourth quarter. The center hiked the ball to me at the forty-yard line and then, with a sudden moment of clarity, I realized that not only was I literally the only one holding the vital pigskin in my hands, but I was the only one holding it figuratively as well.

Okay, so I didn't think about it exactly in those terms since I probably didn't know what literally or figuratively meant until college. But I understood that win or lose, the outcome of our team rested on my shoulders as the quarterback. Sure, our little linemen had a job to do keeping the defense away from me; the receivers had to catch the balls I threw to them, and the running backs had to do their parts, but *I* was ultimately the lynchpin. Our success or failure was on me.

It was a lot of pressure to put on a seven year old, and my first inclination was to run screaming like my ass was on fire to the parking lot and toss my cookies. My second inclination was to do whatever I had to do to win. Thankfully, the second was much stronger. My competitiveness reared up and beat back the nervousness with a sledgehammer until there was no more fear or doubt. All that remained was a confidence in myself to utilize everything our team had been practicing and get the job done.

The coaches and my father told me I had an incredibly powerful arm. I was a lot bigger and stronger than all the other kids my age, standing half a head taller than most. Looking over the top of my opponents' helmets, their backs all to the goal posts, the end zone was in my sights alone, mine for the taking.

From that moment on in the game, my throws were dead accurate, perfect spirals. Our receivers were tough and fast. And the Hawks were no match for the Bulldogs that day.

I may have been young and foolish; hell, I'm still young and foolish, but even back then I was wise enough to know without a doubt that nothing would *ever* feel as magnificent as leading my team to a win. The admiration, the cheers, and praise of my performance is still exhilarating, addicting even. Which is why I work my ass off to be the best damn quarterback I can be for my team.

My only problem as the starting quarterback for the Wilmington Wildcats is that my professional success now comes with even greater levels of anxiety before I take the field.

Tomorrow is the first real game of my fourth season playing professional football, and already my palms are sweating, and my heart is ricocheting around in my chest like a pinball game thanks to the nervousness. As much as I love to win, my position as the leader of my team is a double-edged sword. If we lose, it's all on me. And when I fail, I let down my parents, my fifty-two teammates, the dozens of coaches and management staff, and the millions of fans. That's why I absolutely abhor losing and why I had to chug half a bottle of Pepto-Bismol half an hour ago before I could eat dinner.

"Do you think we should just shave our heads?" Lathan Savage asks me, interrupting my struggle to keep down the steak we grilled out on my oceanfront deck before turning on the State versus East Carolina game in my living room.

Blinking in confusion at my best friend and tight end, I try to figure out what the fuck he's talking about. When he runs his fingers through his blond Mohawk that's identical to my jet black one thanks to a bet we both lost a few weeks ago, understanding finally dawns.

"You know, just take it all off and start over from scratch?" he clarifies.

"I'm not shaving my fucking head," I tell him, reaching up to stroke the velvety sides of my new do. "My melon is too lumpy for that shit. The rest of our hair will grow back soon," I assure him. While I always cut my hair as soon as it starts curling around my ears, Lathan's was nearly brushing his shoulders when our teammates chopped it off, so he had a lot more of it to miss.

"I think I might shave all mine, you know, since my mom's starting to lose her hair again," he says sadly while keeping his eyes on the television.

Dammit.

I am such an insensitive asshole. Here I am having a pity party about winning a freaking football game tomorrow while Lathan's over there wondering if his mom will live through Christmas. I should've realized he wasn't thinking about shaving his head for vanity's sake, but I'm not the sharpest knife in the drawer, especially when my head is so incredibly far up my own ass. Lathan's mom just started going through chemo and radiation again after the cancer in her kidney's spread to her pancreas.

"I'm sorry, man," I tell Lathan sincerely, meaning for my ignorance and for what he's going through. "How's she doing?"

"From bad to worse," he answers. "At least there's a game tomorrow to give me a distraction."

As if on cue, like a gift-wrapped present sent from the good Lord above, my doorbell rings.

"How about a distraction *tonight*?" I ask Lathan as I get to my feet. "I don't know who it is, but I'm sure she has hot friends."

"Seriously? Another booty call?" he scoffs with an eye roll.

"I can't help it if the ladies always come back wanting more," I argue.

It's no secret that I thoroughly enjoy sex or that I've had a lot of lovers. In fact, I don't even have to try to get a girl into my bed anymore. Like the sun rising over the ocean each morning, it just happens naturally. Which is why I recently started playing a little game I like to call "Cheesy, Sleazy and Easy." Lately, when a woman comes on to me, I try and break out the stupidest, most arrogant pickup lines that come to my mind to repulse them, to encourage a slap to my face rather than have them bend over and beg me to slap their asses. So far I'm oh-for-forty-five.

Did it hurt when you fell from heaven?

If I could rearrange the alphabet, I would put 'u' and 'i' together.

Well, here I am; what are your other two wishes?

Your lips look so lonely. Would they like to meet mine?

No shit, those are just a few horrible examples that would never work for any other man, but they, unfortunately, worked for me. So it sucks that I've never won a round and been turned down. I don't like losing, especially to my own stupid self.

I'm not a complete dumbass. I know that the women who sleep with me are only using me, whether for my money, fame, or good looks. I'm simply an object to be acquired. They all have ulterior motives. Why else would they want to fuck me simply because of my name? I can be an enormous asshole or a complete sleazeball, and they'll still lead me away by my dick and do all manner of naughty things to me.

It's depressing really, not to have anyone just want me for me. Take away my millions, my superstar career, fancy cars and beach mansion, and I'm just a decent-looking guy of immense stature and below average intelligence.

But I do have millions, and I am a superstar, so, for now, I guess I'll have to endure the meaningless fucks until I find a woman who refuses my sexiest pickup lines, calls me out for being an asshole, and finally presents me with a worthy challenge. There's no fun in having a slut throw herself down and spread her legs for me without making me work for it. I want the thrill of wearing a stubborn woman down, one who fights me tooth and nail while I slowly chip away at her resistance until she finally submits.

"You're disgusting, and one day your skanky ways are gonna catch up to you," Lathan calls out.

He's likely right, but there's a ginormous chasm between my playboy ways and his celibacy, though. Instead of agreeing with him, I head to the door and simply reply over my shoulder with, "I think it's time for you to lose the V-card, man. You're almost thirty."

"No, I'm not! I'm only twenty-four," he calls back.

"Like that's any better," I mutter with a shake of my head.

If nothing else, a quick fuck is a helluva good distraction to take my mind off the anxiety before a game or the depressing loss afterward. Lathan sure as shit could use a distraction with everything in his life he's currently dealing with. I get that he has self-esteem issues or whatever from his fat camp days, but that's all in the past. I'm not sure how he hasn't gone apeshit from bottling up the natural urges for this long. Men need to get laid, or they go crazy. I'm cranky if I go more than a week without a release, especially with all the stress during football season.

I don't even have to make booty calls, they just appear like magic on my doorstep. And tonight's unexpected guest will be a welcome relief to my oncoming panic attack.

As I approach the mostly glass front door, I don't see any lust-filled beauties waiting for me on the other side, so I unlock it and open it wide in welcome, greeting tonight's surprise romp before she disappears.

Unfortunately, there's not a woman waiting for me with open arms.

No. Instead, there's only a seat-looking thing on the cement stoop with a tiny, snoozing baby inside, next to a black bag. I glance back out over the yard and find the driveway empty except for Lathan's truck. There are no cars coming or going on the silent street either.

Huh. Someone just rang the doorbell, so they have to be close by, maybe on foot.

I step outside barefoot in my jeans and gray Wildcats tee and walk to each end of the porch looking for who the hell is fucking with me, but there's not a soul in sight.

Okay, so this must be one helluva prank. Lathan's always harping about my manwhorish ways, just as he was only seconds ago, so he's obviously the one fucking with me tonight.

Leaving the door wide open, I stomp back into the living room and ask him with my hands on my hips, "What did you do, man? Borrow someone's baby to screw with me? Ha-ha. Hilarious. Now tell them to come back and pick it up."

Rather than bust out laughing, Lathan simply stares at me silently for several long moments. "Huh?" he finally asks.

"Bravo," I tell him with a slow clap of my hands. "Nice touch with the poker face and all, but seriously, dude, someone needs to come get their damn baby. It's getting chilly outside."

"What the hell are you talking about, Quinn?" Lathan asks.

I heave a heavy sigh. "Are you fucking with me right now?"

"I swear I don't even know what the fuck I would be fucking with you about," Lathan replies, getting to his feet. "Who was at the door?"

"A baby."

"A babe? Do you need me to go ahead and leave then?" he asks.

"Because there's no way in hell I'm gonna lose my virginity to some random jersey chaser."

"No, man. A *bay-bee*. Baby."

With a creased forehead, Lathan walks past me and toward the open front door. I follow behind him.

"Holy shit! There's, like, a baby out here!" he turns around and exclaims while pointing back at the kid. That's when I start to believe he didn't set me up. "Why is there a baby on your porch?"

"No clue. I thought you were fucking with me," I tell Lathan.

"Shh! Watch your mouth!" he scolds me, holding a finger to his lips. "You can't say *fucking* around a baby."

"Um, dude, you just said *fucking* in front of the baby," I point out.

"Shit," he mutters, running his fingers over his Mohawk. "Dammit, I probably shouldn't say shit either."

"Or dammit," I opine with a sigh.

"Why is there a baby on your porch?" he asks again.

"Now you sound like a broken record," I tell him, throwing my hands up in the air with exasperation. "I have no clue why there's a baby here!"

"Be quiet before you wake it up," Lathan steps back inside the house and lowers his voice to warn me softly.

"Forget waking it up. Should we bring it inside?" I ask.

"I guess," he answers with a shrug. "We definitely can't leave it out there."

"Okay then, pick it up."

"Nuh-uh. You pick it up," Lathan argues, shoving his hands in the pockets of his jeans. "It's on your porch!"

"Fine," I grumble.

Marching over, I bend down and lift the bottom of the seat in my arms and carry it into the living room where I place it in the middle of the hardwood floor.

"Now what?" I ask Lathan after I hear him shut and lock the front door.

"Oh shit," he mutters. When I look over, he's holding the black bag that came with the baby in one hand and a white sheet of paper in the other.

"What?" I ask, going over to stand beside him so I can read over his shoulder. It's a handwritten note that says, *"I can't do this anymore. He's yours, I'm certain of it. You would have known about him sooner if you read your mail."*

Two words stand out more than the others.

He's yours.

"Fuckkk," I groan while squeezing my temples as I try to think. "That's impossible, right? I mean, I haven't knocked anyone up! I'm not stupid. I always use condoms. *Always!*"

In response to my rambling, Lathan bends over at the waist and just starts laughing. When he eventually recovers enough to straighten, he says, "I believe the words I'm looking for are, *told you so!*"

"There's no way. He doesn't look anything like me," I reply, gesturing toward the tiny, sleeping baby.

"He's a baby. Babies don't look like anyone but babies," is Lathan's unhelpful response.

"What the hell are we gonna do?" I ask him frantically, my chest tightening with a lack of oxygen in what I know from experience is the makings of a full-blown panic attack.

"You mean, what are *you* gonna do?"

"Yes, what the fuck am I gonna do?" I ask while pacing in front of the sleeping kid, breathing in through my nose and out through my mouth to try and calm the mounting anxiety.

"Oh shit, man," Lathan whispers. "Now it's looking at us."

My pacing stops at his words, and then the two of us start inching closer to the seat. Pale blue eyes blink open and stare up at us, right before the face scrunches up and turns red, its mouth opening in a loud wail.

"Shit. Now, look what you've done. You've got to pick it up!" Lathan declares with an elbow to my side.

"I'm not picking it up. You pick it up," I tell him.

"Oh, for fuck's sake," he says while pulling out his cell phone.

"I thought you said we shouldn't say fuck," I remind him.

"I'm calling Roxy," he tells me over the increasing cries. "She'll know what to do, right?"

"Maybe. Hopefully"

"Shit, she's not answering," Lathan informs me. "Let me try Kohen. Maybe they kissed and made up or whatever."

"Maybe," I agree with a wince as the crying grows louder

"Yo, Kohen! Do you know where Roxy is?" Lathan shouts into the phone, his index finger pushed into his free ear so he can try to hear. "Yeah, does Roxy know anything about making them, like, stop crying? Can you and her come over to Quinton's? There's a... situation."

While he talks, I collapse into my leather recliner as the reality of the situation starts to hit me. Someone actually thinks I'm the father of this kid, which is insane and impossible, but now it looks like I'm stuck with it.

"Yeah, you won't believe this, but someone dumped a freaking baby on Quinton's doorstep with a note saying it's his," Lathan continues to explain to Kohen. "Tiny little guy. We were just watching it sleep in its plastic seat thing, and then all of a sudden it woke up and started wailing. Now it won't stop!"

What the hell am I gonna do with a baby? I've never even held one before, and someone thinks *I'm* the appropriate caretaker for this unknown kid?

"Thanks, Kohen!" Lathan shouts into the phone before hanging up, and then says to me, "They're on the way."

"Thank God," I grumble.

The crying continues, increasing in volume and intensity while a continuous loop of mostly hazy female faces flash through my mind. All the one-night stands that were fun but fleeting. I don't even remember all their names, only recognizing them by the idiotic things that came out of my mouth before we ended up naked.

Now it's not so funny.

Did I fuck up and not use protection? Did a condom fail me? I can't count all the times a woman has tried to slip it in without wrapping it up, because it happens so often. Getting knocked up with my baby would mean more than just a big-ass child support paycheck. It would mean owning me.

Never gonna happen.

I always refused sex when I realized what those women were up to, usually pushing their pretty little heads down and coming in their mouths just to be safe.

This kid's mama has to be mistaken.

When the doorbell finally rings a few minutes later, I jump up to answer it, but Lathan reaches it first with me right behind him. Fuck, I just hope it's Kohen and Roxy and not another kid.

The blonde woman standing before us in a blue dress should be deemed a goddess as relieved as I am at the sight of her.

"Help?" I beg.

"Why me?" Roxy asks. "Do you just assume that I know what to do with a baby because I'm a woman?" she asks, crossing her arms over her chest. Our team's new kicker, the first female in the league, tries to be tough, but I know she's a softie on the inside and isn't really upset.

"No. Maybe. Yes!" I shout, covering both of my ears with my palms to momentarily drown out the noise, so I can think. "You're the only one I trust not to break my son," I say, and then my jaw falls open when I realize my slip. Just because someone dropped him off on my porch doesn't mean he's really mine. I've *always* been careful. "I mean if he really is my son. Even if he's not, it wouldn't be cool to break someone else's baby, right?" I ask Roxy.

"Explanation accepted," Roxy replies before pushing past us and moving further into the house. Kohen is right behind her and nods at Lathan and me in greeting.

Kohen and I haven't exactly been friends since I joined the team and accidentally slept with his fiancée, but I think we're working on it. He's learning to trust me more since I've had the opportunities but haven't made any moves on Roxy. Never will, because while we may be good friends, it's clear that Roxy started falling for Kohen from the first day they met, as shitty as that was when she ran Kohen over. In fact, it's good to see Roxy holding Kohen's hand, which I take to be a sign that they've officially made up. The two had their own trust issues to work through, and I'm glad Kohen pulled his head out of his ass to fix things with Roxy.

"Whoa. So this is, what, like official now?" Lathan asks Kohen in reference to their relationship while we all make our way to the screaming in the living room.

"Official," Kohen yells to be heard.

"And Quinton said you both get to stay on the team?" Lathan asks him.

"Yep. And Roxy's starting tomorrow," Kohen tells us with a smile.

"Congrats!" Lathan yells to Roxy as we reach the living room.

"Thanks," she raises her voice to reply. "Has he been in that seat the whole time?" she asks, gesturing toward the gray baby car seat with blue trim still sitting in the middle of the floor.

I nod in the affirmative.

"That's at least one reason he's crying. He wants out; wants to be held," she informs us.

When Roxy steps around to the front of the seat, she gasps and falls to her knees despite the fact that she's wearing a dress.

"Oh my goodness!" she squeals. Letting go of Kohen's hand, she starts unbuckling the straps over the crying baby's chest. Once she's done, she scoops him up in her arms with zero hesitancy, telling me that, thankfully, she has taken care of babies before. The kid even dials back the volume of his screams when he's resting in her arms. The woman's a miracle worker, as evidenced by the three men she has crowding around her on the floor in awe.

"Did he come with a bottle by chance?" Roxy looks up and asks us.

"I think so," Lathan says. He gets to his feet, goes over to grab the black diaper bag from the sofa and brings it over before retaking his seat on the floor.

"Wow, he's little," Kohen says. "No bigger than a football."

"Yeah, he's probably just a few days old," Roxy tell us.

"That can't be my kid, right? I mean, my baby would be, like...ten times his size," I point out since my mother likes to remind me that I was over ten pounds when I was born, requiring her to have an emergency C-section.

"Actually, genius, even big men start out as little babies, otherwise how would women push them out?" Roxy explains.

"Got a bottle, but it's empty," Lathan says, holding a little one in the air before I can respond. "Can't you, like, you know, whip it out and let him eat?" he asks Roxy.

"Oh my God," she mutters, rolling her green eyes in exasperation. "My jugs are empty. Only having a baby fills them up. Jeez."

"Ohhh," we all mumble in understanding. You would think that with as many tits as I've sucked on I would already know that.

"Okay, Lathan, look through the bag and see if there are any containers that say infant formula," Roxy tells him slowly.

"How do you know all this baby stuff?" Kohen asks her.

"I babysat in the offseason around our neighborhood when I was a teenager," she explains, looking down at the baby who is already a little mack daddy, rooting around the top of her dress in search of her titty. Okay, so maybe he *is* my flesh and blood. "Babies were my favorite," Roxy says to Kohen. "I mean, I don't want one. Well, not right now or anytime soon because my kicking career would be over, but someday..."

"Yeah, me too," Kohen replies, his eyes on hers.

They're so sweet I could puke. Nope, that's probably the anxiety.

"Found it!" Lathan shouts, holding up a small canister. Unfortunately, his loud voice makes the baby start fussing again. "Shit, sorry."

"Okay, all we need now is water. Quinton, you got any filtered or purified water?" Roxy asks me.

"Ah, yeah, the kitchen faucet has a purifier on it," I tell her.

"Good. Why don't you do the honors since you'll be here alone with him tonight?" she suggests with a smile.

"What the fuck?" I exclaim. "No, you guys can't leave him here with me! I don't even know how to, like, pick him up or whatever. He'll just scream, and we've got our first game tomorrow! I need to be rested and ready!"

We can't lose the first game, or it will haunt us the *entire* season. My rookie year we lost not only the first game but the first six. It was awful to try and stop that cycle. By the time the team got our shit together, we were out of playoff contention.

"Calm down," Roxy tells me. "I'll show you how to do everything you need to know before we leave. Then we'll come back over in the morning to check on things before we go to the stadium, okay?"

"Who's gonna watch him during the game?" I ask since I sure as fuck can't play with a baby strapped to my chest.

"Guess we've got a few calls to make tonight," she answers with a shrug. "First, take the bottle to the kitchen, put four ounces of water in it and then however many scoops the container says to add for four ounces. Easy, right?"

"Um, yeah," I mutter as I get to my feet. Grabbing the bottle and canister from Lathan, I take them into the kitchen, reading the label on the formula as I go.

First, it tells me to wash my hands. I figure the bottle needs to be washed too, so I take the lid off and clean it. Now for the tricky part. Since the bottle has a four on the side, I fill it up with water, assuming it holds four ounces. The instructions say that I need two unpacked scoops of powder shit for that amount of water, so I pop the top on the canister and measure the powder out with the little plastic scooper before screwing the lid back on the bottle.

Done.

That wasn't so bad.

Back in the living room, Roxy says to me, "Great, now shake it until you can't see the powder chunks floating around and have a seat on the sofa."

I do as she says, shaking it like a Polaroid picture before sitting next to the armrest. Roxy stands up and carries the baby over in her arms. God, this all seems so surreal. Just this morning I woke up in a random woman's bed after a night of hot, sweaty sex, not a care in the world other than the season opener tomorrow, and now here I am, stuck with a kid.

When Roxy starts to lower the baby toward my lap, I snap back to reality.

"What are you doing?" I ask her frantically.

"Showing you how to hold a baby," she answers. Placing the kid in the crook of my right arm, she removes hers from him completely.

Oh shit, I'm holding a baby!

"There, you're doing it," Roxy declares proudly.

She's right. I am doing it, and he's not screaming his head off quite as loudly anymore. I say it's a *he* based on the blue one-piece outfit and blue and white striped hat he's wearing. He looks so delicate and small. Fragile. I hope I don't accidentally hurt him. My outstretched palm is probably about the size of his whole entire body.

"Wow. He's so...light and warm," I mutter while looking down at the little guy. Holding him isn't as scary as I thought it would be. While I'm still worried I might break him, I can't help but think he's kind of...cute.

"Let me see your phone," Roxy says to Kohen, who hands her the device. She snaps a few quick photos before she lifts my left hand that I forgot was still gripping the bottle and brings it up to the baby's lips. The little guy opens his mouth and instantly starts sucking.

"He was hungry. He's a growing boy," Roxy says while snapping a few more photos with Kohen's phone. "Especially if he's gonna be six feet six like his daddy."

I don't know who the hell dropped him off with me, but I'm pretty sure they've made a mistake. A huge one, in fact, by leaving their kid with someone who doesn't know shit about babies.

"He may not be mine," I remind Roxy.

"If it turns out he is yours, do you have any idea who the mother may be?" Roxy asks before taking a seat on the sofa next to me. Kohen eases down on the other side of Roxy like he can't stand to be more than a foot away from her.

"No. No name on the note," I answer her question. "All it said was, *I can't do this anymore. He's yours, I'm certain of it. You would have known about him sooner if you read your mail.*"

"Wow. Okay. So first thing's first, let me call the local hospitals and police department just to make sure we don't have someone's stolen baby," Roxy suggests, which is pretty smart thinking. "Then, you'll need to go get a DNA test on Monday, probably take him to a pediatrician and get him checked out too."

"Yeah," I reply, wondering how long it will take to get back the results. A few days probably. What the fuck do I do with the kid until then? My parents are coming in for the game tomorrow, so maybe they can stay and help out.

"In the meantime, try to think of who you may have slept with around nine months ago, so the end of December? If he was born a few weeks early, maybe the first of January?" Roxy offers, trying to be helpful. There's no way I'll admit to her that I can't even recall exactly how many women I slept with during those two months.

"Ugh, don't remind me," Lathan says when he slumps down into my brown leather recliner. "January second we lost big time in the first round of the playoffs."

"Aw, fuck," I groan and lean my head back against the sofa at the god-awful reminder of the night we lost the playoff game. "That was a bad night. I got shitfaced doing a bar crawl with Cameron and Nixon. I made them both drink a shot for every dropped pass of mine, and I had to do a shot for every interception I threw. For the *entire* season. We all lost count around the tenth or eleventh one. I woke up the next morning naked except for my shoes in the back of a cop car with three different club wristbands on."

"Shit, dude. I didn't know that. Did you get arrested?" Lathan asks.

"No, but only because the cops were apparently big fans. They said they picked me up on an indecent exposure call when I was wandering around Nixon's neighborhood. Since they recognized me, they drove me around until I woke up and gave them my address. When I got home, I signed some jerseys and shit to thank them for not throwing my sorry ass in jail or selling me out to the paparazzi."

"So you think the mother is someone you hooked up with that night?" Roxy asks.

Goddamn it.

The one night of my life that I get blackout drunk and I knocked someone up?

"Maybe," I answer honestly on a sigh. "That's the only night of my life that I don't remember all the shit I did."

"And since you didn't keep it in your pants, now you've got a baby on your doorstep," Lathan says.

"We still don't know for sure that he's mine," I remind him.

"In the meantime, though, he's your responsibility," Roxy tells me. "Once he finishes eating, I'll show you how to change him. Kohen, can you and Lathan go to Target and buy some newborn diapers and a pack and play?"

"A pack and what?" Kohen asks, and I'm glad I'm not the only one who doesn't know jack about kids.

"I'll send you a text with pictures," Roxy tells him with a kiss on his cheek.

"Okay, but when I get back, you and I are going home," Kohen says when he stands up. "Sorry, Quinton."

"Yeah, yeah. I'll make Lathan stay to help out," I reply.

"No way, bro," Lathan argues. "At least one of us needs to be fresh and ready tomorrow; and since my dick is free and clear in this situation, it's gonna be me."

A snort escapes before I can help myself at the sad reminder that he's never actually been inside a woman. "I'll take a crying baby any day over your long, miserable years of suffering with your virginity."

Roxy gasps in surprise over hearing about the twenty-four-year-old virgin at the same time Kohen pipes up and says, "Amen."

"While I would rather you keep your big mouths shut about my personal shit, I'm not ashamed," Lathan says, although his cheeks are a nice new shade of red. "If this baby is yours, you'll have to spend the rest of your *life* taking care of him," he says, causing me to wince at that dick slap of truth to my face. "And, Kohen, you nearly lost your million-dollar career because of your dick. So, tell me again what I'm missing out on by *not* sleeping around?"

"I approve, Lathan," Roxy tells him. "One day, you're gonna make a woman fall in love with you even harder when she finds out that you waited your whole life just for her. She'll feel cherished and special."

"Thank you," Lathan says, flashing Roxy an appreciative smile.

"Hopefully she won't have already worked her way through an entire football team before she finds you," Kohen responds with the more realistic scenario before Roxy elbows him in the gut making him release an "Ow."

"Don't you have some baby shopping to do?" Roxy asks Kohen with raised eyebrows.

"The sooner we get this done the sooner we go home, so I can remind you how cherished and special you are," Kohen replies, giving Roxy a kiss that nearly goes into PG-13.

"Don't forget the condoms!" I remind them, effectively ending their make out session.

"Mood killer," Kohen says before he and Lathan finally leave.

"I THINK HE'S DONE EATING," Roxy says a few minutes after the guys take off to the store. "Now you need to burp him."

"He can't burp on his own?" I ask before handing her the bottle. "And, fuck, we don't even know if *he* has a name."

"Aww," Roxy says with her bottom lip out. "That's so sad. We should give him one, even if it's only temporary."

"Yeah," I agree. "Any suggestions?"

"Possibly your kid, so your call," she says with a grin.

"Right," I reply on an exhale as I study the little guy. I sit him up to get a better look.

"Don't do that without –" Roxy starts right before the kid goes straight *Exorcist* on me. Yellowish, nasty-smelling, regurgitated formula erupts from his mouth, soaking his outfit and my shirt and jeans.

"Dude, that wasn't cool," I say to the baby while gagging from the stench.

"I was gonna say, don't sit him up without a burp rag," Roxy informs me as she pulls a white cloth from the baby's black bag and brings it over to try and mop up the mess.

"I am so out of my league here," I tell Roxy as she takes the baby from me. "We've got to find his mother ASAP."

"I don't think it's gonna be that easy, Quinton," Roxy says sadly as she spreads a blanket on the floor and lays the baby down on it. "If she dropped him off on your doorstep…no offense, but she must have been desperate to get rid of him." Roxy starts undoing the snaps that go down the center of his outfit with practiced ease. "Come here and watch so you can do this next time," she glances up to tell me.

Kneeling down on the floor beside her, I watch as she pulls the kid's arms free and then his legs before she changes his diaper.

"Easy, right?" she asks. "Just be gentle with pulling his arms and legs through the clothes holes, and make sure you always support the back of his head whenever you pick him up."

"I can't do this Roxy," I confess, getting back up so I can pace, the stinky puke on my shirt making it impossible to think straight.

"Sure you can. It'll just take a little practice…"

"No, I mean, I'm not ready to be a father," I clarify.

"Mr. Competitive Quarterback, are you actually backing down from a challenge?" she asks with an arched blonde eyebrow that causes my feet to stop.

"Hell no," is my automatic response since giving up or quitting isn't ever an option for me. "I just mean my life is too busy and hectic for a kid, if he's even mine."

"Some of the other players have kids," Roxy points out as she finishes redressing the baby.

"Yeah, and they also have wives or at least ex-wives who stay home to take care of them."

"Then I guess we just need to find you a wife," she teases.

"Find me the one woman in the great wide world who actually turns me down, and I'll put a ring on it," I joke.

"Oh, that's right!" Roxy exclaims. "You're waiting for the lady who would rather slap you than kiss you to come along so you can begin the challenging process of sweeping her reluctantly off her feet."

"Exactly," I tell her. "And I may be old and feeble in a nursing home before that day ever comes."

"I wouldn't doubt it," she replies, followed by a laugh. "Now come practice picking him up."

"Why can't you just toss him to me?" I joke.

"He's not a football to be tossed. And you need to practice since he's gonna be with you until we get DNA results or find his mother."

"Fine," I grumble. "But let me change first."

Once I'm in a clean, laundry-scented shirt and jeans rather than vomit-covered ones, I head back into the living room. Reaching down, I start to scoop the baby up from the floor, but Roxy raises her hand to stop me. "Remember to cradle the back of his head."

"Got it," I say as I wedge one of my big palms underneath his head and the other beneath his narrow backside. Since he doesn't weigh much, he's easy to lift. "Now what?" I ask Roxy while holding him out in front of me.

"Bring him closer to your body so that he's resting against your chest, feeling your warmth," she says, demonstrating with her empty hands. It takes a few tries before I finally get him twisted around.

"Like this?" I ask.

"Yeah, but you can move your hand from his head since it's propped up on the crook of your arm," she tells me, which makes holding him easier and frees up my right hand. "Now sit down and let's give him a name."

Taking my favorite seat in one of the oversized recliners, I get comfortable. With the baby in one arm and the TV remote in my other hand, I'm all set. Maybe this won't be so bad after all.

"So...any ideas for what to call him?" Roxy asks before plopping down on the sofa.

"I dunno," I say on a heavy exhale as I try to think.

It's not like I've ever considered the names I would give my son since I've never really imagined having kids. I love my life, playing football and being a rich bachelor with plenty of women to keep me busy. But I guess if I were to have a kid I would probably want to name him after a great football legend, since I would want him to follow in my footsteps and play. Actually, now I can even picture myself teaching my son how to throw a perfect spiral in the backyard after school and taking him to games on Sundays...

"How about Emmett or Troy?" I ask Roxy. "Maybe Brady?"

"Football players?" she asks, followed by a giggle. "Okay, fine. I guess Brady would be a pretty good name."

"So we'll call him Brady, you know, until we figure everything out," I tell her.

"Sure, Quinton. Whatever you say," Roxy replies with a smile.

About an hour after Lathan and Kohen come back with the baby supplies, we finally get the baby bed thing put together while Roxy holds a sleeping Brady. Already the name is sort of growing on me like it fits him. I'm sure his mother gave him a name, and he probably has a birth certificate somewhere. Too bad I don't even know who she is. Roxy made some calls, but no one knows anything about the baby or his mother.

"I can't believe someone could just leave their baby behind, especially one as adorable as he is," Roxy says after we put the little guy down to sleep in his new bed.

"Yeah, and I'm clearly the wrong man to pick for the job," I reply, taking a seat on the foot of my bed. There are five other bedrooms in my enormous house, but it didn't seem right to put the baby in one all alone tonight.

"You'll figure it out," Roxy assures me with a squeeze to my shoulder. "And who knows, maybe she'll show back up in a few days."

"Maybe," I respond doubtfully.

Tomorrow morning my parents are coming into town, so I called and asked if they would babysit for a friend during the game. They gladly agreed, so I figure I can explain in person what's really going on when I see them. Hopefully, my mom can even stick around and help out for a few days until we get the DNA results back. Which brings me to another problem I hadn't really considered. What happens to Brady if I'm *not* his father and we can't find his mother?

"Well, I'm gonna head out," Lathan tells us as he starts for the hallway. "See you all tomorrow. Good luck, Quinton."

"Thanks," I reply.

"We better get going too," Kohen turns and says to Roxy.

"Yeah, it's getting late," she replies hesitantly while still watching the sleeping baby. "But now you've got my number, so you can call if there's an emergency," Roxy tells me.

"Okay, thanks, Roxy," I say before getting up to give her a hug of gratitude for helping me out. "Thank you too, Kohen," I tell him, offering a fist bump, which he hits.

"No problem. See you in the morning," Kohen says before he leads Roxy into the hallway with his palm on her lower back.

The anxiety of knowing I'm about to be alone with a baby for the first time has my chest constricting and my palms sweating again. Of course I get nervous before a game, but this is different. It's an actual life that depends on me to not fuck up.

I'm about to freak out and chase down Roxy and Kohen before I hear Kohen's voice call out from down the hallway.

"Changed our minds! We're staying, Quinton," he shouts.

"Thank God," I mutter in relief.

Now that the current crisis has been averted for the moment, I flop down on the bed and pull out my cell phone to call up Nixon. I want to see what he remembers about the night we lost the playoff game.

"Yo, man, this better be important," Nix says when he answers.

"You busy?" I ask.

"Ah, yeah. My head's between the legs of a beautiful woman, so what the fuck do you want?" he barks.

Surprised, I say, "What about your whole no sex before a game rule?"

"My dick is staying in my pants until tomorrow night after we win and she can return the favor."

"Right," I say with an eye roll.

"So what's up, QB?"

"Someone left a baby on my porch tonight," I tell him.

"Nice! Lathan pranking you?" he asks.

"Ah, no. There was a note that said he's mine. And since he's been here for hours, I'm starting to think it's legit."

"No shit?" he mutters. "Who did you knock up?"

"No clue; that's why I'm calling you."

"Sorry, man, but I don't keep a running tally of all your bedroom TDs."

"I know," I tell him. "It's just that, do you remember the night when we got shitfaced after losing the playoff game?"

"Fuck, man. You're killing my mojo. Don't remind me of those three drops, two of which were in the end zone, or I'll have to get shitfaced again tonight to forget."

"I know, it was one clusterfuck after another. But if this kid is mine, and that's a big *if*, then that's the only night I think it could've gone down."

"Oh, shit," he mutters. "You forgot to wrap it up?"

"Dude, I forgot everything other than drinking with you and Cameron and then waking up in the back of a police car. Do you remember any women I may have hooked up with?" I ask.

"Hmm, most of the night was a blur to me too, man," he replies. "But didn't you go off with some tatted up chick when we were at *Limelight*?"

"I left with a woman with tattoos?" I ask.

"I think you disappeared for a little while with her. Before that, you kept slipping Benjamins down the front of her skirt and asking for a private lap dance."

"*Limelight* is just a nightclub, not a strip club, right?" I ask in confusion.

Nixon chuckles. "Yeah, that's why it was so hilarious! She was our waitress, serving us those lime green Jell-O shooters, but I'm betting she ended up giving you more than a lap dance."

"Fuck," I groan softly while eying the bed with the sleeping baby.

"Guess now you're wishing you would've gotten a blowjob instead," Nixon remarks.

"Do you remember her name or anything else about her?" I ask. "I've got to find her to figure out whether or not this kid is mine."

"Nah, man. No clue. It was loud as shit in there, and I was drunk off my ass."

"Yeah, okay. Well, thanks for the info. I'll call Cameron and see if he remembers anything else and let you get back to your pussy," I tell him.

"Thanks, she's getting all impatient wanting more than my fingers inside her," he replies.

"I didn't need to know that, dude," I say before hanging up.

Finding Cameron's number in my phone, I call him up next.

"What the hell, Quinn? I was sleeping. Why aren't you?" the other starting wide receiver for the Wildcats asks when he answers.

"Sorry to wake you, but it's sort of important," I start and then tell him the quick version about the kid getting left with me. "Nix said he thought I may have hooked up with a waitress, one with tattoos. Do you remember her?" I ask.

"I remember that God-awful playoff game," he grumbles. "And yeah, I think I remember a waitress sitting on your lap. She had these blue streaks in her raven hair, Japanese tattoos of, like, koi fish and water or some shit on her arms. Wasn't that at *Limelight* when we started throwing back all those Jell-O shots?"

"Yeah, that's what Nixon said too," I reply, excited to maybe have a lead. "Do you remember her name by chance?"

"Nope, but by the end of that night I didn't remember my own name," he answers.

"Well, thanks for the info. Get some z's, and I'll see you on the field in the morning."

"All right. Sorry about the kid, Quinton. Later," Cameron says before hanging up.

So it looks like I can add a visit to *Limelight* to my list of things to do after tomorrow's game. With nothing else to be done tonight, I change into a pair of sleep pants and turn off the light before crawling under the covers to try to get a few hours of sleep.

When the baby wakes up crying just two hours later, I start to get the feeling that it's gonna be a *lonnnng* night.

CHAPTER TWO

Callie Clarke

I startle awake to the sounds of a crying baby, which is rather concerning since I'm absolutely certain that I didn't have any kids in the house hours ago when I fell asleep.

Sitting up in the middle of the bed, I push my sweaty blonde locks out of my eyes as I try to catch my breath and get my bearings. That's when I realize that it was all just a dream. My house is empty. No babies crying. No husband. Just me and my tiger-striped cat Felix, who is not in his usual spot, curled up asleep at the foot of the bed.

Now that I'm feeling wide awake thanks to the urgency in the dream, I decide to get up and grab a glass of water to soothe my dry mouth before trying to lay down and get comfortable again.

Even with only the faintest bit of light shining in the windows from the street lamps, I'm easily able to find my way around the bed in the familiar room. Only when I'm less than a foot away from my reading chair, do I see the shape of a man sitting in it.

A scream is reflexively pulled from my throat without a thought before common sense returns. The next second I'm running around the side of the bed where there's a landline phone.

"Callie, it's just me," the man quickly says, and I recognize the voice of my husband, or soon to be ex-husband, after I've picked up the receiver. Not reassured in the least by that information, I keep hold of the phone, my finger poised over the backlit number nine, ready to punch in the three digits that will bring police assistance.

"What the hell are you doing here, lurking around in the shadows while I sleep?" I yell at John, squinting when he suddenly flips on the blinding overhead lights.

"I just miss you," he says sadly. And when I'm able to blink my eyes fully open, I see that his words match the fallen expression on his slender face. Tonight he's dressed in dark sweatpants and a baggy sweatshirt, so it's hard to tell if he's healthy and clean or using the excess material to hide his emaciated body that's been sacrificed thanks to his very nasty drug habit.

"Get the fuck out of my house!" I yell at him, pointing the way to the front door in case he forgot between now and when he snuck in.

"It used to be my house too," he says.

"That was before I found out you were giving my sister drugs in exchange for sex!" I shout, tears prickling my eyes and burning my throat at the reminder of waking up in the middle of the night to find him in the guest bed with my sister. The sounds of their naked bodies slapping against each other, the grunts and groans of their betrayal was the biggest wake-up call of my life.

"One time!" John exclaims in response as if a single occurrence rather than multiple ones makes it any better. "That only happened one time, and I told you I was sorry. I just needed…"

"Save the bullshit!" I warn him, already knowing what he's gonna say from hearing it so many times before --- that him having an affair with my sister was all *my* fault because I was pressuring him to get me pregnant. And that after failing to get the job done in seven years, sex with me was nothing but a chore; that I blamed him for our infertility and didn't act like I loved him or wanted him anymore, blah, blah, blah. "And if you think I'll ever believe it was only *one* single time you fucked her and got her pregnant after *years* of not having any luck with me, then you're a bigger fucking idiot than I already thought you were!"

"I swear I didn't knock her up," he says. "She seduced me that night! You know damn well that the whore will fuck anyone to score a hit!"

Without even thinking about it, I toss the phone down and storm over to slap the shit out of his face.

"Bianca is no saint, I know that," I snarl at him, my palm still stinging by my side. "But she's a desperate addict that needed help, and all you and those other bastards do is just take advantage of her!"

Rubbing his dirty blond scruff where I hit him, John says, "In our eight years of marriage I had *one* moment of weakness that you're gonna punish me for forever, but yet you'll forgive Bianca?"

"No, I haven't forgiven her. But she's my sister, and she needs help! You are a rat bastard that I never want to see again!" I tell him without an ounce of sympathy. "Now get the fuck out of my house before I call the police. And you better believe that Monday morning I'll have a restraining order against your ass."

"Come on, Callie," John whines, giving me big, brown puppy dog eyes. "We can start over if you'll just give me a second chance."

"Never. Gonna. Happen," I tell him slowly so that it will maybe finally penetrate his thick skull. "Hell could someday freeze over," I say while giving his shoulder a shove that propels him down the hallway. "Pigs could eventually evolve and start to fly." Another shove to his chest in the living room causes him to stumble backward closer to the door. "But one thing I know without a shred of doubt in my mind is that *we* are done!"

Unlocking and unchaining the front door, I open it and push him, forcing him out before slamming it shut again. Slumping with my back against the door, I close my eyes and take a deep calming breath, trying to lower my heart rate to an acceptable level. Monday I'll get the locks changed, and then I'll go to the police department to fill out the paperwork for a restraining order because I am so sick of this bullshit happening. John suddenly pops up out of the blue every few weeks, but this was his first late night visit. I wasted too many years of my life being tied to that asshole. Never again.

I finally pour that glass of water I wanted before settling back into bed. As expected, after the weird baby dream and the ordeal with an uninvited guest, it takes lots of tossing and turning before I'm able to drift back to sleep.

The next time I wake up, it's to the sound of the doorbell ringing.

"Ugh! Are you fucking kidding me?" I roll over and groan to the ceiling. I consider pulling the pillow over my head and ignoring him, but then I realize John has a key, so why would he bother with the hassle of the doorbell?

Lumbering out of bed, my feet shuffle toward the door where I unlock and open it. A gasp escapes my parted lips at the sight of two uniformed police officers with matching grim expressions on their faces.

"What's happened?" I ask them, wrapping my arms around myself to brace for the news.

"Sorry to wake you, ma'am," the older, robust one starts. "Do you by chance know Bianca Williams? This address was listed on her driver's license."

"Yes, she's my sister. Why? What has she done now? Is she okay?" I ask, looking back and forth between the two of them.

"I'm so sorry to be the one to tell you this, but Miss Williams was taken to the hospital earlier tonight for a suspected drug overdose."

"Oh God," I mutter, resting the side of my head against the door frame. "Is she gonna be okay? Oh, no! What about the baby?"

When the two officers look at each other silently without answering me, I know it's bad. "We can give you a ride to the hospital if you would like."

"S-sure," I say, blinking back tears. "Just, um, give me a second to change," I tell them before shutting the door for a moment of privacy.

And then I give myself thirty short seconds to cry before I have to wipe away the tears and pull myself together to deal with Bianca's newest catastrophe.

CHAPTER THREE

Quinton

"Hey, Mom. Hey, Dad. Come on in," I tell my parents, greeting them each with a hug when I open my front door bright and early Sunday morning.

In fact, the sun is so bright it's making my migraine worse. The one caused by getting up every two hours or so last night because of the hungry, crying baby. Out of the four times I got up, Roxy left me all alone except for the first one. Still groggy from sleep, she found me in the kitchen and made sure I remembered how to fix the bottle before turning tail and crawling back into bed with Kohen.

And yeah, while I wish Roxy would have taken over and just let me sleep, I know the baby is my responsibility and not hers. Kohen and her left half an hour ago to go home and get ready to head to the stadium.

"You look like shit, son. Party too hard last night?" My dad asks with his salt and pepper eyebrows raised in disapproval.

"Ah, yeah. It was a two-person party in here all right," I mutter sarcastically as I lead them into the living room.

"TMI!" my mom groans from behind me.

"It's not what you think," I assure her, waving my hand toward the baby, who is awake inside the bed thing I moved from the bedroom to the living room this morning. He's lying flat on his back, just like Roxy told me to do when I put him down.

"Why is there a baby bed in your house?" Mom asks, tiptoeing closer in her jeans and Wildcats sweatshirt until she can peek over the edge of the bed. "Oh my goodness!" she exclaims before she reaches in and picks him up, a hand carefully cradling the back of his head. Guess I shouldn't be all that surprised that my mom knows what she's doing since my parents obviously raised me.

"Quinton, why is there a baby in your house?" my father asks, repeating my mother's question as he inches closer to my mom.

"Last night someone dropped him off and ran, leaving me a note that says he's mine. Until I get a DNA test, though..."

"You don't know if he is or not," my dad finishes. "This could be one helluva scheme for your money."

"I don't really think so," I tell him honestly while scratching my head. "I mean, she didn't even leave me *her* name. If she wanted money, why not wait at the door while holding him and demand child support instead of just...leaving him?"

"How could a mother do that?" my mom asks as she stares down at the baby in her arms, rocking side to side. "And what were *you* thinking, son?" she looks up and scowls at me with narrowed blue eyes, the same as the ones I see every day in the mirror.

"We don't know for sure he's mine," I remind her. "But there was this one night back in January..."

"Quinton! I am so disappointed in you," my mom says with a shake of her head, making me feel even shittier.

"Yeah, I know. Look, I really need to get a shower and head to the stadium to start warming up. Can you take him to the game and watch him until this afternoon?"

"Yes, of course," my mom answers.

"There's his bag with his bottle and diapers or whatever," I tell her, pointing to the black bag on the floor beside the bed and car seat. "And Roxy said the bottom of that car seat thing has to be latched down in the backseat."

"Have you been taking care of him all night?" my dad, who has been rather quiet, asks.

"Yeah. Roxy, our new kicker, showed me how to do everything and stayed over last night in case I needed her help. But Brady kept me up all damn night..."

"Brady? His name's Brady?" my mom asks with a smile. "Oh, I love it!"

"It's temporary," I tell her. "For all I know, he already has a name and a father out there somewhere."

"*Or*," my mom starts. "He could be yours. Ours."

"Well, he's yours for today," I tell her. "Have fun."

"Oh, I'm sure he'll be a perfect little angel," she replies.

I take her word for it and start down the hallway to grab a quick shower and get my tired ass over to the stadium.

"He looks like you," she calls out, stopping me in my tracks. "Smaller, but the squinty eyes and pointy chin are yours and your father's."

"He looks like a baby," I turn around and argue. "And wasn't I, like, ten pounds and gigantic when I was born?"

"Yes, but you were also two weeks *late*. I bet you would've been this size if you had come on time. But you were stubborn even then," she replies.

"Didn't Quinton wake us up every hour to eat the first three weeks?" my dad interjects.

"Yes, I believe so. My milk didn't come in fast enough, so we had to use bottles," she answers.

"TMI," I mutter, slapping both of my palms over my ears.

Without a doubt, Sunday afternoon I played one of the worst games of my life against the Atlanta Lions.

My reflexes were so slow that I got sacked five fucking times. I only completed twelve out of twenty-seven passes with zero touchdowns through the air. It was a brutal game.

Thankfully, our defense was on fire, scoring on two takeaways from Atlanta, and then Roxy came through for us with three field goals, including a game-winning one. My team picked up the slack and seriously saved my ass today.

I feel like a zombie by the time my parents hand Brady back to me outside the stadium. They said they were sorry, but they can't stay longer. Both have work and appointments they can't miss back home up in Roanoke, yadda, yadda, yadda.

To make the day worse, as I'm driving us home in my Land Cruiser with Brady fastened in his car seat in the back, the foulest odor known to man begins to fill the car. I'm gagging before I get all the windows rolled down. And then I'm forced to pull over in a shopping center when I start dry heaving from my close proximity to what is obviously toxic waste.

Jesus, if they could bottle up this smell, it could be used as a deadly weapon.

Last night Roxy handled the one shitty diaper Brady had while we were putting together his bed, but I can't call her tonight since she and Kohen are having dinner with her dad and her friend Paxton, who are here from out of town to celebrate her first real game. I'm fifteen minutes away from my house, and there's no way I can drive any further without throwing up.

Not knowing what else to do, I glance around the shopping center, looking for a place to get down to business. That's when I spot the purple sign with the word "Babies" in it.

Fuck yes.

With my head sticking out the driver side window like a dog, I steer the car toward the beacon of light that will hopefully be an answer to my prayers.

I pull the front collar of my t-shirt up over my nose and mouth before I throw Brady's bag over my shoulder and then extract the stink-miester's seat from the back to carry him inside.

"Hi, welcome to Babies & Company. Is there anything I can help you with today?" a young, bubbly sales associate in a purple shirt asks as soon as I walk through the door. She's cute with long brown hair and a curvy body, eyeing me up and down like she wants to climb me. And any other day I would be throwing out cheesy lines, but I'm not up for playing games today. I'm not sure if it's the god-awful smell or the fact that I didn't sleep any last night because of the possible result of a one-night stand, but right now I don't think I'd even get a half-stiffy if this woman was talking to me with her mouth full of my cock.

"Hey, how's it going? Do you have, like, one of those table things to change him on?" I ask, hefting up the car seat.

"Well, sure, right this way," she says, beckoning me with a hand before she turns around and heads toward the back of the store. "You look familiar," she tells me over her shoulder. "Where have I seen you before?"

"Ah, maybe on the football field?" I offer, trying to keep up with her speed walking when all I want to do is pass out in my bed.

"Right! You play for the Wildcats, don't you!" she exclaims in recognition. While some women are familiar with the various positions, usually I'm just "that football player" to most.

"Right," I answer. "Quinton Dunn. Nice to meet you..."

"Kelsey," she supplies as we turn down an aisle. "Didn't you have a game today?"

"We did. Won it too," I answer.

"Awesome, congrats!" she replies. "Okay, so here are the changing tables we currently have in stock. We have these in white, oak, cherry and espresso."

"This one will work great," I tell her, setting Brady's car seat down in front of the first one we come to, a white one, to start unstrapping him.

"Good choice," Kelsey says cheerfully. "It's usually three-twenty nine, but it's on sale this weekend for just two hundred and seventy-five dollars."

I grab a diaper and the pack of wipes that are getting low and place them on the table and then lower Brady to the wooden structure as the sales associate continues talking.

"This one has three spacious drawers and a cabinet underneath, making it great for storage too. In fact, once he outgrows the changing table, it can be converted to a regular dresser...ah, what...what are you doing?" she asks when I start unsnapping the one-piece outfit Brady's wearing. "Oh, whoa!" she exclaims, reaching up to hold her nose once she gets a whiff of his stink.

"I swear I didn't feed him any rotten milk or anything," I tell her as I pull my shirt over my face again and start undoing the diaper.

"Wait, you're changing him, like, here?" she asks, sounding nasally like Fran Drescher since her nose is still plugged.

"Well, yeah. That's what they are for, right?" I ask as I take a handful of wipes and try to mop up the brown mess, not without more gags and dry heaves.

"But, sir, you can't..."

"Oops," I say when some of the runny poo splatters onto the pristine white changing table.

"Oh my God," the associate mutters when I pull the diaper out from underneath the kid.

Looking around the floor with my hand holding up the nasty, poop-filled diaper I ask, "Do you have a trash can around here? I can't just leave him."

"Sir, these tables are for sale, not for actual use," Kelsey tells me belatedly.

"Too late now," I tell her. "Can you watch him while I find a trash can, or do you want to take the shitty diaper?"

"Um, yeah, okay, straight back and to the left are the bathrooms," she tells me, putting a hand on Brady's stomach, not that he's going anywhere or anything.

After I dispose of the hazardous waste, wash my hands and return to the changing table aisle, Kelsey has thankfully diapered and redressed Brady and is now holding him on her shoulder.

"Thanks for your help," I tell her.

"No problem," she says with a smile. "You do know that you have to buy this table now, right?"

"What? But I just used it once," I argue.

"Yeah, and you got your son's poop on it."

She makes a valid point.

"Fine," I exhale in agreement. "I think it should fit in the back of my Land Cruiser. Can you watch him while I pay and load it in my SUV?"

"Yeah, of course," she replies with a smile.

"Oh, and do you have more of those butt wipes?" I ask.

"We sure do."

"And that's his last clean outfit, so I probably need some tiny clothes for him," I tell her. "I mean, it could take days to do the DNA test and get the results back, so I probably need more of that milk powder stuff too."

"Oh, so he may not be your son?" she asks with a creased brow.

"Not sure," I answer honestly and then cringe. "And can I beg you not to tell anyone about any of this whole ordeal?"

"Sure," she replies. "Your secret is safe with me."

"Thanks, Kelsey."

"If you want to take him up front to pay, I'll grab some wipes, a few newborn outfits, and formula and meet you there. Anything else you need while you're here today?" she asks.

"Do you have something to make him sleep longer?" I ask. "He woke up every two hours last night, and I really need some sleep."

"Is he drinking from four-ounce bottles?" she asks.

"Yeah."

"Does he finish them during a single feeding?"

"Oh yeah, like he can't guzzle them down fast enough."

"Then maybe he needs more at each feeding so he can sleep longer without getting hungry."

More to eat equals sleep longer? Hell yes.

"Oh my God. You're a baby genius," I tell Kelsey. "Let me get some bigger bottles."

"Sure," she says with a smile. "And babies like to be swaddled when they sleep, are you doing that?"

"What the fuck is a swaddle?" I ask her.

"I'll grab some of those too," she replies with a giggle.

"Thank you. You're a lifesaver, Kelsey."

"You're welcome! Give me a few minutes to grab a buggy and load up; then I'll see you up front to watch him while you load up," she says before walking away.

I get Brady buckled into his seat, all the while feeling a little more optimistic about everything. In fact, Kelsey seems to know a lot about kids...

At the front of the store where the registers are, there's only one other person in line, so I wait behind them while an older woman rings up a woman and her toddler.

"Hi, did you find everything you need today?" the older, rotund lady asks when it's my turn.

"Yeah, Kelsey's rounding it all up for me and said to meet her here," I explain.

"Oh good," she replies with a smile.

"Has she been working here long?" I ask.

The lady considers my question for a moment. "About a year I believe."

"And did you do, like, criminal background checks and all on her?"

The lady looks confused, blinking her eyes silently at me for several seconds before she answers. "Well, of course. We thoroughly vet every applicant before hiring them. I can assure you that you and your son are safe when shopping with us."

"And how much does she make, you know, like an hour?" I ask.

The woman's jaw falls open in shock that I would ask something so personal.

"You'll have to discuss Miss Kelsey's wages with her directly," she finally responds stiffly. Then the rest of the wait is spent in silence.

Finally, Kelsey appears with a shopping cart slam packed with baby goods and parks it behind me.

"All set, except for the changing table," she tells me over the pile.

"How much do you make?" I ask her.

"Ah," she looks from me to the other sales associate, who I assume is her boss. "You want to know how much money I make? Why?"

"Just wondering."

"Around fourteen an hour."

"And how many hours a week do you work?" I ask.

"Thirty or so," she answers with a shrug.

"I'll pay you two thousand to come work for me day and night this week," I offer her.

"Holy shit! Doing what?" she asks. "You play football."

"Yeah, and in order to play football, I need a babysitter. You seem to know your baby shit, and this lady said they checked you out before they hired you, so... what do you say?"

"Oh my God. Sure, I mean, yeah. That would be awesome!" the young girl exclaims before turning to her boss. "Can I please have a week off?" she begs.

"Well, I suppose...wait, are you that quarterback for the Wildcats?" the lady asks me.

"Ah, yeah. I can get you tickets to our next home game if you want," I offer.

"Wow, my husband will be so excited," she says. "Now let's ring you up."

As they begin to unload the buggy and start scanning items, I look down at the sleeping baby at my feet and can't help but wonder if I'm going a little overboard. If Brady's not mine, then I can always donate the baby items, right?

That reminds me of tomorrow's to-do list: DNA test, take Brady to see a pediatrician and try to track down his mother.

CHAPTER FOUR

Callie

"Dear Heavenly Father, with heavy hearts we come to you," the chaplain begins from the other side of the hospital bed. "Our hearts are heavy because of a life that is leaving us. Death engulfs us, Lord. Thank you that Jesus knows the way through this dark shadow. Take the hand of our dearly departed sister and make yourself known. Guard our hearts and minds in Christ Jesus. Keep that which is your own and take it into eternity to be with you always. Amen."

I lift my bowed head, and my eyes automatically go to my sister's prone form in a sea of white sheets. My first thought seeing her naturally blonde hair dyed black and spread over the pillows is that she looks like a sleeping Snow White. My second thought is that I'm a horrible person because more than the grief of losing her, greater than the sadness of knowing I'll never speak to her again, is my anger and hate.

Early this morning on the way to the hospital, the policemen finally told me the heartbreaking news, and I realized that my nightmare was just beginning.

Bianca was no longer pregnant and didn't have a baby with her when she was found alone and unresponsive in an alley. I was completely devastated, more so about the baby than Bianca's dire condition.

My sister didn't survive the night. The excessive amount of heroin in her system caused too much damage to her heart, lungs and other vital organs before she received any medical treatment. The effects were irreversible once she was brought to the hospital.

It's more than just the affair with my husband now that has me so angry at Bianca even in death. No, I hate her because she knew how badly I've longed to be a mother, and she carelessly ended the life of her child rather than leave him or her with me.

I can't help but wonder if she thought to herself, *I fucked Callie's husband, so what can I possibly do to top that? Oh, I know! I'll take the life of my baby before I OD just to rub it in her face that she'll never be a mother while I easily got knocked up by the only man she's ever loved. Yes, that should do the trick to stomp on Callie's already broken heart.*

I'm a horrible person.

Months ago, if I had been able to forgive Bianca, maybe I could've taken her in, kept her off drugs while she was pregnant, and convinced her to let me raise the baby. Hell, I bet she would have given the baby to me in exchange for a few thousand dollars in drug money. Sure, I wouldn't be able to look at their baby without being reminded of the ultimate betrayal, but he or she was completely innocent. The poor thing didn't get to pick who his or her fucked up druggy mother and asshole addict father would be, or to be conceived in an act of adultery. It didn't deserve to die. So that's why I'm standing over my sister's dead body, hating her with an unholy vengeance.

Our father is a truck driving alcoholic with kids in all fifty states.

He never gave a shit about us, and our mother was murdered four years ago in a drug deal gone bad. Bianca and her baby were all I had left of a family, and now they're gone too. I've never felt so lonely or miserable in my life.

"Do you need anything else, Mrs. Clarke?" the decrepit but kind hospital chaplain asks me.

"No, sir. She'll be cremated without any funeral services, but thank you for the final prayer," I tell him before he nods and limps out of the room.

Bianca had her cell phone on her when they brought her in, and I've called to notify a few of her friends that she's gone. Other than that, there's no one else. I don't even know where her belongings are, where she's been living the last few months. All I know is that she's gone and she took an innocent life with her.

I touch my sister's lifeless hand one last time before I say goodbye and leave her. Instead of heading home, I walk down the hospital corridor and take the stairs to the third floor. From there I check-in at the neonatal intensive care unit, or NICU, nursing station before washing up and putting on a clean pair of scrubs over my clothes.

A few afternoons a week I volunteer as a cuddler. Some premature babies are kept here at Dobson Memorial for months while their parents are in different cities or states, having to continue working their full-time jobs to keep insurance. Research has shown that the babies do better when they're held regularly. Since the nurses are so busy, they let volunteers come in to help out, after a full background check, of course. Today more than any I need the warmth and care just as much if not more than the babies.

"Hi, Callie! How's it going?" Tina, one of the young nurses, asks when she sees me pulling on the green scrubs in the sterile room.

"Not so good," I reply. "I need some cuddles."

"I've got a few takers," she says with a smile. "I'll get the first one ready."

"Thanks, Tina," I say. "Oh, and, um, you haven't had any babies of Bianca Williams or unknown mothers in the last few days, have you?" I ask even though it's pointless.

"Who's Bianca Williams?" she asks.

"She's my sister. *Was* my sister," I correct with a sniffle. "That's why I'm here this morning. She passed away from a drug overdose. The doctors said Bianca had recently delivered...but there was no baby with her when she was found."

"Oh God. I'm really sorry, Callie," Tina replies before wrapping her arms around me. "I'll check the registry, but that name doesn't sound familiar. So sorry for your loss, hon."

"Thanks," I tell her. "Figured it was worth a shot to ask."

A few minutes later, I'm in one of the white, wooden rocking chairs, holding a swaddled preemie with all sorts of cords attached to him, fighting for his life in my arms. Tears race each other down both of my cheeks while I mourn the loss of my sister, who I feel guilty about pushing out of my life. But mostly I cry for the innocent baby who was never given a chance to fight.

I knew Bianca had an addiction. She would steal money from my wallet whenever she had the chance, which I never really cared about. Mostly it bothered me that she wouldn't just ask me for the cash instead of being deceitful. Then there was her affair with John. They were the only two people in my life who I loved, and they both managed to crush me at the exact same moment.

When Bianca told me she was pregnant, I was angry, but mostly I was jealous. There she was, a drug addicted, lying thief and she had the one thing I've always wanted. And what did she do with the precious gift she was given? She threw it and her life away like it meant nothing.

And it's all my fault.

If I would have pushed aside my pride and broken heart, I could've tried to help her instead of leaving her to fend for herself. She's dead because I gave up on her.

I'm starting to think that maybe I don't deserve to be a mother if I couldn't save my sister.

Ever since I was a little girl, it's all I've wanted, to hold my own baby in my arms. Not just because I'm a woman, and it's what everyone says I'm supposed to do, but because being a mother is my soul-longing desire. It's what I thought I was meant to do with my life, the reason I worked so hard to have a career with a flexible schedule so I could stay home, why I set aside every penny I possibly could into a savings account...

Maybe I'm wrong, and I was never meant to become a mother. Pregnancy happens so easily for teenagers and women like Bianca who don't want the responsibility but simply make bad decisions that leave them with the consequences. So why is it so hard for me unless it's just never meant to be?

Is that why I was cursed with endometriosis? To ensure that I would never have the opportunity to nurture and love my own child?

I've done everything the doctors have told me to do. I had the surgeries. I take daily prenatal vitamins, eat right and exercise, running several miles a week. I don't touch alcohol and have never smoked a cigarette in my life. I can't remember the last time I had a caffeinated beverage. Yet, years have gone by, and I didn't even need to take a single pregnancy test because I faced the evidence of my disappointment each and every month without fail. There's been no close calls. Just the agonizing cramps that mark the beginning of another missed opportunity.

Now, I'm a thirty-six-year-old divorcee, and I'm running out of options. The sand is pouring into the bottom of the hourglass while I sit back and watch helplessly.

Adoptions were a possibility, but only when John and I were married. He resisted the idea and wanted it to be a last resort. Now that I'm single, the agencies ignore me and won't even return my calls despite the fact that I'm financially secure and have been mentally and emotionally prepared to be a mother for nearly a decade.

The chances of me meeting another man and falling in love again seem rather slim. Thanks to my cheating husband and sister, I don't know if I'll ever be able to trust someone again. Without trust, there's no possibility of marriage and definitely no babies.

So not only am I mourning the loss of my sister and her baby today, I'm also mourning the loss of possibility. It's time to give up and face the fact that I'm just not destined to have the family I've always wanted.

CHAPTER FIVE

Quinton

This morning the pediatrician examined Brady and assured me that he is absolutely healthy, even though he thinks he may have been born a few days early. He said the bigger bottles were fine for him too as long as he didn't yack up constantly, which he hasn't done since I figured out how to burp him right away after a feeding.

From the doctor's office, Brady and I went to the testing lab. I'm really glad that the DNA test was nothing more than a quick swab of both our mouths.

Now comes the hard part --- waiting.

According to the clinic, it will take at least three days for the test results to come back, so maybe by Thursday I'll know whether or not I'm really Brady's father.

I'm extremely thankful that Kelsey has agreed to come stay at the house as a live-in babysitter for the week since it's gonna take longer for the results than I expected. Last night she was right about Brady being hungry and needing more than four ounces despite being only a few days old. The little guy was starving. Once he had the bigger bottle, he slept for four long, sweet, peaceful hours, which I was grateful for. Kelsey even got up and changed him at two and six while I fixed his bottle. Although I insisted on getting up to feed him, it was nice of her to be there and be willing to help.

Tonight, Kelsey is staying with Brady while I drive downtown, hoping that the staff at *Limelight* can give me some information about finding the woman who could potentially be his mother.

Since it's a Monday, the bar is having some sort of cheap beer night to try and lure in college kids and fall tourists. At nine o'clock the place is still pretty empty, though, so I walk up to the bar and immediately get waited on by the bartender with long auburn hair and a low-cut, white see-through shirt that draws in the eye. Obviously, she's a veteran who knows how to work her tits for more tips.

"What can I get you to drink tonight, Mr. Dunn?" she asks familiarly with a broad grin when she recognizes me. I can practically see the dollar signs flashing in her green eyes.

"A beer, make it your choice, beautiful," I tell her, encouraging her flirting if it will get her talking to me.

"Well, in that case, only the best for our star quarterback," she answers before turning around to grab a bottle. After popping the top, she places a beverage napkin in front of me and puts the beer down. "Can I get you anything else, hon?" she asks while leaning forward on her elbows to give me a fantastic view of her cleavage while her words hold the unmistakable, much more salacious offer behind them.

My dick is apparently still angry at me for the lack of sleep and refuses to take the bait, so I decide to get on with my purpose in coming here tonight.

"Actually, some teammates and I were in here back in January, and, well, one of my buddies can't stop talking about this girl he met. I'm trying to find her for him," I tell the bartender, making up the story because I'm still trying to keep the whole baby daddy drama out of the press. "Do you by chance know the name of a waitress with Japanese tattoos and black hair with blue streaks so I can put him out of his misery?"

"Hmm," the bartender mutters while tilting her head to the side in thought. "You said that was all the way back in January?"

"Yeah, around the second. We lost a game, but she apparently made him feel much better," I joke.

"Then that would probably have to be...oh shoot, what was her name?" she asks herself while snapping her fingers. "She up and quit in, like, April or May, and I haven't seen her since."

"Is there a manager around who may remember and could give me her contact information?" I ask.

Pulling out my wallet from the back pocket of my jeans, I remove five crisp twenty dollar bills and slide them across the bar to her.

"Give me just a second," she says with a wink before sweeping up the cash and slipping it into her front apron. Then she saunters off toward the back of the club.

I sit and sip my beer, waiting patiently and hoping the bartender brings me something worthwhile back.

A few minutes later she appears in the dark hallway and crooks a finger at me, beckoning me to come to her. I take another long pull on my beer before I set it down and climb off the stool, heading in her direction. Taking my hand without a word, she leads me into an empty office where she shuts the door behind us.

"Found it," she says, looking up at me while biting her bottom lip. Her hand slowly slips a piece of paper into my front jean pocket. She could've just handed it to me, but then she wouldn't have had the chance to let her fingers seek out the length of my cock through the thin material of my pocket lining. "Found something else too," she informs me as if I weren't already aware of her groping.

So what do I do? Now that I have what I came here for, I try to think fast and come up with the foulest thing I could possibly say to see if she'll back off or if she has her sights set on banging the Wildcats quarterback regardless of how much of a jerk I am.

"It's big, but I think you can fit all of it in your dirty mouth just fine," I say while staring at her cleavage and running a finger up her neck. "How's your deep throat? You look like a girl who could suck a dick like a porn star."

"God, yes," she replies right away, pressing her full, soft tits against my chest. "I'll give you the best blowjob you've ever had."

Annnd I'm oh-for-forty-fucking-six.

What sort of woman would offer to get me off with her mouth minutes after meeting, knowing she won't get anything in return? After I practically called her a dirty whore? One who only sees a name, a jersey, dollar signs, any or all of the above as the end game.

Normally I would've already had my pants unzipped while gladly pushing the woman whose name I don't even know to her knees, feeding my famous cock into her mouth that she wants so badly. Whether it's sleep deprivation or having the possible consequence of a one-night stand thrust into my life, tonight I'm just not interested in getting off for the hell of it. I mean, of course my cock twitches with interest because, fuck, she's full on stroking the shit out of it now through the front of my fly. He likes the attention and her big tits, but it feels all...wrong.

Reaching for her wrist, I remove her hand from my crotch and place a kiss on the center of her palm to try to take the sting out of my rejection.

"I really need to get going tonight, but maybe we can pick this up some other time?"

Like never.

"Aww," she says with a fake pout once I let her wrist go. "Well, I put my number on there too. Call me anytime," she says before patting my pocket again and swiping her hand over my hardening cock.

As if she couldn't get even more pathetic, she's apparently content to offer herself up to me like a twenty-four-hour, on-call slut delivery service.

How could I possibly decline such an offer, right?

What man wouldn't want to call up this woman, have her come over and blow him whenever the hell he wanted?

I'm just so fucking sick of it.

Not the blowjobs. The blowjobs are great.

I'm so tired of these women. Before my car leaves the lot tonight, I'm sure this nameless one in front of me will be telling one of her friends we did a lot more than talk in this room. I'm just a trophy fuck. Some want bragging rights, others think they can fuck me so good I'll keep them around. They're all so clueless.

Sure, I would like to think I'm a better lover than the next man, but the fact is I'm probably not. I happen to be an amazing quarterback who gets paid a lot of money; and for some reason, they think that makes me an incredible catch. It doesn't occur to the jersey chasers that I could be the biggest asshole on the planet; and if it actually does, they don't care because *who* I am doesn't matter to them. Only *what* I am gets them hot and wet, salivating for my dick.

In six or seven years, if I'm lucky and don't get hurt sooner, my football career will end. The money will start to dry up, and then I'll be a normal guy once again. Is it too much to ask to want someone who will still want to be with me even then?

I'm not psychic, but I'm almost certain that I'll never have a future with a chick who'll gladly suck my dick without me even knowing her name.

"Have a good night," I tell the bartender over my shoulder while quickly making my escape out of the office and the bar.

Only once I'm sitting in my Land Cruiser do I turn on the overhead light and pull out the small sheet of paper from my pocket. Inside is what I assume is the bartender's name, Natasha, above her phone number, and below that is the name Bianca Williams and a Wilmington address about ten minutes from my house. I assume Bianca is the girl I'm looking for.

Bianca.

Nothing about that name rings any bells which makes me feel

like shit. How could I have unprotected sex with a woman and not remember her face or name?

Never again will I get drunk again. And I should be seriously thankful that my STD tests from June all came back clean.

I decide to wait until tomorrow morning before hunting down Bianca Williams, telling myself that it's late and I'm fucking exhausted. But the truth is I'm not in as big of a hurry as I was before to get rid of Brady. Actually, I'm rather hesitant about taking him back and leaving him with a mother who abandoned him. Can she actually be trusted with him?

Tomorrow morning I'll go see her, and we'll talk about custody. Tonight, I'll prepare myself for the possibility that she may refuse to take Brady back.

I don't know which is scarier, wondering if she'll want him or not.

Setting the car seat down on the porch of the cute little one-story cottage home Tuesday morning, I'm feeling a mixture of nervousness and a little excitement, thinking of finally seeing what could be the mother of my son again.

Watching Brady sleep soundly in his seat since, you know, the sun is up and he's obviously nocturnal, I realize that I'm gonna miss having the little guy around all the time if Bianca has changed her mind. We'll probably have to settle on joint visitation, although it will be nice to sleep fully through the night once again. In such a short time, though, I realize that I've already grown attached to him.

For the first time in my life, someone has depended on me to take care of them, to keep them safe and fed. He was more than just my responsibility. I actually enjoyed being the one who provided for him, and more and more often I find myself thinking about someday teaching him how to walk or how to throw a football…

But I'm not cut out to be a full-time dad.

My schedule is too stressful, and I'm constantly traveling. It wouldn't be good for Brady to grow up getting carted off from one stadium to another. Like the pediatrician said to me yesterday, babies need routines or whatever. Not to mention the fact that the media hounds would always be drooling to get a peek at him to earn a few bucks for some tabloid photos. It's a miracle that we've kept it quiet this long.

Besides, a baby needs a mother in his life, even if she occasionally makes bad decisions, like dropping him off with a stranger.

Taking a deep breath, I finally reach out and push the doorbell, hearing the chimes echo from inside the house.

I'm expecting a raven-haired, tattooed girl to open the door, the one that I only vaguely remember thanks to my friends' description of her.

Instead, I come face to face with a tiny, sweet-looking lady in her late twenties or early thirties wearing very feminine pink and white striped satin pajamas. Her blonde hair is cut short so that with it pushed behind her ears, it's even with her chin. Not wearing an ounce of makeup, she has high cheekbones, and her tan skin is flawless, nearly luminescent. She's just one of those natural beauties, but her big, stormy grayish-green eyes are red-rimmed and sad as they blink up at me, *waaayyy* up at me since I'm towering at least a foot and a half over her.

"Can I help you?" she asks, crossing her arms over her chest with an unimpressed frown on her face. It's a much different greeting from the usual flirty smile and batted lashes women typically give me. I guess the bags under my eyes are not very attractive, and my blue wrinkled tee and jeans are unimpressive.

"Hi, I'm, ah, looking for Bianca. The *Limelight* said that this was the, um, address she listed, you know, on her employment application or whatever," I try to explain, but it comes out somewhat tongue-tied, which is definitely a first. I'm sure it's just the lack of sleep slowing down my tired brain.

"Who are you?" the lady asks with an annoyed sigh and tilt of her head like her neck is hurting from looking up at me for so long.

Everyone knows who I am, especially in this city. In fact, I don't remember the last time a woman *didn't* recognize me right away as some sort of professional athlete. Obviously, this little fairy princess is not a football fan, which I have to admit is a damn shame.

"Why are you looking for Bianca?" she prompts, moving her hands to her hips impatiently while I continue to stare down at her, remaining uncharacteristically mute.

"Oh, well, ah, funny story," I start, choking out a gruff chuckle that I try to cover up as a cough. "A few days ago, I believe Bianca may have left something of hers behind on my doorstep."

"What? What did my sister leave?" she asks in annoyance.

Stepping aside so that my large frame is no longer blocking the view of him, I wave a hand in the direction of the sleeping baby.

Taking a step forward, the woman gasps and sinks to her knees in front of Brady, reminding me of Roxy's initial reaction. After she slaps a palm to her gaping mouth, her eyes begin to leak, which for some reason makes my chest ache for her.

With a shaky hand, she reaches out and gently soothes her fingertips over Brady's chubby cheek and then down to his little, balled up fists. Her touch is so loving and reverent that I almost feel guilty for intruding on such a private moment.

"Are you...are you his father?" she eventually asks, getting back to her unsteady feet while drying her face with the sleeves of her pajamas.

"No freaking idea," I answer with another chuckle. "Still waiting on the DNA test results, but I guess it's possible since I don't remember shit about that night with Bianca..."

That's the last word I get out of my mouth before the petite, sad, dainty-looking woman sucker punches me with her tiny fist, right in my fucking face.

"Ow! What the hell?" I ask while clutching my now throbbing chin. Sure, I get hit by three-hundred pound men all the time, but not smack dab on my pretty face thanks to the helmet and facemask I wear during games. "Why the hell did you hit me?"

"This is all your fault!" she exclaims.

"My fault?" I repeat. "I was drunk that night, but Bianca wasn't, not that I remember. So I contend that this clearly falls fifty-fifty on the responsibility scale," I argue. "And wow, it may not even be my kid! We won't know until we get the results back Thursday or Friday. Who are you anyways?"

"I'm Bianca's sister," the feisty fairy woman answers. "I don't know what she was thinking. She should've brought him to me!" she shouts before she bends over and picks up the car seat that's half her size.

"Whoa, whoa, whoa," I say, growing protective of Brady when she starts to walk back into the house with him. "Is Bianca here? Because no offense, but I think this is between her and me."

"Thanks to you, she's dead! And *no offense*, but you can join her for all I care," she says before slamming the front door in my still aching face.

Holy shit.

"Bianca's *dead*? When? How?" I ask, completely confused since Brady's only a few days old.

The wooden structure in front of me doesn't answer any of my many questions, so I start pressing the doorbell, ringing it over and over again until I can get some answers.

CHAPTER SIX

Callie

I can't believe he's alive and healthy! A beautiful little boy!
Unfastening his harness, I pull him out and hug him to me while sitting on the floor, not caring if it wakes him.

I was so fucking furious with Bianca for abandoning her baby, but now I feel guilty for thinking the worst of my drug dependent sister. I figured she had aborted him, or gotten high and tossed him carelessly in some dumpster.

I'll always feel terrible for not forgiving my sister, for not doing more to save her, for kicking her out of my house after I found out about her and John's affair, and then refusing to help her once she told me she was pregnant. But I'm so thankful that she didn't harm her son. She should've left him with me, not some stranger, but I know I brought this on myself when I pushed her out of my life.

Vaguely, I notice that my doorbell is ringing continuously in the background. After it rings for more than a handful of minutes, I finally give up. The Jolly Green Giant outside is obviously not going away anytime soon.

Marching across the living room floor, I open the door with the baby still clutched to my shoulder.

"What?" I ask him.

"You can't just drop that bomb and walk away from me, woman!" the Giant says with narrowed blue eyes.

"Yes, I can," I tell him.

"Please tell me what happened to her," he begs, looking so miserable that I cave on a sigh.

"Fine. You, if you are his father, stupidly knocked up my sister, who was a heroin addict. Since he seems healthy, I'm guessing that she stopped using while she was pregnant. But then after she had him, Bianca went and overdosed late Saturday night. She passed away Sunday. Therefore, her death is on you!"

"On me?" he asks with his jaw hanging open. And yeah, I can't help but notice he has a handsome, sculpted diamond shaped face to match his stunning blue eyes. It's easy to see why Bianca slept with him. Not only is he attractive; but even in jeans and a wrinkled tee, he looks rich, which is right up her alley. The Land Rover parked at the curb confirms as much.

"How is the fact that your sister overdosed *my* fault?" the Giant asks.

"You're just like all the rest she screws for money," I tell him. "How much did you pay her for sex?"

He cringes, telling me that despite his attractiveness, he actually *did* give Bianca money to fuck her. Ugh, that's so disgusting. I start to close the door in his face again, but he quickly lunges forward and slaps a hand on it before it shuts.

"I don't pay women to have sex with me," he replies. "But yeah, okay, I may have given her some money that night, but I was drunk and confused. My friends said I thought I was in a strip club asking for a lap dance. I'm sorry I did that, and I'm sorry I slept with her. I'm...I'm also sorry that she's gone."

"Save your apologies since they aren't worth a shit," I reply with a scoff. "Now leave before I call the police."

"Ha!" he laughs. "Go ahead. Try it. I'm sure they would love to stop by and get my autograph."

"Autograph?" I repeat.

"Yeah. I take it you're not a football fan."

"No, not really," I answer honestly since I've never really been into any type of sports.

"Well, I'm the starting quarterback for the Wilmington Wildcats," he says while puffing his broad chest. "Last year I was the second best in the league."

"Wow. Impressive," I reply sarcastically with a roll of my eyes. "Now leave."

"Fine," he says. "I'll leave, just as soon as you give me the kid back."

Gasping in horror at the thought of letting this baby go after just getting him back, I release the door to hold him to me tighter with both arms around him. "Not gonna happen," I tell the giant.

"Then I'm not leaving," he says as he enters the house, causing me to take a few steps backward so that I can look up at his face without getting a crick in my neck.

"You said you may not even be the father!" I respond with a huff.

"Bianca left him with me because she obviously wanted me to take care of him," he says, his words hitting me like a slap in the face. Or a punch, sort of like the one to his hard chin that left my knuckles swollen and aching.

"I'm her next of kin, so I'm *his* next of kin unless you turn out to be his father, which I wouldn't be so sure of. If that is the case, then I'll see you in court," I warn him.

"You can't be serious," he mutters, running his hand through his jet-black hair that I now notice looks vaguely like a Mohawk. On anyone else, the hairstyle would probably look ridiculous, but on him, well, it doesn't make him less attractive.

"Look, hot shot," I start. "I appreciate you bringing him by, but your job here is done. Go back to getting drunk, fucking random women, or whatever else you do."

"Hotshot?" he repeats with raised eyebrows and the right corner of his lips lifted in a smirk.

"Whatever," I answer. "Yesterday I had to say goodbye to my twenty-three-year-old sister before they cremated her. I thought she had the baby and tossed him in a dumpster or...or traded him for drug money, so I'm relieved that you've kept him safe. But now he's my responsibility, not yours."

"Unless I'm his father," he replies. "And if so, how do I know that you're gonna take care of him? With everything you've got going on, you seem rather emotional and unequipped to look after a baby. So, I'll just hang on to Brady until the test results come back," he says before reaching for the baby on my shoulder.

"Remove your hands from him, or I will bite them off," I warn him.

Ever so slowly he drops his hands and stares at me for several long, silent moments.

"What do you say we compromise?" he asks. "We should talk, get to know each other. Let me take you out to lunch, and Brady can come with us."

"You want to take me *out*? What, like on a date?" I ask skeptically.

He nods in response.

"Hell no. Are you as delusional as you are tall?" I scoff. "I don't even know your name."

His reaction is definitely not one I was expecting.

Chuckling, the giant raises his fists in the air and exclaims, "Yes, finally!"

"Finally?" I repeat.

"Yeah, *finally*," he answers.

"What does that mean?" I ask.

"That means, game on, baby," he replies, followed by an enormous grin and a wink that warms me up from head to...well, not down to my toes, but a much lower spot, giving new, literal meaning to the phrase "panty-melting smile."

And then I can't help but wonder who the heck this man is and what the hell I've gotten myself into.

CHAPTER SEVEN

Quinton

"Who are you, anyway?" the cute pixie lady asks as I follow her further into the house, refusing to leave despite her repetitive demands.

"Quinton Dunn," I say. And when she finally faces me again in the quaint little living room, I offer her my hand to shake. She hesitates before quickly removing her palm from Brady's back to take it. Brady's palm can't be much smaller than hers.

"Callie Clarke," she responds in a rush that I barely catch. "How long have you had him?" she asks, taking a seat on the sofa.

"Since Saturday night," I tell her, lowering myself onto the seat across the coffee table from her.

"And Bianca...she just...left him with you?" she asks, looking down at the baby on her shoulder as if she already loves him and can't imagine a mother doing such a thing.

"Yeah, he was in the seat, and there was a bag with food and a few diapers, along with a note that said he was mine. She didn't even put her name on it."

"And let me guess, you had no idea which of your many...romps he came from," she assumes correctly. But I decide to try and minimize the truth, because for some reason I don't want her to know the full extent of my manwhore ways. She already dislikes me, has punched me in the face and rejected me, so why make it worse?

"Sunday I had a game, and last night it was getting late, but it only took me a day to track Bianca here. So I don't have as many *romps* as you think," I reply, withholding the fact that it was my friends who remembered what her sister looked like and not me. Without Cameron and Nixon, I would've been so fucked.

"So, Cassie, do you live here, you know, alone?" I ask while glancing around the living space that's definitely all feminine.

When my question is met with silence, my eyes finally meet her cloudy gray ones that still look irritated at me, like I'm a dirty, mangy, stray dog that won't leave.

"It's *Callie*, and do you really think I'm gonna open up and give you, a stranger, the intimate details of my life?" she asks with an indignant huff.

She thinks I'm a stranger, the man millions of people recognize on sight.

Nice.

"Guess not," I reply with a smile I try to hide since her reaction to me is exactly what all other women's should be. Getting to my feet, I tell her, "Well, it's been great meeting you, *Callie*, and I'm really sorry about Bianca, but I should get him back to the house."

"You can go, but he's staying," the woman looks up and says, clutching Brady to her shoulder.

"Look, there's no reason to be difficult. Just like we don't know if I'm his father, we don't even know for sure if Bianca is the one who left him on my doorstep, right?"

"She was found after she had just given birth, but there was no sign of the baby. So I think it's safe to assume..." she argues with moisture filling her eyes.

"Well, I think we should get a DNA test for you too to make

sure," I challenge, not to be an ass but because I don't want there to be any doubt.

"You can't be serious!"

"I'm very serious, woman. This is a kid's life we're talking about. We can't just bounce him around from one person to the next."

"You're right," she says while standing with Brady and walking toward the kitchen. I follow behind her and see her pick up her cell phone from the counter. "We need to get attorneys to figure all this out. I'll call mine."

"Holy shit," I mutter, running my fingers over my Mohawk. "I didn't say we had to pull out the big guns."

Leaning against the counter with Brady still on her shoulder she says to me, "I don't know who the hell you are, but you're *not* leaving this house with my nephew. I'm guessing you don't know a thing about babies either, do you?"

"I'm learning," I reply defensively. "And I have help, a full-time nanny."

"Some stranger you're just gonna leave him with all day while you go gallivanting around? I don't think so."

"Gallivanting?" I repeat with both my eyebrows raised in offense. "I think you mean *working*."

"I thought you said you're a football player."

"I am."

"So then you can't really call that *work*," she remarks, making me gasp.

"Woman, did you seriously just insult my profession?" I ask. "You have no idea how hard I work, the hours and effort I put in to be one of the best quarterbacks in the entire country!"

"It's still just a game," she raises her chin defiantly and answers with a shrug.

"A game they pay me millions of dollars to play," I argue, but she doesn't even flinch at the mention of my bankrolls or look impressed. "So you know what that means, don't you?" I ask.

"What?" she asks on a heavy sigh. "You have more money than sense?"

"I have a shitload more money to spend on lawyers," I say while pulling out my cell phone from my pocket.

"You're such a giant prick!" she shouts, loud enough to cause Brady to wake up and start fussing. "Get out of my house!"

Having a woman try to get rid of me is a completely new experience. Getting insulted is a first too.

"Give me back my s...supposed son, and I'll leave," I say, barely catching my slip of calling him mine until those results come back. "And lower your voice, woman. You're upsetting him."

"Ugh! I'm calling the police to report you for trespassing!" she threatens while her fingers start pressing buttons on her phone.

"And I'm calling the police to report *you* for *kidnapping*," I counter while scrolling through my contacts to find my contract attorney's number. I doubt he will be of any help in this situation, but hopefully, Brian can get me a quick referral.

Noticing the time on my phone, I realize just how fucked I am. It's almost eleven o'clock. I'm supposed to be at the stadium watching tapes with the rest of the team in three hours.

Maybe I'm wrong, but I have a feeling that it's gonna take more than three hours to settle a custody dispute for a baby without a legal name.

Wandering off down the hall, I find an empty bedroom for some privacy, doubting the woman would let me back inside the house if I step outside to make a call. I try Lathan first since he's also a team captain, but he doesn't answer. Nixon doesn't either, so I reach out to Roxy. She thankfully answers on the third ring.

"How's it going, baby daddy?" she asks.

"Not good. Can you tell Coach that I've got a...situation that needs to be handled and I'll be in early tomorrow morning to watch the films before practice?"

"Oh, so you want me to be the one he yells at and loses his shit on?" she asks.

"Yeah, sorry," I tell her with a cringe. "I tracked down Brady's mother…"

"Oh good!" she exclaims.

"She's dead, Roxy," I tell her softly. "After she left Brady with me, she overdosed Saturday night."

"Oh no! That's awful."

"It is," I agree. "So now I'm here at her sister's house, and she's refusing to let me leave with Brady. Since I don't want to play tug of war with the kid or leave him here until I know whether or not he's mine, we're gonna have to get attorneys to figure it all out."

"Wow, that sounds rough. I'll cover for you, but you better get in here tomorrow morning, or you're gonna be screwed."

"I will," I promise her. "God, I can't wait for those results."

"How much longer do you have?" Roxy asks.

"Probably until Thursday or Friday. I don't know what I'm gonna do with this woman until then. She's…feisty."

"Feisty?" Roxy repeats.

"She socked me in my mouth!" I reply indignantly. "And, um, she turned me down for a lunch date. First time in the last forty-seven attempts since I've been keeping count."

"Some woman *hit* you *and* turned you down?" she repeats. "Is she old and ugly?"

"Neither."

"You mean the mythical creature who doesn't swoon at the sight of Quinton Dunn actually exists?"

"She does. I mean, she's cute and petite, and she *really* doesn't like me. I'm afraid things might get ugly, and she'll claw my eyeballs out."

Roxy giggles. "Sounds like you've met your match."

"I definitely have my work cut out for me."

"That's what you wanted, right? A challenge? The thrill of the chase?"

Just the thought of having to woo, to pursue a woman who hates me, has my blood pumping with an excitement that rivals stepping out onto the field before a game. I wanted Callie before she turned me down. What man wouldn't? She's sexy as hell. The problem is, I slept with her sister, who she just lost. She blames me for knocking Bianca up, and that's not gonna be something to easily overcome. But hell if I'm not anxious to try.

"What do I do?" I ask Roxy.

"What do you mean, what do you do?"

"I haven't asked a woman out since my senior prom. How do I get her to change her mind?"

"I don't know. Be nice to her? Don't use any of your ridiculous pick-up lines? Let her get to know you? Try and get to know her?" she suggests.

"Yeah, okay. I'll try all that," I say.

If every other woman in the world wants me, how hard can it be to convince this one woman to cave?

Callie

"Your honor, my client is better suited to be appointed the custodian of this child. As you'll see on the exhibits I've submitted, Mrs. Clarke has been previously vetted carefully for numerous adoption agencies, who all deemed her more than fit to be a mother," Amy Eastwood, my attorney, argues while we stand in an emptying courtroom late Tuesday afternoon.

The gray fox of a judge clears his throat before responding. "While I can certainly understand your position, counselor, the fact is that this court doesn't have any grounds on which to *allow* custody to Mrs. Clark nor Mr. Dunn until the DNA test results are submitted. Therefore, unless the two parties can agree to an out of court arrangement until then, I'm afraid I'll be forced to place the child in the custody of the State-"

"*NO!*"

The jerk and I both shout, interrupting the judge with our strong disagreement for that particular outcome. Even the cocky asshole is obviously aware of how god-awful it would be for that poor baby to be handed over to an overcrowded, shitty social services office.

"Your honor, Mr. Dunn has an endless amount of resources with which to take care of the child rather than putting more stress on our state's already depleted public service," the giant prick's attorney argues. "Mr. Dunn immediately sought the evaluation of a board-certified pediatrician who estimated that the child in question is only days old, much too young and fragile to enter the custody of the state."

"While I certainly appreciate your enthusiasm for your client, Mr. Billingsley, I cannot grant custody to a party based on financial means alone," the judge argues, looking over his bifocals at us. "Now, I'm going to recess court for fifteen minutes; and when I get back, I hope both parties will have disappeared so that I won't be forced to put a newborn in child protective custody."

"All rise. This honorable court will remain in recess for fifteen minutes," the bailiff calls out as the judge stands and then disappears through the door behind the bench.

"I'm sorry, Callie," Amy sits back down in her seat and says quietly to me. "You and Dunn need to figure something out because I would hate to see this little guy get lost in the system. The fact of the matter is, as of right now, *neither* of you have any rights to him. We don't even have a birth certificate for chrissakes."

"Ugh, why did my sister have to go and pull this shit?" I grumble. "Bianca should have brought him to me, and we wouldn't even be standing here!"

"Well, if the DNA says that Dunn is the biological father, he has a right to full custody of his son," Amy whispers quietly. "Basically you have two options, Callie. Either you can keep throwing away your money on my legal fees with a very good chance of walking away empty handed on anything but maybe infrequent visitation, or you can make nice with Dunn. See if you can convince him to voluntarily agree to some type of custody arrangement while simultaneously digging for as much dirt on him as you can. Unless we can provide evidence to the court for why Dunn shouldn't have custody, you're shit out of luck, girl."

Groaning, I lower my face into my palms, fighting back the tears that burn my eyes.

Dammit, Bianca! You knew how much I wanted a baby, how long I've tried to get pregnant! Is that why you did this? To hurt me more than you already have by destroying my marriage?

With an exhale, I lift my head and look at my nephew, who is sleeping peacefully in his carrier, while trying to figure out my next step. I don't care what the DNA tests show. Even if he came from the sperm of some rich, foolish playboy, this baby belongs with me, far away from a life that's probably nothing but partying and screwing random women...which gives me an idea.

"What kind of evidence would you need for me to win custody?" I ask my attorney while staring across the courtroom at the arrogant football player dressed in a suit that probably cost more than my car.

"Anything that would make him unfit to be a father," Amy answers with a shrug as she stands up and starts packing up her files into her briefcase. "You know, something serious like heavy alcohol or substance abuse, blatant promiscuity, child abuse or neglect..."

The hamsters in my head all jump on their wheels at the same time as a plan begins to form. There's nothing I wouldn't do to make this motherless boy mine. I already love him after only spending a few hours with him today, and I can't imagine handing him back over to a stranger.

"When you say evidence of those things, you mean, like, proof? Pictures, videos, witness statements?" I ask Amy.

"Exactly," she says with a nod. "But for now, let's find an empty conference room so we can try and negotiate a temporary resolution."

CHAPTER EIGHT

Quinton

"My client insists that he retain custody in his residence until we receive the test results," my attorney, Joseph Billingsley, says to the two women sitting across from us, Callie and her lawyer whose name I've already forgotten.

"Your client has to be willing to compromise, or we'll go right back in that courtroom—" Callie's attorney starts to argue before Callie places her hand on the sleeve of the woman's suit jacket to interrupt her.

"It's okay, Amy," Callie tells her attorney softly, the anger from earlier absent from her naturally beautiful face. In fact, her stormy green eyes now look...calculating. *Oh fuck.* "I can agree to those terms with certain conditions," Callie declares unexpectedly.

"Well, okay then. What conditions?" Joseph asks, leaning across the table on his forearms to show his interest in her offer.

"I want Mr. Dunn to allow me unrestricted, unlimited access to the baby," Callie clarifies while her eyes are locked on mine.

Joseph turns to face me with his eyebrows raised in questions, so I nod my agreement.

"We can agree to that, but only during the hours of nine a.m. to –" Joseph starts.

"No, she can see him whenever she wants," I interrupt. "Until we come back to court next week with both sets of test results, and as long as he remains in my custody."

"Agreed," Callie answers almost too easily.

"And are you two sure you can behave yourselves? Because I would hate to end up back here with the judge taking the baby away," Callie's attorney says.

"No more squabbling from me," Callie replies with her palms raised in the air.

"Good. Me either," I agree.

"Well, I'm glad we got this worked out. Amy, can you draft up a document for both of them to sign?" my attorney asks.

"Sure," the woman replies with a fake smile. "I would be happy to do your job for you, Joe."

"Hey, now!" Joseph starts, but I clear my throat in warning.

"You and your client can stop by the office on the way home," Callie's lawyer says as she and Callie stand to leave.

The attorney is already out the door while Callie stares silently down at Brady sleeping in his seat for several long moments before she walks out reluctantly.

"Wow, that went easier than expected," Joseph tells me.

"Yeah, a little too easy," I agree as I recall the angry, shouting woman from earlier. That Callie wasn't as scary as the one who just agreed to leave Brady behind with me.

"You didn't have to agree to anything," Joseph says. "That woman doesn't have a leg to stand on, and her attorney knows it."

"I don't mind. Her sister just died suddenly, so it doesn't feel right to take him away from her too," I reply.

"Well, just watch your back. Domestic cases can get ugly, especially where child custody is concerned. I wouldn't put anything past a woman who has spent years trying to adopt without success before filing for divorce. She's obviously desperate to have children."

"Whoa, divorce?" I repeat in surprise. "You mean Callie was married?"

"Nope," Joseph answers with a smile. "She *is* currently married. According to the court docs I dug up this afternoon, she and her husband have been separated for almost a year. The divorce should be finalized soon."

"Huh," I mutter in surprise. "Did it say why they're divorcing?"

"The same reason most marriages end," he tells me. "Adultery."

Damn. Callie's husband cheated on her? What an idiot. And then her sister up and dies from a drug overdose, leaving behind her baby with me, a stranger rather than her own blood. No wonder the woman was so angry this morning.

I don't like seeing Callie upset. She deserves some happiness in her life after all she's been through. And now, more than ever, with all the odds stacked against me, I want to wear her down until she actually agrees to date me. I'm a competitor at heart, and no one has ever said no to me before today. Or punched me. That was definitely a first I think as I reach up to rub my still slightly aching chin. Thank goodness she's not a very big woman or I would probably have one hell of a knot by now.

Callie's feistiness is hot, and I'll do anything to get her into my bed, anything except give her the one thing she wants, full custody of my son. If he's mine, I'll let her see him whenever she wants, which means I get to spend time with her too. But how long will it take before she turns against me for not letting her have him?

This might be harder than I thought to pull off.

A few hours later, Callie, Brady and I walk back into my house and are instantly greeted by Kelsey and the delicious smell of...

"Did you cook a roast?" I ask Kelsey as my stomach growls. After our long day, I've barely had anything to eat since the breakfast she made me.

"Yeah, with carrots and potatoes. Hope that's okay?" the young girl asks shyly.

"Hell yeah, that's okay. You're the best, Kelsey," I tell her.

"How did everything go?" she asks, looking between me and Callie, Brady's car seat sitting on the floor in between us.

"Brady's staying here for now. And, Kelsey, this is Callie, potentially his aunt, so she'll be visiting..."

"Brady? Why do you keep calling him that?" Callie turns and asks me. "I thought there wasn't a birth certificate."

"There's not, but I wanted to call him something other than *him*," I clarify.

"That's a horrible name," the woman says, more of her annoyance from earlier dripping through her momentary agreeability.

"I like it," Kelsey jumps in and says in my defense. "It's a cute name."

"Thanks," I tell her with a wink.

"Do you want me to get *Brady* changed? When did he last eat?" Kelsey asks as she starts toward his car seat to scoop him up.

"I'll do it," Callie snaps at her, bending down to pick up the car seat first. Kelsey gives me a wide-eyed, confused and questioning look, but I just shake my head and hand her the diaper bag to refill.

"The formula is running a little low and so are the diapers," I tell her.

"I'll get it restocked," she says before Callie jerks the bag from my hand.

"I've got it," she answers. "Now where's his room?"

"That would be in my room," I tell her. "Let me show you the way. Kelsey, can you go ahead and get some plates and everything out for dinner?" I ask her since I already know after just a few days together that the girl likes to constantly be helpful. She just runs around the house in circles if I don't give her something to do.

"Sure thing, Boss," Kelsey says before speed walking in the direction of the kitchen.

"You don't have to be so rude to her. She's just trying to help," I tell Callie as I show her the way down the hall to the master bedroom. I even let her carry Brady in the car seat since she's made it abundantly clear she wants to do it herself.

"Taking care of a baby isn't that big of a deal. It doesn't require a full-time, slutty nanny," Callie says in a huff.

"Watch it, woman," I abruptly spin around in the middle of the hallway to warn her. We're so close that her sweet, fruity smell invades my senses, temporarily distracting me before I recover and remember my indignation on Kelsey's behalf. "I get that you have a lot going on and that you don't particularly like me, but there's no reason to badmouth a nice girl who is just here trying to help me out," I snap at her.

"Whatever," she replies, lowering her stormy eyes in what I hope is a little humility.

Turning around and stepping inside my bedroom, I flip on the lights.

"So, here's his changing table. Extra diapers, wipes, and clothes are in the drawers," I tell her.

"Thanks," she mutters softly as she takes Brady out of his seat and lays him down on the table. "And I'm, ah, sorry about what I said."

"No problem," I say as I walk out of the room with a satisfied smile.

CHAPTER NINE

Callie

I'm feeling more than a little overwhelmed.

In fact, as soon as we walked into the waterfront mansion, I was so intimidated that I lashed out, forgetting my plan of playing nice to get some dirt on the football player. There was also something else bothering me that I wasn't expecting.

The young nanny is so pretty, and she was fawning all over Quinton. While I had no right to make assumptions about her, the first thing I thought was that her responsibilities probably include more than just taking care of the baby. Knowing a man like Quinton, well, make that *any* man but especially him, he probably wouldn't discourage her to give him a little more personal attention. Which is fine and none of my business, so why does the thought of her and him bother me?

As I'm changing the baby, I realize that instead of being a tad jealous of her, I need to be nice to the nanny, try to win her over and see if she has any secrets of Quinton's I can use in a custody case.

After we eat what I have to admit was a decent meal, Quinton takes Brady to feed him, not that I'm agreeing to use that name, and then I'm alone in the kitchen with Kelsey.

"So, how do you like working here?" I ask, trying not to sound too nosy while wiping down the table as she starts on the dishes.

"It's great. Quinton's really nice and pays me well," she answers.

"Well, that's good," I say. "Do you sleep here in the house too?"

"Yeah, and I get up when I hear Brady at night, but Quinton is usually already fixing his bottle," she says, which I have to admit is rather surprising. I assumed he would depend on the nanny to do everything for the baby, especially the late-night feedings.

And now that I think about it, the way she answered didn't sound like she's *sharing* a bed with Quinton, but I decide to delve deeper.

"So, you're not, you know, sleeping with him?" I ask.

"God, no," she exclaims, and then lowering her voice she says, "I mean, I would in a heartbeat if he asked, but he hasn't."

"Oh, well, is he seeing someone?" I ask.

"Not that I know of. There haven't been any women coming by other than Roxy."

Before I can inquire as to who this Roxy is, Kelsey informs me.

"Roxy's the team's new kicker, and she's seeing Kohen Hendricks. He usually comes by with her."

"Oh," I reply. "I thought football players were all about wild parties and lots of women."

"*Sorry to disappoint.*"

I jump when Quinton unexpectedly walks back into the kitchen cradling the baby in his arms. "Brady didn't want much of his bottle, so I'm gonna change him and put him to bed," he says to Kelsey, handing her the nearly full bottle to wash. "Then, I'm probably gonna try and get some sleep myself. Tomorrow morning I have to be at the stadium at eight a.m. to watch the films I missed today before practice starts."

"I guess I'll head home too," I tell them.

"I assume you'll be back in the morning?" Quinton asks me with a crooked smirk.

"Yeah," I agree.

"Do you have a job or what?" he asks.

"I work from home as an accountant," I reply. "The busiest times of year are January to April during tax season, so I have a lot of time off in the fall and winter..."

Quinton closes his eyes, throws his head back and pretends to snore. Loudly.

"Sorry," he says when he opens his bright blue eyes again, the usual lopsided grin on his face. "Just the job description put me to sleep."

"Well, not everyone can have careers as exciting as playing a game one day a week," I remark before I go over to press a goodbye kiss to the baby's forehead. "See you tomorrow."

"What? No kiss for me?" Quinton teases.

"I've got something you can kiss, all right," I mutter with a shake of my head before letting myself out the front door.

Later that night when I finally lay down in bed, it's impossible to fall asleep thanks to the excitement of the day and the emotional roller coaster of the week.

After rubbing Felix for a while, I finally give up on sleep, and I get up to start crocheting the new project idea I had earlier today. Years ago when I was bored, I went into a craft shop and picked up a beginner kit. Ever since, I've been hooked. Weaving the yarn in a repetitive pattern is a relaxing, stress relieving activity. And I've been doing a lot more of it since the divorce. Mostly I make pink and blue hats for the NICU babies, but I've also made a few blankets too.

Tonight, I need the hobby to help me get my mind off the baby. I miss Brady and hated having to leave him at Quinton's. It's not fair that I would give anything to be a mother, but fate always has other plans. Ones that involve letting a man who doesn't know the first thing about being a father have custody of my sister's son over me.

There has to be something I can do to convince Quinton that the baby is better off with me. His life is probably hectic and crazy, traveling all the time when I'm right here in this house ready and able to care of the little guy day and night.

And yeah, I can admit that Quinton has what appears to be a few good qualities and seems like a decent guy. He's just being so damn stubborn about custody. Maybe he's not even the father, and my sister had it all wrong. If that's true, there's no one but me who can legally have him. Unless John is later tested. I can admit that I would prefer Quinton as the biological father.

I guess we'll just have to wait for the results and see. Until then, I'll have to try to be cordial with Quinton and his nanny. The man's certainly easy on the eyes, incredibly tall, buff and handsome. There's something else about him that I can't put my finger on that makes him seem ridiculously desirable. Maybe it's the fact that he just looks like a virile man capable of impregnating dozens of women to repopulate the Earth after an apocalypse nearly wipes out all of mankind. It's a crazy notion since I have to assume that if Brady is his son, he's Quinton's *only* offspring and he doesn't really have an army of baby mamas.

Then, I can't help but wonder if I've never gotten pregnant because I was sleeping with the opposite type of man Quinton is. John is lazy and has no drive to succeed in anything except procuring drugs without me finding out. Oh, and sleeping with my sister. Thinking of them side by side, my money is on Quinton being the father of Bianca's baby. There's no way John could be responsible since his sperm obviously takes after him.

I blame those foolish thoughts for causing me to wake up in the middle of the night with my hand in my panties thanks to a fantasy involving a giant football player having his way with me. In fact, I'm so far gone that I bite my bottom lip and continue to let myself imagine being pinned down by the strong, sweaty man pumping into me while promising not to stop until he gives me a baby.

FEELING ONLY a smidge embarrassed by my naughty dream last night involving the man I currently loathe, I ring his doorbell around eight-thirty, expecting the nanny to answer. Instead, a frazzled looking Quinton with his black Mohawk all askew opens the door and walks back into the house, barely acknowledging me.

Once I step inside and shut the door behind me, I realize why.

The baby is screaming at the top of his lungs.

"What's wrong with him?" I ask Quinton as I jog to catch up with him on the way back to his bedroom. "And aren't you supposed to be gone by now?"

"He's been like this *all* night," Quinton tells me once we reach the room where Kelsey is pacing the floors, bouncing the baby on her shoulder, her hair also unbrushed.

"Is he hungry?" I ask, holding my arms out to take him from Kelsey, who passes him to me with a relieved sigh.

"No," she answers, nodding to the full bottle on the dresser. "We keep trying, but he's barely eaten since last night."

"He slept a lot yesterday. I had to wake him up to feed him," Quinton says with his phone in his hand. "The pediatrician's office should be open now. I'm gonna call and get him an appointment."

"Good," I say before I start bouncing Brady on my shoulder and making a shushing sound to try and soothe him. It doesn't work.

Quinton has to walk out of the room to make the phone call since the baby is crying so loudly.

"I feel so bad. I told Quinton I could take him to the doctor so he wouldn't miss practice, but he insisted on staying," Kelsey says.

"Yeah, he should go, and I can stay with you," I agree. "We'll be fine."

"Well, maybe you can convince him," she tells me. "I'm pretty sure he's not supposed to miss any time with the team."

I start to say it's just a freaking game but refrain since that wouldn't be very nice or helpful.

"What's wrong, little boy?" I ask the baby. He doesn't respond. I put my palm over his forehead to check and see if he's running a temperature, but he doesn't feel feverish.

"Okay, they can see him at nine-thirty," Quinton tells us when he walks back in the room.

"Kelsey and I can take him if you need to head to the stadium," I assure him.

"I don't know," he answers with a shake of his head. "What if there's something wrong?"

"Let me get your cell phone number; and if so, I'll call you right away. Otherwise, it's probably just gonna be a lot of sitting around and waiting on the doctor."

"Yeah, I guess," he replies, running a hand over his head. "If you're sure, then I should head on in. Maybe I can leave early..."

"We'll be fine," I tell him with a wave of my hand. "Go."

"Kelsey can give you my cell and the numbers to have them page me at the stadium and practice field," he says, just before I experience temporary blindness.

Quinton swiftly yanks his white t-shirt over his head and then walks shirtless over to the dresser to pull on another one. The man in my imagination last night was a sorry substitute for the real thing. I knew he was obviously muscular underneath his clothing, but I didn't expect all the smooth, tan skin or chiseled abs.

"Tell them to bill me for the visit," Quinton says, barely penetrating the hypnotic trance I'm under as he drops his pants and pulls on a pair of jeans just as quickly over his red boxer briefs. Way too quickly. "They have my information on file from when I brought him in for a check-up on Monday. I swear they told me he was perfectly healthy."

When my lips suddenly go dry, I realize my mouth is hanging wide open, so I make a point to shut it before he sees. A glance over to Kelsey reveals that I'm not the only one in awe of the giant's body.

"Call me after you see the doctor and let me know what they say," Quinton tells us while shoving his feet in a pair of athletic shoes.

"We will," I assure him, feeling much more agreeable than usual toward him. Must have been the partial glimpse at his nudity.

As Quinton comes closer, I finally notice that his normally bright, blue eyes not only look heavy with weariness but are also full of worry. Leaning down, he places a gentle kiss on Brady's head and then surprises the shit out of me when he cups my jaw, the same one that was only moments ago hanging open at the sight of his amazing body.

"Thank you," he says softly before pulling his enormous palm away.

He says something to Kelsey as well over the crying baby as he leaves the room, but my brain is all fizzled out, my cheek still warm and tingly from his caress.

"Wow," Kelsey mutters, and then she dramatically faints onto Quinton's unmade, island-sized king bed. "Is it just me or does he smell absolutely edible?" she asks while actually sniffing the man's sheets. And yeah, if there weren't any witnesses, I might do the same for another hit of Quinton's clean, masculine woodsy scent.

"If you say so," I tell her offhandedly, trying hard not to sound affected. "We better start getting Brady's bag packed up."

"Yeah," Kelsey says, rolling and rutting around in the sheets like she's making snow angels before she eventually gets to her feet with a dreamy smile on her exhausted face. "Don't tell him, but I would've worked for him for free."

"Your secret is safe with me," I reply with an amused eye roll.

"Do you mind if I grab a quick shower? It won't take me but like ten minutes, and then I'll get his diaper bag packed."

"Sure," I say, glad to have a moment alone to do some snooping through Quinton's room.

Once Kelsey leaves, I wait until I hear the shower come on down the hall; and then, still holding the crying baby to me, I head for the bedside table. A gasp leaves my mouth as I take in all the objects --- a mountain of supersized condoms, some lube, a pair of fuzzy handcuffs, and a vibrator. Wow. While those are rather shocking to find, it's nothing really out of the ordinary for a single man who likely has a revolving door of women in his bed. And yeah, I feel sort of stupid and embarrassed for being nosy. Also, a little curious about what he does with those items...

Shutting the drawer, I go around the bed to search the other side table's drawer. In that one, I find nothing but boring sports magazines. Well, that's not nearly as exciting.

There has to be some sort of dirt on Quinton that I could use in court.

For now, my investigating will have to wait because my head is already pounding from the baby's constant cries near my ear. I feel terrible for the little guy and wish I knew what was wrong. Hopefully, it's nothing serious.

CHAPTER TEN

Quinton

My eyes try to focus on the screen in front of me as I sit in the stadium's viewing room, but my mind isn't really processing what I'm seeing like it should be.

Instead, I keep glancing down at my phone, checking the time and waiting for messages from Kelsey or Callie. In my gut, I know that something is seriously wrong with Brady. The kid wouldn't just scream all night, refusing to eat if he was fine. Without knowing shit about taking care of babies, I'm certain of that.

"Quinton? Are you paying attention?" Coach Griffin snaps at me, pausing the video.

"Ah, yeah, Coach," I answer, jerking my head up, focusing harder on the screen.

"Then how many seconds did you hold the ball on that last play?" he asks.

"Um, long enough to get sacked," I answer.

"And did you see that Cameron was open down the field?" he asks, rewinding the play to point out the huge opening I missed. "He had five steps on Atlanta's corner and could've ran that in for a touchdown."

"You're right," I say in agreement at the same moment my phone starts to ring from an unknown caller. "Shit. Sorry, Coach, but I've gotta take this," I tell him before answering. "Hello?"

"Hey, Quinton," the sweet feminine voice says, and it only takes me a second to realize it's Callie.

"Hey, what did the doctor say?" I ask.

"They did some bloodwork, and Brady's bilirubin level was high–"

"His *what* levels?" I interrupt.

"Bilirubin. He has jaundice," she explains. "The doctor said it's very common and sometimes doesn't show up until a few days after birth. His levels have doubled since they checked on Monday."

Jaundice? That sounds serious.

"So, now what?" I ask her. "Do they give him medicine or something to make it better?"

"Ah, no," she replies. "We're on the way over to the hospital–"

"The hospital?" I shout as I get to my feet.

"They're just gonna admit him to do some phototherapy, you know, put him under a special light. He may even get to come home with a wearable light tomorrow if his bilirubin levels come down enough..."

"So, wait, they're *admitting* him into the hospital overnight?" I ask in concern.

"Yeah, just for a day, maybe two to get the levels down quickly."

"Okay, I'm on my way. Which hospital?"

"Dobson Memorial on West Waterford Drive," she answers. "But you don't have to come right now –"

"See you in a few," I tell her before ending the call. "Sorry, Coach, but I've gotta go. The baby's being admitted into the hospital with jaundice."

"Quinton, all of us have families too, but this is your team. You're one of the captains and the rest of the team depends on you to help us win games."

"I'll be ready to play Sunday," I assure him as I start for the door.

"He may not even be your kid!" Coach argues.

"Maybe. Maybe not," I turn around and answer. "But his mother left him with me to take care of him. Until we have answers, he's my responsibility."

"Don't miss practice this afternoon!" he calls out to my back. "If you do, I'll have no choice but to bench you."

"You can't be serious!" I yell at him, my anger battling its way out to overcome the exhaustion. "I have given *everything* to this team for three years, and now I just need a few days -"

"Your personal life has gotten out of control, Quinton, and you know it! If that *is* your kid, then you were reckless months ago, just like you're being irresponsible now."

Coach's unexpectedly harsh words pull me up short, hurting even more because I know they're the truth. That doesn't mean I'll back down on this particular issue.

"Bench me. See if I give a shit, because you know the only chance this team has of winning is with me playing," I tell him through clenched teeth. "I hope whatever point you're trying to make here is worth losing."

On the short drive to the hospital, the realization of what I just did hits me.

Did I seriously just walk out on my team?

Yes, I believe I did.

And while football has always been the most important thing in my life, the one and only thing I'm good at, there's not an ounce of regret in me for what I did.

Last night I maybe only got two hours of sleep and not just because Brady was crying but because I was worried about him. I knew something was wrong, but I didn't do anything. I should've taken him to the emergency room instead of waiting all damn night.

Now, they're putting him in the hospital. It was my responsibility to take care of him, and I let him down.

Right before I pull up in the hospital's parking lot, my phone thankfully dings with a new text message from Callie telling me they've checked in and are getting settled in the room on the third floor in the NICU center.

Right off the elevators, I spot a nurse at the front desk. "Hi, I'm looking for...Brady Dunn's room," I say, hesitating over his name since it's the first time I've ever spoken it aloud. It's the name I wrote down on all the paperwork at the pediatrician's office Monday since he doesn't have any other name.

The middle-aged brunette looks up at me, and her eyes widen in recognition. "You're Quinton Dunn," she says with a gasp.

Shit.

For the first time, I realize how bad this will be if this gets out, a baby that may or may not be mine from a woman who overdosed on drugs. Callie doesn't need that shit on her right now, the media badmouthing her dead sister. And while some of the coaches and a few close teammates know about Brady, I had hoped to keep everything quiet in the press until we get the paternity results back and we know for certain. I really don't want to deal with any of that crazy shit right now since there's enough to worry about with Brady being in here.

"Could you please not tell anyone...?"

"Of course we won't tell anyone," the nurse responds with a huff. "But you should be careful coming in and out of the hospital. Anyone could see you, and you're very recognizable."

"You're right, I know," I admit.

"I'm the supervising nurse, and I'll talk to everyone on the floor to remind them patient information is HIPAA protected. And if anyone asks, we'll just tell them you're visiting with some of your pediatric fans," she replies with a wink.

"Thank you," I reply, hoping I can trust her. And then a thought hits me. "Do I...do I have pediatric fans here?" I ask.

"Of course. You're Quinton Dunn! There are several guys and girls battling cancer who I bet you could cheer up with a quick visit."

Damn, that's sad as shit. I freaked out when Callie told me Brady has jaundice, so I couldn't imagine how the kids and parents deal with something as life threatening as cancer.

"I'll, um, I'll ask my manager to bring by some jerseys, footballs and stuffed wildcats if you can give me a list of how many I need," I tell her.

"Why, Mr. Dunn, that would be so generous of you," she says with a smile. "I'll get right on it."

"It's the least I can do," I tell her, feeling sort of bad for not thinking of doing something for the kids here sooner. "For now, can you show me where to find Brady? How's he doing?" I ask.

"Sure, and we just got him all settled in. First, you'll need to get a bracelet that matches his. Only family can see him," she tells me as she types on the computer in front of her. "Let me print you one up real quick, and then I'll take you back."

A few minutes later and I'm finally stepping into Brady's room for the first time.

Holy shit.

The little guy looks so tiny and fragile inside the enclosed plastic container, lying underneath a bright blue light. He's completely naked except for his diaper and a dark blindfold over his eyes.

"Hey," Callie says from off to the right. I look over to see her getting up from the sofa against the wall.

"Hey," I reply. "How is he?"

"They just laid him down," she tells me, coming over to stand beside me to see into his bed. "The warmth must feel nice, or he finally gave into the exhaustion, because he stopped crying and fell right to sleep."

"Good," I reply on a relieved exhale. "Has he had anything to eat?"

"About two ounces while we were waiting for the doctor," she answers. "His weight's gone down about half a pound since Monday, but the doctor said he'll probably want to eat more tomorrow. They're gonna draw blood to check his bilirubin levels every twelve hours."

"So they think he's gonna be okay?" I ask.

"Of course. They see this all the time. I think the doctor said that about three in five babies become jaundiced. It's very common."

"Good," I reply, some of the stress and tension leaving my body. "Now we just...wait?"

"Yeah. I can stay with him if you need to go –"

"No!" I growl, cutting her off. "I'm staying, and that's the end of the discussion!"

"Sorry, I just wasn't sure..." she trails off, taking a step back from me.

Rubbing a hand over my face, I take a deep breath to try and calm down. "I didn't mean to snap at you. It's just been a rough morning, and last night was horrible. I'm worried and tired and cranky..."

"Well, then why don't you come sit down and rest? Try to take a little nap while he's sleeping," Callie says before she takes my hand in hers and leads me to the vinyl sofa.

"You sure?" I ask her. "I feel like...I dunno, like I need to be doing something."

Taking a seat, she pulls me down next to her. "The light is all Brady needs right now, so get some rest."

With a heavy sigh, I lean my head back on the sofa cushion but don't let her hand go yet. Surprisingly, Callie doesn't try to pull away from me either. I've never been much of a hand holder, but I can admit that it's nice and comforting right now in this moment, like my anchor during a hurricane, keeping me from getting lost at sea.

"Where's Kelsey?" I roll my head toward Callie to ask, mostly just because it gives me a reason to look at her beautiful face again.

"She took my car back to the house to get some sleep. The poor girl was a zombie," Callie says with a small smile. She doesn't sound the least bit hostile toward Kelsey; unlike she did yesterday when she first met her.

"You like her," I point out with my own grin.

"She's a nice girl."

"Yeah, she is."

"And she has a huge crush on you, by the way," Callie says, making me bark out a laugh.

"Oh yeah?" I ask.

"Like you didn't know," Callie huffs with an eye roll.

"I didn't," I reply while looking back over to check on the brightly glowing baby. "And even if that's true, she's a little young for me. Besides, I'm currently taking a hiatus from women thanks to that little glow worm."

"A hiatus?" Callie asks. "Yeah, right. Like that will last more than a week."

"It'll last," I assure her, because the woman currently holding my hand is the only one I've wanted since I first saw her yesterday morning. The one woman who has ever actually turned me down. "Wanna place a bet?" I ask her.

"Sure," she says. "If I win, you let Brady stay with me for an entire weekend."

"Deal," I say, even though it's possible that in a few days, based on the results of a test, he could be spending every day with her. I try not to dwell on that possibility. There's no point worrying about something I have no control over. Either he's mine, or he's not. We'll find out soon enough and deal with the results when the time comes.

"If I win," I start while stroking my thumb back and forth over her knuckles without looking at her. "You have to let me kiss you."

From the corner of my eye, I see Callie's head turn away from me, glancing out the hospital window as I hold my breath waiting for her response.

"Fine," she eventually agrees. "One kiss. Now get some sleep before you say anything else crazy."

And so I finally close my eyes and give in to the exhaustion, feeling a little more optimistic about everything than I did ten minutes ago.

CHAPTER ELEVEN

Callie

When Quinton's head falls limply onto my shoulder about fifteen minutes after he closed his eyes, I try not to flinch and wake him. He's tired and needs the sleep. It's not like it's all that uncomfortable to have a giant man resting on me. Still holding my hand while he's slumped on the uncomfortable sofa, his long legs spread wide in front of him, he sort of reminds me of a big baby who is just looking for a little comfort.

That opinion changes a few minutes later when he pulls my hand over to the top of his thigh, right up against his very big cock. Looking at his face, I try to determine if he's actually awake and just messing with me or not, but his blue eyes are sealed shut; long, dark lashes resting on his cheeks. Just like Brady's.

I'm starting to believe Quinton really is his father; and if so, that means my chances of getting custody of my sister's son are dwindling rapidly. And while my heart is already breaking with the truth of the matter, I realize that trying to make Quinton look like an unfit father is going to be much harder than I originally thought. Perhaps it's even impossible.

Speaking of harder...my knuckles are currently being dragged up and down the growing length next to the fly on Quinton's jeans. And I would be lying if I said I wasn't impressed or...a little turned on, imagining the place between my legs made just for such a long, thick object. I blame my fifteen-month celibacy for the reason my heart begins to speed up and why my thighs clench at the idea of having him inside me. Fifteen long months of my deteriorating fertility wasted after catching my worthless piece of shit husband cheating on me with my sister.

It's not as if sex with John was ever...good. No, it was just a means to an end, one he could never successfully fulfill. So many years with him wasted, and now time is running out.

On the other hand, the Jolly Green Giant beside me looks, and now I am all too aware that he feels too, like he was made for the sole purpose in life for procreating. Is that why so many women swoon over him? Because their ovaries know he's the epitome of virile?

"Mmm," Quinton moans in his sleep at the same time he squirms further down into the seat. After that, the pressure he places on my hand pumping his cock increases like he needs more. Which is why I'm not all that surprised when he releases my fingers interlaced with his in order to cover his bulge with my palm. For curiosity's sake only, of course, I squeeze his shaft.

Wow.

Quinton should've played baseball instead of football because he's swinging a freaking bat between his legs. Watching the room door for signs of the nurse, I may or may not start stroking his growing shaft to see how much bigger it will get. Apparently, I'm not jerking him fast enough since Quinton's giant hand covers mine to move it quicker while his hips start to lightly thrust, getting involved in the action. And the throbbing between my own legs says I'm not as unaffected by him as I thought.

"Come on, Callie. You won't break it," Quinton mumbles, startling me, but his eyes are still shut. He's having a dream obviously; and in that dream he's with me, of all people? No, that's impossible.

I don't get the time to dwell on his words, though, because his hand squeezes mine harder before he lets go to rub his thumb over the head of his cock through the denim. His muscular body shudders, and then I realize he's coming in his pants, all thanks to my hand job.

Surprisingly, that doesn't make him wake up either. If anything, he heaves a sigh, like all the tension has been released from his body. I ease out from underneath him, laying his head back on the seat. Standing on wobbly legs, I look in the cabinets for a blanket, which I thankfully find, mostly to hide the wet spot on his jeans that I feel a little guilty about rather than to provide him with the warmth. With a quick check on Brady, who is still sound asleep, I escape from the room, jog down the stairs and head out the front doors of the hospital to grab some fresh air.

What the heck did I just do?

~

Quinton

I WAKE with a horrible crick in the right side of my neck, so I try to roll over and get more comfortable. Thankfully, my quick reflexes allow me to catch myself before I land on the floor. Sitting up, I see the bright blue glow across the room and remember that I'm in the hospital with Brady, who has jaundice. Guess I passed out when I sat down with Callie after going three nights without much sleep.

Just as I start to stand up to stretch and check on Brady, I notice the blue blanket on my lap, the one covering quite a big wet spot on the crotch of my jeans. A very sticky wet spot.

Are you fucking kidding me?

I had a wet dream in the middle of the day in a hospital room? Who does that?

Although, I can admit that I don't feel nearly as frantic and anxious as I was when I first found out Brady was here. Now I'm just embarrassed as shit.

Then, I remember holding Callie's hand and sitting down next to her on this sofa. Oh, God. She must've been the one who covered me with the blanket. Was she still in here when I came in my pants too?

As uptight as that woman is, she'll never forget this or forgive it. Thankfully, she can't read my mind, or she would probably be even more pissed because I'm pretty sure I was having a dream about her. Yeah, she was lying in my bed wearing a white, cock-teasing negligee, but she refused to let me fuck her despite how much I begged. Instead, she declared she could only give me a hand job, hence the mess in my pants.

Fuck.

I'm about to stand up to check on Brady before trying to do damage control in a bathroom when the room door opens, and Lathan and the nurse from the front desk walk in. I lean back against the sofa again, deciding to keep the blanket on my lap.

"This man claims he's your brother," the nurse tells me with a skeptical scowl as she comes over with a piece of paper.

"Ah, yeah. He was adopted," I reply with a grin. "See, we have the same haircut."

"Right, well, he can stay as long as you're here with him. And here's the list you asked for," she says, handing over the paper before leaving the room again.

"Whoa," Lathan mutters as he walks up to the plastic container where the baby is sleeping. "He looks so pitiful in there," he glances over to me and says, echoing my sentiments.

"Yeah, but he's stopped crying and is finally sleeping, so I think it's good for him," I reply, folding the list of kids' names and setting it beside me so I can call Wilson and ask him to bring by the items after Lathan leaves. "Thanks for coming by."

"Sure," he says before he strolls over and takes the seat next to me.

"I had a quick nap," I explain with a tug on the blanket. "He didn't sleep at all last night, and not much the two nights before."

"So sleep deprivation is your reason for pissing off coach and getting benched for the first quarter Sunday?" he asks me with narrowed green eyes.

Ah, so I guess Coach Griffin decided on my punishment. He's gonna make me sit out the first quarter while my backup probably plays like shit. That way all the fans and my teammates can be angry at me when they realize I was benched for missing practice.

"Brady's my responsibility, at least for now," I explain. "Without a birth certificate, he can't go on anyone's insurance. I'm paying the medical bills, so they'll do what they have to for him and not worry about costs."

"What about that nanny you hired?" Lathan asks, sounding slightly less angry.

"She's at home asleep since she was up pulling her hair out with me while we tried to figure out what was wrong with Brady all last night. Kelsey is young, and this is too much to put on her. She took him to the doctor for me this morning."

"I get that you're worried and all, but the team has to be your priority, or we all suffer," Lathan tells me. "Do you know how many times I've wanted to be with my mom at her doctor's appointments or take care of her after the chemotherapy sessions? But I stayed here because we don't get the luxury of sick days or personal days."

"That's different," I tell him and wince, instantly regretting my words. "Sorry, man, I just meant that your mom has your dad to look after her. This kid doesn't have anyone except for me and maybe Callie, if he's her sister's baby."

"He's also a baby who won't remember any of this shit. So what does it matter if it's you here or the nurses?" he asks. "Especially if it costs you your spot on the team."

"You don't get it, and there's no way for me to explain," I say, leaning forward to bury my face in my hands. "Being someone's father or *possibly* their father is different. His *life* is in my hands, and that's not something I'm just gonna casually pass off on a nanny or nurse or someone else. If something bad happens to him...that's all on me."

"Sorry, I'll, um, come back."

I lift my head as soon as I hear Callie's voice, but she's already disappeared out the door.

"Who was that?" Lathan asks.

"Callie, Bianca's sister, so possibly Brady's aunt," I reply.

"She's hot," he says, stating the obvious. And just like that, whatever ire I had at him is gone. "Does she have wings and pointed ears too?" he asks, making me chuckle.

"None that I've found yet," I answer, not that I haven't wanted the opportunity to get her naked for a more thorough check. "Or maybe she just uses her fairy dust to hide them."

"You're fucking her and the nanny both, aren't you?" he asks.

"No!" I exclaim.

"Just one of them?"

"Neither. I haven't fucked either of them," I answer.

"Wow, that's a first," Lathan says in surprise.

"Tell me about it," I reply.

I'm blaming the mess in my pants on my recent drought. I haven't slept with a woman in five days, which is sadly a new record for me. It's not like I even have to work for sex. Women walk up to me out in public and suggest we find somewhere to bang less than five minutes later. I've fucked women in nasty men's bathrooms with other men watching, in random storage rooms or coat closets, the dressing rooms of retail stores. You name it, and I've probably done it there.

Sure, I could turn them down like the bartender at *Limelight*, but I'm a normal man with simple needs. Or maybe my needs are greater than the average. Either way, I like sex and enjoy it. So when a woman suggests we find a quiet place to do the nasty, I usually don't decline, especially before a game to get rid of the nervousness. Or after a bad loss to make me forget I let everyone down. Especially not after an amazing win when the adrenaline's still pumping through my veins, and I want to celebrate my success.

So maybe I use sex as a coping mechanism. It works better than antidepressants or anxiety medications and is a much healthier pick me up than comfort food or illegal drugs that would make me fat or get me suspended. The way I see it, there's nothing wrong with two consenting adults getting their rocks off as long as we use protection and don't end up on the front page of a tabloid.

Obviously, I may have to work on the whole using protection thing when I'm drinking if Brady turns out to be my son. I pull out my phone to check for any missed calls from the testing facility but don't have any.

"So when do you find out if you're his father?" Lathan asks as if reading my mind.

"Tomorrow or Friday hopefully," I reply.

"And if he's not?" Lathan asks.

"Who the hell knows," I answer honestly. "Then we'll wait and see if Callie's his aunt. She'll have her results by Friday or Monday at the latest."

"Well, good luck," Lathan says before he gets to his feet. "I don't mean to give you shit; I just don't want you to forget what's important."

"I know," I tell him simply, because there's no way I can explain to him that Callie's right. When it comes to taking care of my son or playing football, at the end of the day, one is still just a sport.

CHAPTER TWELVE

Callie

I wait until Quinton's friend leaves the room before I step back inside. He was obviously a football player too, big and muscular with even the same Mohawk type haircut as Quinton.

Once I'm inside, I walk up to the baby's container and put a hand on it when I see his eyes are open.

"Hi, Brady," I say, the name starting to grow on me.

"He's up?" Quinton asks from the sofa. He stands, but then sits back down again with the blanket clenched to his lap. I bite my lip to try and hide my smile.

"Yeah," I tell him. "I'm gonna let the nurse know, so maybe she'll let me take him out of there to feed him."

"Okay, thanks," Quinton says. "I'm gonna go...find a bathroom."

"There's one right across the hall," I tell him with my face turned away as I leave so he won't see my grin.

The white-haired nurse at the front desk thankfully agrees to let me take Brady out long enough to give him a bottle. So I get the formula ready while she opens up his container and does her required check of all his vitals and draws blood for tests.

I also change his diaper before I wrap him in a hospital blanket and sit down with him in my arms to try to feed him. When he starts greedily sucking down the bottle, I'm relieved.

Despite my order for my eyes not to drop to the man's crotch when Quinton walks back into the room a few minutes later, they do it anyway, taking in the dark wet splatters on his denim.

"The sink sprayed me," Quinton says when he notices my attention to that particular part of his body.

"I didn't say anything," I mutter, looking back down at Brady.

"How's he doing?" Quinton asks when he sits down next to me and runs his hand over Brady's sparse head of dark hair.

"Hungry, which is a good sign," I answer.

"Good," he replies on an exhale. "Could I hold him when you get finished? Before they put him back in there?"

"Yeah, of course," I agree, his sweet request causing tingling flutters in my belly. And strangely enough in my breasts as well. That could also be remnants from just half an hour ago when I was stroking Quinton's long, hard cock while he slept.

Sneaking a glance over at the giant football player, I have to admit to myself that I'm attracted to him, more than just his magnificent manhood. Not that I would ever let someone like him in my panties; but I'm certain that if I did, it would be fantastic. He's just so big and masculine with a gorgeous face. More than simply sex on a stick, this man is a walking positive pregnancy test, as evidenced by the baby in my arms. Most likely his son, depending on the results we should have soon.

And then I remember the words I overheard him saying to his friend that nearly made my ovaries melt into a puddle. *"Being someone's father or possibly their father is different. His life is in my hands, and that's not something I'm just gonna casually pass off on a nanny or nurse or someone else. If something bad happens to him...that's all on me."*

I'm starting to think I was wrong about Quinton. He's beginning to realize what it takes to be a father, more than just piles of money or having someone babysit while he's away. It's an enormous responsibility, and I'm pretty sure he doesn't intend on taking that job lightly.

CHAPTER THIRTEEN

Quinton

I wake up with a warm, soft body pressed against mine. Mmm. My cock likes that a lot as evidenced by the way he's trying to bust through my jeans to get closer. Especially when the softness starts to wiggle against him, urging him on.

Slipping my hand over her hip, I flatten my palm on her clothed stomach to press her closer. Wait, why are we wearing clothes in bed? I find the hem of her shirt and ease my hand underneath so that I can encounter her smooth, warm skin.

The soft body gasps loudly, and it's music to my ears. Moaning would be better, but I'm getting around to that part. Just as my pinkie disappears into her waistband, her hand grabs mine at the same time she says my name. Not in the "Oh, Quinton" way but in the "Quinton, what the fuck?" way.

My eyes fly open, and that's when I remember it's Callie sleeping in front of me on the pullout sofa in Brady's hospital room.

"Fuck. Sorry," I mutter, removing my hand from her body to reach down and adjust the bulge of my jeans.

Callie rolls to her back so that I can see her flawless face, her cheeks painted rosy red. "No, it's my fault. I, um, got too close," she says while licking her lips, which I feel in the tip of my cock that her hip bone is now pressed firmly against.

Since she didn't jump up, I assume she wasn't too offended by getting poked with my morning wood. And now she's still here, lying next to me, the tempting swell of her tits within reach, her mouth only inches from mine. Her eyes are watching my lips while her hand rubs her stomach where my own just was.

Is she waiting for me to kiss her?

I lean down to close the distance between us just as the phone in my pocket begins to vibrate against my leg and hers.

"Oh shit," Callie mutters before she does jump up, straightening her clothes as she goes over to check on Brady.

Damn phone.

I pull it out of my pocket to answer and see who the hell interrupted our moment so I can go kick their ass.

"Hello?" I say gruffly into the receiver.

"Mr. Dunn?" a polite lady's voice asks.

"This is him," I reply, expecting her to launch into some telemarketer scheme.

"Hi. This is Christine from the testing lab. We have your paternity test results if you would like to come by–"

"I'm on my way," I say quickly before ending the call and scrambling to my feet. "Can you stay here with Brady for a few minutes?" I ask Callie. "The test results are back."

"Of course. Go," she says, just as she did last night while I spent a few hours handing out signed merchandise and visiting with the kids on the other side of the hallway. Rather than make me feel sad for them, those tough guys and girls inspired me. They're stronger and more courageous than I'll ever be. I gave my contact information to the supervising nurse and told her to let me know if she ever needs me to stop by again to visit. In fact, I would like to start coming here more frequently.

"Good luck?" Callie asks, reminding me of where I need to get going. Her two words are spoken as a question like she's not sure what I want the results to say. Or maybe she's reluctant to find out if I'm Brady's father. My attorney has made it clear. That would mean she wouldn't have a chance at any type of custody, only visitation as I allow it. The court couldn't force me to let her see him, but I would never keep her away from him.

"Thanks," I tell her simply before walking out the door.

On the short drive over to the lab, I try to figure out which way I'm leaning for the results, but it's not quite as clear-cut as a few days ago when I was tested. At the time, I assumed Brady's mother was alive and well but mistaken in her claim that I was his father. I'd only had him for about a day, still didn't know what the hell I was doing fixing bottles or changing diapers, and I was cranky as fuck from not playing my best game thanks to the lack of sleep.

But now, three days later, it feels like everything has changed.

I've gotten used to having the little guy around, so much so that I panicked when Callie told me he had to be admitted into the hospital. I've been worried sick about him and hate seeing him lying in that container. My first thought when I saw him was that I wanted to pick him up and hold him to make sure he was okay.

So, while I never intended to become a father, or ever really thought about having kids, I'm not opposed to taking on the responsibility suddenly thrown at me.

When my heart begins to race the closer I get to the lab, I realize that I'm afraid the results will say I'm *not* his father and the chance to take care of him will be ripped away from me.

I walk into the testing facility like a zombie, both in a rush to find out but also wanting to delay it. Once I know the results, there's no going back.

After I show my ID to the woman at the front desk, she retrieves a letter size envelope and offers it to me with a smile. Taking it from her is the first time that I realize my hand is shaking. This is one of the most important decisions in my life.

The envelope is sealed, of course, so I walk back to my car with it instead of opening it in public where someone could recognize me and take photos or videos of my reaction. Nothing is sacred when you're a sports celebrity.

Once I'm locked inside the safety of my car again, I tear off the end of the envelope and dump the single sheet of paper out into my lap.

This is it. The moment of truth.

As soon as I unfold the letter my eyes start scanning. I get to "Quinton Dunn is not" and don't have to read anymore.

Fucking...goddammit!

I crumple the sheet of paper into my fist and toss it over my shoulder. Screw it. I don't care what it says. Bianca left him with me, and I'm gonna take care of him. At least until Callie gets her results probably tomorrow. Then, if he is Bianca's, Callie will take Brady from me, and I'll never see either of them again.

If he's not, well, then maybe there's a chance I can adopt him if his mother doesn't come forward.

Fuck. If neither of us are blood relatives, the court would probably take Brady into the state's custody until all that shit gets figured out. Picturing underpaid and overworked staff ignoring his cries because they're too busy or too swamped to feed him almost does me in.

Throwing my head back against the seat, I close my eyes and take slow deep breaths in through the nose and out through my mouth after my lungs seem to forget how they're supposed to automatically function. My throat begins to burn like someone's pouring scalding water down it.

No, there's no fucking way I'm gonna let them take Brady into child custody.

Then, I remember at the court hearing when Callie's attorney mentioned that she had been previously approved for adoption. Even if Brady's not Bianca's, maybe Callie will still want to adopt him. I know she already loves him regardless of what the test says. If so, maybe she would still let me see him. Hell, I could easily pay her enough child support to take care of him.

Feeling a little bit more optimistic about things after getting crushed, I start the car and drive back to the hospital.

CHAPTER FOURTEEN

Callie

I'm feeding Brady, snuggling him in his blanket when Tina, the NICU nurse I know, comes in the room.

"Morning, Callie. How's he doing? Taking a few ounces?" she asks, sitting down her laptop on the counter to type.

"Yeah, he's draining this four-ounce bottle down," I tell her with a smile. "That's a good sign, right?"

"It is," she answers. Once she's finished typing, Tina washes her hands in the sink and comes over to sit next to me.

"He's precious," she says. "And I think he's gonna be just fine."

"Good," I reply with a smile.

"So, you think he's your sister's baby?" she asks.

I nod. "Yeah, I believe so. There's no record of his birth here?"

"Nope. But we couldn't find any photo ID on him, so it's hard to be sure," she jokes. "Your sister definitely wasn't admitted here. Maybe she had him at another hospital?"

"Maybe."

Leaning in closer, Tina whispers, "So, the rumor floating around the nurse's station is that Quinton Dunn is possibly the daddy. Any truth to that?"

"It's possible," I tell her since there's no reason to lie about it. The fact that Quinton's been here is a pretty good giveaway that he may be the father.

Fanning herself, she says, "God that man is...*mmm*."

"I guess," I reply with a shrug.

"Guess? There is no guess. He is the hottest man I've ever seen in person. And jeez, based on the size of his hands, he *has* to be well-endowed."

"If you say so," I mutter trying not to remember in great detail how he felt in my hand yesterday or pressed against my bottom this morning, ready to go.

"But he's not just a pretty package. He's a big softie too," Tina gushes, her hands over her heart.

"How do you know that?" I ask.

"Because of what he did yesterday," she answers, like I know what the hell that means.

"What did he do?" I ask in confusion.

"You didn't hear?" she replies. "He went around and visited with all the pediatric patients and their families, even the babies, giving them signed jerseys and stuffed animals. Everyone was so excited to see him. All the nurses were tearing up, especially since we had heard about this little guy being here," she says, reaching over to rub the top of Brady's head.

"Quinton did that? You're sure?" I ask in disbelief, remembering when he disappeared for a few hours last night. I'd assumed he had gone out to grab something to eat.

"Yep, all of the nurses came in to see him, even the ones not on duty," she answers with a slow nod. "So freaking sweet. And he only asked that the hospital not notify the media."

"Wow," I mutter, trying to put that information together with the playboy image I have of Quinton.

"So now the yucky part," Tina says when I sit Brady up to burp him. "I've got to go weigh him and draw some blood."

"Aww. Poor little guy," I say, giving Brady a kiss on his forehead before I pass him to her.

"I'll be right back, and we'll get him under the lights again while we wait for the results. He may be able to go home soon," she says when she gets up to leave with him.

"Fingers crossed," I reply, holding up my twisted fingers.

Quinton returns a while later after Brady is back under the light. He was gone longer than I expected; and based on the crestfallen expression on his handsome face, I can't tell what that means.

Is he upset that he's Brady's father, or is he sad that he's not?

The unjolly giant shuffles into the room, coming to a stop in front of Brady's bed but doesn't speak.

"Hey," I say to him in greeting.

"Hey," he mumbles before coming over and flopping down on the seat next to me, right where we both crashed for a few hours last night, and I awoke to his massive hand underneath my shirt and erection poking me in my ass. I hadn't wanted him to stop, and I can't exactly blame that on the drowsiness. I knew what was happening and where we were, but I'm not entirely sure Quinton did.

When Quinton doesn't immediately spit out the information I'm desperate to hear, I decide not to rush him. Instead, I give him an update.

"So, good news. While you were gone, they checked Brady's blood work, and it looked good. We get to take him home with a smaller glow light that he wears," I tell him.

"That's great," Quinton says with a small, crooked smile.

"As soon as we get the discharge papers for you to sign, I'll get him dressed; and then we'll be ready to go."

"I'm not his father," Quinton blurts out. "I mean, of course I'm gonna cover all his medical expenses. I just meant...he's not mine."

"He's not?" I gasp in surprise, turning toward Quinton to try and read his face.

While I'm secretly thrilled because that will make it so much easier for me to be awarded custody of Brady, at the same time I actually feel bad for Quinton. And I instantly recognize the saddened look on his face. It's the same expression I would see reflecting back in the mirror every single month that John and I tried to get pregnant, but failed.

He's disappointed.

"I should be relieved, right?" Quinton meets my eyes and asks sadly. "You made it clear I'm not cut out to be a father, I know that. But I still wanted to...try."

"I'm sorry, Quinton," I tell him sincerely while reaching over to cover the top of his hand with mine.

"Even if he's not Bianca's, I want to help you get custody," he says, shocking the ever-loving shit out of me. "I'll pay for your attorneys; and either way, I'll give you child support so you can have everything you need..."

Wow, that's the nicest thing anyone has ever offered me. He's sad and maybe even mourning the loss of the baby he thought was his own, but even so, he's being nice to me, despite all the things I've said and done, taking him to court Tuesday for custody. And now I feel even guiltier for snooping around his house, trying to dig up dirt on him to make him look bad.

I was wrong about him. Quinton's a good guy, and one day I think he'll make a pretty good father.

"Thank you for the offer, Quinton, but you don't have to do that, pay me child support or whatever," I tell him. "I've been saving for a baby for years; and believe it or not, I actually make pretty good money at my boring job. Plenty for me to take care of him, so you don't have to—"

"I just, I want to, okay?" he suddenly exclaims before getting to his feet, keeping his back to me when he stalks across the room. "I want to make sure he's taken care of."

"He will be," I assure him, more certain of that than anything in my entire life.

"What if he's not Bianca's? I don't want him to end up in foster care," Quinton says as he braces his hands on the sink counter and hangs his head. "He deserves better than that."

"I agree," I tell him. "And if he's not Bianca's and he's not yours, no one has to know, right?"

Spinning back around, I catch the wetness on Quinton's cheeks before he quickly wipes it away, and it nearly breaks my heart. "What do you mean?" he asks, his voice huskier with emotion.

"I mean, if neither of us report it, we could just keep him, right?" I explain, not missing the fact that I said "we" like we're a team or...or a couple. "If he's not Bianca's, his mother obviously didn't want him either. So, can't it just be our little secret?"

"Yes," Quinton says with a grin. "We'll do that. You're a genius, Callie."

"Nah, I just refuse to give him up," I reply with my own grin, walking over to his bed to watch Brady sleeping, and wishing it was that easy. But I know deep down that it's not. He'll have to have a birth certificate and Social Security number someday. I don't know how it will all work or what we'll have to do, but I'll do whatever it takes to make it happen. Besides, Quinton looks like he needs some good news.

Before he can say anything else, Tina pushes open the door and comes back in with her small laptop in her hands. "So, are you guys ready to take him home?" she asks with a smile.

"Hell yes," Quinton looks at me and says with a wink that solidifies our agreement to do what it takes to give Brady a home, even if we have to lie or keep the truth a secret.

"So will we see you later this week?" Tina asks me after all the paperwork is signed and she tells us that a home nursing agency will send someone over to Quinton's house later to put on the portable light therapy device.

"Um, yeah, probably," I tell her.

"Great. I don't have the research to prove it, but I think the babies you cuddle get out of here faster than the others," she tells me with a smile before she leaves.

"What was that about?" Quinton asks as we get Brady dressed in his footed coveralls.

"Oh, nothing. I just volunteer a few afternoons a week," I tell him, packing everything up in Brady's diaper bag.

"Volunteer? Like as a nurse's aide or something?" he asks.

"No, as a cuddler," I respond, somewhat embarrassed to be admitting that to him.

"A cuddler?" Quinton repeats, trying to bite back his smile.

"Go ahead and laugh, but it's good for the babies, and it makes me happy," I tell him defensively.

"I didn't say anything," he replies as he picks up Brady's car seat and we start for the elevator bank. "And I think it's sweet."

"Please drop it," I tell him as I wave goodbye to a few nurses at the desk who I recognize. Ones who are blatantly staring at Quinton. Who could blame them?

Once we get off the elevator and step through the sliding doors at the front of the hospital, I inhale a deep breath of fresh air after being cramped up inside the antiseptic fog of the hospital since yesterday.

"I don't know about you, but I could use some greasy breakfast comfort food after these last few hellish days," Quinton says when we get to his huge, and very safe looking, Land Cruiser.

"Yeah, breakfast sounds good," I agree. After snacking on vending machine foods for the past twenty-four hours, I could use an actual warm meal.

Quinton snaps Brady's seat into the secured base in the backseat, and I climb into the back next to him since the seat's rear facing and I still worry about the little guy.

After Quinton shuts the door and climbs in the front, I notice the crumpled ball of paper on the otherwise, clean, spotless floorboard and reach down to pick it up. The testing facility's letterhead instantly grabs my attention; and unable to stop myself, I open it up to read it.

Oh my God!

My hand flies up to my gaping mouth as I reread the typed, bold words over and over again. Words that shatter my heart into a million tiny pieces. Why did I have to read the stupid letter? I was so close to finally having custody of Brady and the disappointment of having this chance ripped away from me is almost too painful to bear.

For one long, agonizing minute I have an internal debate with my conscience, wondering if I should say something or just keep my mouth shut.

But then I remember Quinton's sweet words about how seriously he takes his responsibility for Brady, the tears he shed just moments ago when he was certain he wasn't his father, and I know I could never live with myself if I withheld this information from him. Brady would never really be mine; it would be a lie that would ruin any happiness he may bring me.

"Quinton..." I say before he can back out of the parking spot. Wiping away the moisture from my eyes, I lean forward between the two front seats and offer the wrinkled up sheet of paper to him.

"I don't want to see that again, Callie," he grumbles.

"Quinton, look at it. Read it again," I encourage him, even though it means I lose everything.

"Dammit, fine," he says when he finally jerks the document from my hand and starts to read the words in bold. "*Quinton Dunn is not excluded as the biological father of Brady Dunn.* There, you happy?" he asks, handing the paper back to me.

"Exactly how many times have you been hit in the head, hot shot?" I ask him teasingly, trying not to let my despair show.

"What the hell?" Quinton replies, twisting around in his seat so he can face me.

"Okay. Let's try this instead," I say with a heavy exhale to gather my strength. *This is the right thing to do,* I tell myself. "Do you know what 'not excluded' means?" I ask him.

"Yeah, I get it, Callie. I'm not his father."

"No, Quinton," I say slowly. "You're not *excluded* as his father.

In paternity testing language, that means that you are the most likely biological match. But since it's only like ninety-nine percent certain instead of one hundred percent, they can't come out and say *you are his father*."

"Wait, what are *you* saying?" he says with his dark eyebrows drawn together.

Throwing my hands up in exasperation, I finally shout, "You're his father!"

"Seriously?" he asks with his eyes widening in shock. He grabs the paper away from me again and then starts punching something into his phone. If I had to guess, he's probably doing an internet search to verify my explanation. "Son of a bitch," he mutters.

"Hey, that might be my sister you're talking about," I tease him.

"I'm his father?" he asks, looking back at me again and then the car seat. "He's really mine?"

And even knowing that I just lost any chance I had of getting custody of Brady, I can't help but smile and be happy for Quinton as tears begin to leak from my eyes.

"Congratulations," I tell him, reaching over to tug Brady's blanket up over his chest. It hurts like hell to face the truth, but Brady deserves to be raised by one of his biological parents, especially one who already loves him so much, even if he was unexpected.

"Holy shit," Quinton says, running his fingers through his hair and giving it a tug. "Holy. Shit."

"Might want to work on your explicit language," I warn him, brushing away the wetness on my cheeks with my knuckles.

"Shit, you're right," he says, which makes me laugh, especially since he doesn't even notice what he said. "I've got to call my parents. Hell, I've got to call...everyone."

"Slow down, Daddy. How about you make a few important calls, and then we get that breakfast you offered?" I ask him because I need some time to process all this.

"Thank you, Callie," Quinton says. Reaching for my hand that's in my lap, Quinton brings it to his lips, kissing my still damp knuckles before he presses my palm to his face and I end up stroking the stubble over his cheek. I'm not sure why; it just sort of happens. "Thank you, sweetheart. We're gonna work out custody. You can see him whenever you want. I know how much you already love him too."

Before I can reply with my gratitude, he's letting my hand go so he can turn back around in his seat to start making calls, the first being obviously to his parents since the first words out of his mouth are, "You're a grandma!"

It's sweet to see him so excited after how upset he was earlier. And I'm envious, wondering if I'll ever get to experience the same happiness and to be someone's mother like I've always wanted.

First thing's first, tomorrow or Monday I'll find out for certain if Brady is my nephew. That would be wonderful if he is, but at the same time, in my heart, he'll always be Quinton and Bianca's son no matter how much time I spend with him or how much I love him. In the end, he's not mine, and I have no real claim to him, only whatever Quinton offers for visitation. He loves his son and deserves full custody of him. I'll just take whatever time with Brady he'll give me.

CHAPTER FIFTEEN

Quinton

I'm a father.

I'm a freaking father.

I can't seem to stop saying those words to myself over and over again while Callie and I sit across from each other in the diner's red, vinyl booth, my son sleeping in his car seat next to me.

My son.

I have a son. He's actually mine, which is a completely different possessive feeling than I've ever had before. I've owned things, cars, phones, clothing, a house, all material items that were mine. Things that eventually break down, fade, fall apart, or I eventually give away. Nothing has ever been permanent. Constant.

Of course, there are my parents, who still live in our hometown up in Virginia. But for the past eight years, I only see them occasionally and talk to them on the phone a few times a week, whenever the mood strikes. I love them and know they'll always be there for me whenever I need them, but this, with Brady, is completely different.

Even when I'm away from him for even a short time, I'm thinking about him, worrying about him, wanting to be near him to make sure he's okay. He's my responsibility, his health, his well-being; all of it is in my hands, on my shoulders.

Oh shit.

My chest tightens, and I feel a little dizzy like at the beginning of a panic attack.

How could I ever think the game of football was the most important thing ever when there's this? Fatherhood.

"You okay? You went from smiling like a fool to looking like you're gonna hurl," Callie says, pulling my attention to her beautiful, serene face.

"This is...big," I say, gesturing to Brady.

Breathe in through the nose, out the through the mouth. In through the nose, out through the mouth.

"It is," Callie agrees. "But I think you can handle it."

"Really?" I ask, gasping for oxygen before my lungs explode.

"Yeah. It won't happen overnight, but you'll figure it out," she says while looking over at Brady with a small smile.

"How long have you known you wanted to be a mother?" I ask since it's so obvious from the way she looks at him and holds him, not to mention the fact that her attempting to adopt came up in court. Oh, and I just found out that she volunteers to cuddle the babies at the hospital. It's sweet and...incredibly sad.

"Since I was a little girl," she answers, somewhat surprising me. "I dressed my cats up in baby doll clothes and diapers. They didn't mind too much since I would also feed them milk in real bottles."

"Seriously?" I ask with a grin, imagining a younger Callie holding down a cat to shove a bottle in its mouth.

"Yeah," she answers. "And when John and I got married, we started trying to get pregnant around our one-year anniversary. I couldn't wait to be a mother."

"But you two couldn't..." I start to ask.

"No," she answers with a frown. "I have endometriosis, which can impede fertility. I've had several surgeries in seven years, taken fertility drugs, ate healthy, exercised three days a week, stayed away from alcohol, caffeine, and... none of it worked."

"I'm sorry," I tell her sincerely. "I guess to you it really doesn't seem fair for so many girls to get pregnant with babies they don't want, huh?"

"Yeah, that's why we started looking into adoption about two years ago. I think we were really close when...well, it all went to hell," she says, picking up her water and chugging it.

"Your husband cheated on you?" I ask, and her wide, stormy green eyes flash up to mine.

"How did you know that?" she asks.

"My attorney, he, um, he had pulled the divorce filings before court," I admit, now feeling guilty, like I'm eavesdropping on something that was none of my business.

"Oh," Callie mutters in understanding before a smile stretches across her face. "I'm sort of relieved you're Brady's father, especially if he's Bianca's."

"You are?" I ask with my eyebrows raised in surprise.

"Yeah, I was really hoping he wasn't John's."

"Ah, what? Now I'm confused," I tell her. "John was your husband?"

"Uh-huh," she asks with a slow nod.

"And you thought *he* could be the father of Bianca's baby?" I ask.

"Uh-huh."

"Your husband cheated on you...with *your sister*?" I clarify.

"Yep," she answers. "In my house. I guess it was our house, even though I paid for it. Now it's my house."

"How the hell could they do that to you?" I ask, indignant on her behalf.

"Well, remember I told you that Bianca was a heroin addict?" Callie replies, and I nod while glancing over at Brady, so damn thankful that he's healthy. "She would do *anything* for heroin, including have sex with my husband for a hit," she elaborates.

My jaw falls open. "And you caught them? Together?"

"Yep. It wasn't the happiest day of my life."

"I bet not," I tell her, leaning on my forearms to whisper across the table. "That's horrible, like seriously fucked up."

"Indeed," she says. "Which is why I kicked them both out and asked for a divorce."

"Damn right. You didn't deserve that."

"The last time I saw Bianca was the day she told me she was pregnant," Callie admits, her eyes watering with unshed tears. "I thought it was John's, figured he would ironically knock her up since he couldn't get the job done with me."

"I'm sorry, Callie," I tell her, reaching across the table to squeeze her hand.

"The last thing I said to her was *leave and don't ever think of coming back here* after calling her a whore. I'm a horrible sister. I shouldn't have told you it was your fault she died. It was mine. I pushed her away when she needed me."

"That's not true. It sounds like she didn't deserve you and neither did he."

"Thanks," she replies, turning her head away to wipe away her tears. "Now I'm a thirty-six-year-old single woman. The adoption agencies have shunned me, so I don't think I'll ever get a chance to be a mother."

"You still have plenty of time," I assure her. "Women have babies in their forties nowadays."

"Well, you see, hot shot, to conceive a baby naturally, there has to be a man involved."

"Yeah, I know that," I tell her with a roll of my eyes. "I meant that there's still time for you to find a man who isn't a cheating asshole to give you children."

"The clock's ticking and I'm not just gonna marry the first man I meet so he'll put a baby inside me," she huffs.

Hearing that, my cock twitches beneath the table with great interest, liking the idea of pounding inside Callie until I fill her with my potent seed, as evidenced by the baby on the seat next to me.

"Can we not talk about this anymore?" she asks, which is slightly disappointing. I wanted to hear her talk a little more about the moment of conception or the many, many times the act may take before conceiving.

"Fine," I reluctantly agree, reaching down to subtly adjust my cock that's swollen and cramped behind my zipper. That's when I remember I'm still wearing a pair of cum stained jeans. "I need a shower," I say aloud. "And, shit, I've got practice this afternoon. Do you think you and Kelsey –" I start, but Callie answers.

"Yes, we'll watch him for you. Now, where's our food? I'm starving," she says, looking over her shoulder for the waiter, which gives me a chance to gawk at her rack.

"Me too," I concur, but I'm not just hungry for food.

After a grueling afternoon of practice and excruciatingly long captains' meeting, most likely because Coach Griffin wanted to punish me for my absence earlier in the week, I'm looking forward to getting home and sleeping in my bed. Not that the hospital bed last night didn't have a few perks that the bed in my room is missing. Particularly, a petite, curvy woman with a feisty attitude.

Kelsey has been sending me updates on Brady and how he's doing with his new light, but I haven't heard a word from Callie. Not that she would have any reason to contact me; but still, after spending yesterday and this morning together, I've sort of...missed her. And while I'm anxious to find out if she's my son's aunt, I also want more opportunities to try and win her over, to convince her to go out with me. Or stay in and fuck me. I'm not that picky.

When I pull up to the house, I'm surprised to see that Callie's blue Corolla is still parked in the driveway even though it's after ten o'clock.

Before this week, my routine consisted only of football and the occasional hookup, but usually it meant coming home to a silent, empty house where I might sit on the deck and watch the ocean to wind down for the night before going to bed alone. I've never really thought of myself as lonely since I'm usually surrounded by people most of the day. But now that I know what it feels like to have a son to come home to, I realize just how...empty the house was before Brady. While Kelsey's fun and has been a huge help, I know she's only here because I'm paying her to be.

But Callie, she's here because she wants to be close to Brady. So is it wrong to wish there was a little piece of her that wanted to be here for me too?

Unlocking the front door, I walk in quietly, assuming Brady's already asleep. In the dark house, I find Callie sitting on the sofa next to the lamp, watching TV while wearing a pair of glasses and... sewing?

"I'm sorry, grandma. Do I have the wrong house?" I tease her with a grin. The scowl on Callie's face doesn't seem nearly as amused.

"Grandma?" she repeats.

Okay, so calling her a senior citizen may not be the best way to get in her panties.

"Yeah, grandma," I reply, tossing my duffle bag down in a chair. "But you're the sexiest grandma I've ever seen."

"Watch your mouth," she warns, pointing the stick thing at me. "I'm good with needles and could sew it shut in no time."

"Wow, now I'm a little terrified of you," I admit, collapsing into my favorite recliner.

Finally grinning, Callie removes her glasses and folds them up before she starts putting all the yarn and stuff into a canvas tote bag.

"You leaving?" I ask, disappointed that she's ready to bolt as soon as I walk in the door.

"Yeah, I was just staying to let Kelsey get some sleep. She was still exhausted today," she answers without looking at me.

"Well, you don't have to rush out of here," I tell her. "How's

Brady?" I ask, because I honestly want to know and because I know it will keep her talking to me.

"He's great, eating and sleeping on a normal schedule again and doesn't seem to notice the light he's wearing."

"Good," I say. "As soon as I can find the energy to get to my feet, I'll go check on him."

"Rough day at the office?" she asks.

"Yeah, brutal. But at least I've got tomorrow off."

"Well, have fun catching up on your sleep," Callie says as she stands and throws her bag over her shoulder.

"You may get your DNA results tomorrow, right?" I ask.

She nods and licks her lips as if she's nervous. "Yeah, hopefully. I really don't want to wait until Monday."

"I would like to go with you," I tell her. "I mean, unless you want to go alone, or with someone else."

"Sure, you and Brady can accompany me for moral support," she says while wringing her hands in front of her. "I'm nervous actually."

"Believe me, I know the feeling," I tell her. "Do you think he's Bianca's? Does he take after her?" I ask, because I don't remember what she looked like.

"I hope so, but no, he doesn't look like her," Callie says stiffly. "Oh, and that reminds me. Some bimbo dropped by earlier tonight looking for you. She ran when she saw Brady, so Kelsey and I didn't get her name," she throws over her shoulder as she walks away, and then she's out the door.

Great.

Just when I start to think she and I are making forward progress, Callie throws a penalty flag on the field and we're forced to move backward ten yards.

CHAPTER SIXTEEN

Callie

"What's it say? What's it say?" Quinton asks, practically bouncing up and down while standing next to his open SUV door when I approach with the results.

Instead of climbing in the back with Brady to open the envelope I just picked up from inside the testing facility, I tear it open in front of Quinton, so anxious to know...

"We're related!" I shout in celebration, throwing my arms up in the air. "He's Bianca's."

The next second my feet are lifted off the ground, and Quinton's strong arms are wrapped around my waist as he spins me around in the parking lot.

"This is great, Callie! I'm so happy to hear that," he says against my ear as he hugs me tighter. "We should celebrate."

The front of my soft body slides down Quinton's warm, hard as granite chest when he eventually lowers me. God, Kelsey was right. He smells so good that I could get high on his cedar and amber scent.

When he releases me and takes a step back, I instantly miss the heat and firmness of him pressing against me.

"Celebrate?" I ask once my brain begins firing on all cylinders again. "We celebrated you being his father with a fried breakfast spread, so what should we do to celebrate me being his aunt?"

"Whatever you want," he says, and I know he means it. I could ask Quinton for anything; and with his resources, he would make it happen.

"Can we take Brady to have his newborn pictures made?" I ask while biting my bottom lip hopefully. "I made him something."

"You made him something?" Quinton asks with a smile. "You mean, like, with your grandma yarn stuff?"

"It's called crocheting," I tell him with a playful slap to his chest, mostly just to feel the sexy body part again.

Last night when Quinton got home late from practice, I had already sent Kelsey to bed. While I had been watching Brady with her during the afternoon, I worked on the outfit I had started the night after we had court. I was finishing it up, waiting in the living room for Quinton when he came home and told me I looked like a sexy grandma. If not for the sexy part, I would've been insulted since I'm at least ten years, or maybe more, older than Quinton.

"So, do you know of a place to take the pictures or whatever?" Quinton asks.

"I do know of a studio, one where we bring home the photos the same day. We just need to go back to your place to get one of your jerseys; then swing by my house to pick up the outfit," I tell him. "Oh, and you can meet my cat, Felix. He was hiding under the bed Tuesday when you were there because he doesn't like new people hanging around."

"Felix? Does he wear baby clothes while you force feed him a bottle?" Quinton teases.

"No," I huff, even if I'm inwardly pleased that he remembered that small detail about me from breakfast. "I haven't done that since I was a little girl."

"Good for Felix, I guess," Quinton replies with a chuckle.

"Yeah, it didn't take many scratches for me to learn my lesson," I reply before climbing in the backseat with Brady, who is sleeping peacefully like a tiny angel. It's the first time I've looked at him and known for certain that he's my nephew.

I forgive my sister a little more in that moment. She could've been wrong about Quinton. He could've turned her son into social services, walked away and never looked back. Instead, he gave him a name, took good care of him, and didn't waste time proving Brady was his son. Even if I wanted to kick Quinton's ass when we first met, I still admired his stubbornness in court. Some men would've gladly left Brady behind with me when I insisted on keeping him, just to rid themselves of the enormous responsibility. Not Quinton. He fought tooth and nail for his son before he knew for certain he was the father. Now I'm starting to admire him for being such a strong, caring man.

Quinton

"He's adorable!" the photographer at the studio says when she picks up the camera after carefully arranging my sleeping son.

Brady's head is resting on his tiny arm that's propped up on a football nearly as big as he is. The best part, though, is the handmade blue and yellow beanie he's wearing with the Wildcats emblem on the front. Callie made it for him, which makes it even more special.

Speaking of his aunt, the woman is nearly in tears as she watches the photographer quickly snap photos and rearrange Brady. There are a few photos taken with him sleeping in just his Wildcats beanie and matching diaper stretched out on my jersey, right above my name, which I have to say, makes me a little proud. Maybe Brady will even want to wear my jersey when he's older.

The photographer then situates him inside of a Wildcat's helmet that she had in the studio and places a miniature "Go Wildcats" flag in his clenched fists that's hanging on the outside of the helmet. Even I can admit that it's cute as shit, and I can't wait to show them to… well, everyone in the world. Which reminds me that I need to call my manager.

"Now let's get a few photos of mom and dad with him," the photographer suggests.

Before I can respond, Callie speaks up and backs away saying, "No, I'm just his aunt."

And with just those five words, I can hear and feel her disappointment that she's never been able to have her own daughter or son.

"I think we should get photos of Brady with his aunt, since this was her brilliant idea," I reply, placing my hand on her lower back to urge her forward.

"Fine, but you have to do some too," Callie responds with a huff.

"With the Mohawk? I don't think so," I counter.

"So the hairstyle…it wasn't you trying to be trendy or cool?" Callie asks me with a smile.

"Um, no. I lost a bet," I say while running my fingers down the center of my embarrassment. I also start thinking about the bet Callie and I made on Wednesday, the one about me not sleeping with anyone for a week so that I can get a kiss from her.

Most single men would probably balk at the idea of refusing sex for a week to get a single kiss, but they don't know how badly I want to kiss Callie, or what exactly I have in mind when it's time for her to pony up.

"I can get some close-ups without the hair," the photographer offers, picking up Brady from the helmet and removing his beanie. "Ooh, or we can give dad and son matching hairstyles," she says while trying to get Brady's little patch of dark hair to stand up.

"Let's get some photos of him with his aunt who made his outfit first," I suggest.

"That's really not necessary," Callie protests. "I'm not dressed or ready for pictures."

"You look beautiful," I tell her honestly. "Now get moving."

Knowing there's a significant chance she'll slap me for it, I still swat at her jean-covered ass hard enough to move her toward the photographer.

"Watch it!" she looks over her shoulder and warns me with those stormy green eyes narrowed.

"I am watching it," I tease and blatantly lower my eyes to her ass as she walks forward. Damn, it's a nice ass too, one I wouldn't mind squeezing or smacking bare.

"Stop looking at my ass," Callie hisses.

"Tell your ass to stop flaunting itself in front of my eyes," I counter with a grin.

With a shake of her head, she wanders off while I try to figure out how to make my dreams a reality where that woman is concerned.

CHAPTER SEVENTEEN

Callie

"Okay, now it's Daddy's turn," Beth, our photographer, proclaims. And I sigh in relief that my part is finally over.

Of course I wanted photos of me with Brady, but they didn't need to be professionally taken in a studio. A few quick shots of me sitting on the sofa with my nephew in my arms would have been sufficient.

Now I'll have plenty of memories of when Brady was only about a week old. My favorite shot was of me cradling his dainty head in my palms while leaning down to kiss his cheek. Since it's in black and white, you can't tell I haven't put on any makeup, and not much of my un-styled hair is included in the shot.

"Off with the shirt, Dad. I want some skin to skin shots," Beth directs Quinton, and with only a smidge of shame, I peek over to watch him pull his shirt up and off over his head.

Jesus...fucking...Christ's nipples.

The man is built like a marble statue of Hercules. With his loose fitting clothes on, he looks big and intimidating, but without...wow. He's a sculpted work of art. In high school the football players were the big guys with even larger guts, not highly paid, perfectly conditioned professional athletes like Quinton.

"Um, Callie?" the giant before me asks.

"Yeah?" I respond, and it comes out sounding like an embarrassing sigh.

"I sort of need Brady for the photos."

"Oh, right," I say when I realize I'm still holding the baby. I hand him over to Quinton; and as we make the transfer, there's no way for the back of my fingers to avoid brushing over the warm skin on Quinton's chest and one of his hard nipples.

Since when have I ever been attracted to a man's nipples?

Since now apparently. Did John even have nipples? I don't remember. If he did, I'm absolutely certain that they were not attached to muscular pectorals like these.

Once the baby is secure in his strong, beefy arms, I can't possibly look up at Quinton's face for fear that he'll see my attraction to him... physically. But that's just stupid. He knows he's hot since practically every woman in the world looks at him like he's a chocolate sundae. In fact, when I glance over at the photographer, she's fanning herself and putting her camera down for a drink of water. My mouth is suddenly dry as well.

Beth quickly recovers, though, and begins instructing Quinton on how to stand and hold Brady on his shoulder. The photos of the father and son are sweet and yet still sexy. I'll need to steal a few of these to keep for myself.

Half an hour later, Beth tells us she's finished and that we can either wait around for her to quickly edit and print the photos or come back in an hour or so. Quinton, giant that he is, suggests that we grab some lunch, and I easily agree before we have to get Brady back home and under the light again. In fact, even though we've only had a meal together out in public two days in a row, I like the familiarity of it, and I like having Quinton to myself, unlike at the house where Kelsey is always hovering. Her obvious crush on him is cute, but she's young and naïve. I, on the other hand, know better than to fall for the larger-than-life football player, because there's only one way for it to end --- with heartbreak.

CHAPTER EIGHTEEN

Quinton

"Whatcha got for me?" Wilson Myers, my manager who handles all things PR and shit, asks from where he's standing against his black Mercedes when we meet in the stadium parking lot Friday afternoon as I requested.

"Photos," I tell him, handing him the oversized envelope with one of each of the photos of Brady taken earlier, along with a few of Brady and me together. The ones of Callie and Brady I kept to myself. I've already decided to frame one of the black and white ones to hang in Brady's room.

"Oh shit. How bad is it? You with naked models? Skinny dipping with starlets again?" Wilson asks, knowing me well since we started our business relationship four years ago.

"Much more scandalous," I tell him before he reaches into the envelope and pulls out the...

"Holy shit, Quinton!" he exclaims. "This is yours?"

"He's mine," I confirm with a grin.

"How long have you known? Why haven't you told me? Who

else knows?" Wilson starts firing off questions as he shuffles through the photos.

"I've only known for sure since yesterday. His mother dropped him off with me before she overdosed and died, so I had to wait for the DNA results," I explain. "Only a few players and coaches know about him. Oh, and my attorney, his aunt, his nanny, the doctors and nurses at the pediatrician's office and the hospital, and now the photographer who took these photos."

"Fuck. I've got to move fast before the photographer releases them first!" Wilson shouts. "You're right. This is much more scandalous. You should've warned me there was a chance we would have an illegitimate baby by a druggie ordeal to contend with!"

"Come on, man. It's not *that* bad," I tell him. "Look at how damn cute he is. No one will care who his mother is."

"That's bullshit, Quinton, and you know it!" Wilson argues. "*Everyone* will want to know who the Wildcats QB was stupid enough to knock up."

"Watch it," I lower my voice and warn him. "Spin it however you want, but leave his mother out of it. There's no birth certificate yet, and I'm not even gonna tell you her name to make sure that she stays out of this."

"If you think it's that easy to hide a story this size, then you're crazy. The paparazzi will not stop until they have the answers they know will sell magazines. So do you want the world to know your baby's mama was a drug addict, or do you want to give them some other squeaky-clean mother instead?"

Of course, my first thought of a replacement mother would be Callie, but without asking I already know her answer would be a big, fat no. She seems like a woman who likes her privacy and doesn't want the spotlight on her. As a mama bear, she would likely string up anyone who tried to make a story out of an innocent baby or her sister. And fuck, I still can't believe Bianca slept with Callie's husband. That's so low that I can see why Callie couldn't forgive either of them, but it also means she now has serious trust issues. I'm not exactly the poster boy for a committed relationship since I've never actually had one before. A part of me wonders if I could actually be faithful to just one woman for a long period of time. Sure, this week has been easy with Brady distracting me from my very demanding sex drive, but what about next week or next month, especially traveling for away games? Those are the worst, with women practically jumping on me and piggybacking their way to my hotel room. And if our team loses on the road, the urge to hide my dick in the pussy sand for a few hours to forget how shitty I played is even more prominent.

"I'm not gonna lie about Brady's mother. That will only make it worse if the media figures it out," I tell Wilson; then I remember the note Bianca left with Brady about how she wrote to me. "By the way, where's my fan mail?"

"In my office. I keep meaning to bring it over," he says flippantly.

"Drop it off at the house by the end of the day," I tell him. "I haven't seen any in months, so I want to get started on it."

"Right, sure," he says. "And what's your son's name again?" he asks, pulling out a pad and paper from his pocket. "Brady Dunn?"

"Yep, and don't even try to dig up info on his mother or make up something else," I warn him.

"Suit yourself. Better grab an umbrella, because they're gonna throw so much shit at you, you won't know what hit you."

"Whatever. I'll manage," I tell him as I walk back to my Land Cruiser.

"Oh, and, Quinton?" Wilson calls out just as I reach the car door. "From now on you better be damn careful with your hookups or this shitstorm will rain down on them as the most likely culprit."

"Good thing I'm not hooking up with anyone," I tell him.

"Like I'm gonna believe that!" he calls back, followed up with a chuckle.

"Believe it or not, it's the truth," I tell him before I climb in my SUV and drive away.

Callie

Friday night when I get home, I open up my laptop to check my emails before going to bed and instantly get sidetracked.

Front and center on the headline news is a photo of Quinton and Brady, the one that was just taken a few hours ago.

Wow. News moves fast.

I click on the article and find another photo of Brady in the hat and diaper I made him with one of the celebrity tabloid magazines promising more photos in Sunday's edition. Reading through the article while holding my breath, I make sure there's no mention of Bianca. Thankfully there's not. Yet.

Will they be able to figure out who Brady's mother is?

She's gone, and only a handful of people know, so I seriously doubt it.

Then, just as I begin to relax, I hear it --- the sound of a key being inserted in the front door.

Son of a bitch!

With all that happened with Bianca over the weekend, I forget about my promise to get a restraining order and change the locks on the damn doors!

Felix, also startled, jumps off the back of the couch and takes off down the hall, probably to hide underneath the bed. He's never liked John and used to sneak around to pounce and scratch his bare feet whenever he walked by.

Setting my laptop aside, I get to my feet just as John steps inside the house.

"Get out!" I yell at him.

"Just let me talk for a minute!" he exclaims. "You always did that, jumped down my throat before I could say a word."

"Maybe because I could predict your bullshit and just didn't want to hear it," I counter. "Get out!"

"I talked to my lawyer, and he said that until the divorce is finalized and the assets are divided, this is still my house too."

Shit. There goes my bluff that I'll call the cops on him.

"You're not staying here," I tell him.

"I heard about Bianca," he says. "I wanted to check on you, to see how you're doing."

"How did you hear?" I ask. "There wasn't an obituary in the paper."

When John cringes, I instantly know that he hadn't been prepared to answer that question.

Crossing my arms over my chest, I say, "So, that means you talked to one of Bianca's friends? Or maybe her roommate?" I guess. "You went to her apartment to see her, didn't you? Were you going over to give her more drugs when you found out she died from the last batch you probably funded?"

"I swear I didn't give her any drugs or money while she was pregnant," he responds. "Only...only the other night. She told me she left the baby with his father and needed..."

So that explains why John came over here Saturday night. He felt guilty about what he had just done.

"Needed to get so high she never woke up again?" I finish for him. "You killed her, and you're gonna have to live with that for the rest of your life!"

"I'm sorry, Callie. I swear I didn't know what would happen!"

God, I can't even stand the sight of this bastard, not after finding out the truth, that he likely got a blowjob or who knows what from my sister before he threw drugs or money at her like a whore Saturday, days after she had just given birth to Brady. John knew she was gonna buy drugs if he didn't supply them himself. Maybe he didn't know how much she would do at one time, but he knew what would happen and he did it anyway! I want him gone, and if the police won't remove him from the house, luckily I think I know someone who will.

Walking away from John, I leave him in the living room and head for the kitchen where I charge my phone at night. Thankfully, Quinton and I exchanged numbers back when Brady was in the hospital, so I call him up and pray he answers.

"Is this a booty call?" Quinton says when he picks up. "Because I'll have you know that I having feelings too –"

"Not a booty call. Can you come over? Right now? There's a... situation," I interrupt his teasing to quietly tell him.

"I'm on my way," he says without hesitation, and I hear static on his side like he might be dressing already. "You need to leave the phone on?"

"Sure," I say. "Door's unlocked."

I lay my phone face up on the counter and then ignore it while fixing a glass of water and taking a seat on one of the barstools. John eventually wanders in to continue our lovely conversation.

"You know, the attorney said half of everything in the house and in our joint checking and saving account is mine too," is his first statement, angering me even more.

"Well, your attorney is lying to you, trying to convince you to waste more money you don't have on his legal fees. Because *my* attorney assures me that with the proof of my earnings, which is pretty much ninety-eight percent of the earnings in those accounts, no judge will award you squat."

"We'll see," he says, leaning his elbows on the counter across from me.

"We will. Because if you think you'll get anything from me after your affair, you're dead wrong. I earned that money. I saved it for the baby you never gave me."

"Give me another chance," he pleads. "I'll do everything you wanted me to do, take the vitamins, exercise, stop jerking off, drinking, and using. This time I'll do it all so you can get pregnant."

"Hmm. Such a tempting offer," I mutter as if I'm considering it. "But I'm gonna have to say no."

"This is why our marriage didn't work!" he shouts at me, so close to my face I can smell the alcohol on his breath. "You were such a bitch to me, and you still are!"

"Wow. With all of your kind, sweet words, what was I thinking?" I joke. "There hasn't been a single moment that I've regretted kicking you out on your sorry ass."

"That's not true," he retorts. "I know you regret wasting precious time on conceiving. Now you're fucked, figuratively speaking only. You're almost thirty-seven. Without me, you have *zero* chance of getting knocked up before you hit forty."

His words hurt me, just like he intended, but I refuse to let him see me upset.

"Actually, I thank God every day that I *didn't* bring your spawn into the world. *That* would have been a tragedy. And now I have a nephew to care for and love, so I think I'll be just fine."

"Nephew?" John asks in confusion. "How did you know Bianca had a boy, or where the hell he is?"

"Oh, I know because his father is a nice guy who tracked me down and lets me see him whenever I want. Brady's adorable, which told me right away that he wasn't yours. Thankfully, the DNA proved that fact, so my nephew definitely lucked up on the genetic lottery." Leaning forward across the counter like I'm gonna let him in on a secret I say, "I bet you'll never guess who his father is. Go ahead, try."

Right on time, the front door opens and closes again. Then John's eyes widen and keep moving up when Quinton obviously appears behind me.

"No fucking way," John mutters. "That's...that's Quinton Dunn!"

I glance over my shoulder just because I want to see his gorgeous face for myself.

"What do you know, it sure is."

Quinton's dressed in a plain white tee and dark gray sweatpants, but he still somehow manages to look threatening in the casual attire, or maybe that's the scowl on his face. Shit, is he mad because I bothered him tonight? Maybe I shouldn't have called him. His blue eyes meet mine, assessing me quickly from head to toe on the stool before they go back to John.

When I look over at my soon to be ex-husband again, he's smiling like he's getting ready to meet his longtime hero.

"Hey, I'm a huge fan!" John says.

"Did you ask him to leave?" Quinton speaks to me when he comes to a stop towering over my stool.

"Yep."

"And he refused?"

"Yep."

Stomping over to the other side of the counter, Quinton grabs a fistful of the front of John's shirt, hard enough to yank him to his feet.

"What the –" John starts.

"When I throw you out, you're gonna crawl back into whatever shithole you came from, and you're never gonna show your face here again. Got it?" Quinton asks him, and John reluctantly nods. "If I see you over here or Callie tells me that you came back, I'll beat you bloody; and then I'll let our linemen use you as their tackle dummy. Understood?"

John gives another nod of understanding before Quinton literally drags him to the front door that I hear open and quickly close again, which allows me to finally exhale in relief.

Now to apologize to Quinton for interrupting his Friday night.

I climb down off my stool and start back into the living room when I nearly run into Quinton, who is returning to the kitchen.

"Thanks," I tell his broad chest that smells woodsy and comforting. "I'm sorry I bothered you, but he knew the police couldn't make him leave so..."

"It's fine," he says. Grabbing my upper arms, he holds me away from him to look down at me. "Are you okay?"

"Yeah, just angry and frustrated," I answer on a sigh. I'm so embarrassed that Quinton had to intervene or hear all the shit John said through the phone line that I'm unable to meet his eyes.

"Do you want me to stay or do you want to come back to the house with me?" Quinton asks.

And oddly enough, my first instinct is to say, *yes, stay with me* or take him up on the offer to sleep under the same roof as Brady for a night, but my pride causes me to shake my head instead. "No, I'm fine. He won't come back tonight. And I'll get the locks changed first thing Monday morning."

"You sure?" he asks. "I have plenty of bedrooms."

"I'm sure," I lie. "Go and get back to whatever you were doing before I called."

"Oh, you mean get back to the harem of women I keep in my dungeon?" he teases with his trademark crooked grin.

"Right. I'm sure they're missing you."

"I was actually holding our glow worm and getting ready to watch one of the *Fast and Furious* movies I've seen a hundred times. Not quite as exciting as the harem, right?" he asks, but it sounds pretty exciting and perfect to me.

Wait. Did he say *our* glow worm? I'm sure he just means he and I are Brady's closest relatives.

"How's the home nurse think Brady's doing with the light?" I ask rather than dwell on how happy one word makes me.

"Pretty good. She drew some more blood from his foot tonight, which always makes me want to hurl and nearly chip a tooth from gritting my teeth. Hopefully, if his bilirubin is down some more, he'll come off of the light tomorrow."

"That's good," I agree.

"Kelsey's keeping an eye on Brady, so why don't we turn the movie on here, and I can stick around to make sure the asshole gets the message?" Quinton asks.

"That's not really necessary," I tell him before he pulls away and tromps back to the living room without another word. When I follow him, I see he's holding back the curtain that faces the street.

"His car's still out there," Quinton points out.

Shit.

"Fine. Stay if you insist," I concede before flopping down on the sofa.

"You got any popcorn?" Quinton asks, heading back to the kitchen.

"Cabinet next to the microwave," I shout so he can hear me.

It only takes me a minute searching through the TV guide to find the right movie. And soon the sound of popping and the smell of buttery goodness fill the air. After the microwave dings, Quinton returns to the living room with one big plastic bowl of temptation rather than two. He sinks down onto the cushion next to me so we can share, his considerable weight causing such a large divot that I roll closer to him until our legs are touching.

"Turn it up. There are no babies sleeping here," Quinton instructs, which is all the reminder I need that I probably won't ever have any sleeping babies in my house.

John, the asshole, was right.

In the time it takes to sort through men by dating again, the chances of getting remarried is low, so the likelihood of conceiving after however many years all that takes is highly improbable.

CHAPTER NINETEEN

Callie

"Hey," I say in greeting when Kelsey opens Quinton's front door Sunday morning. Over the past week, I've learned that she really is a sweet girl, but I can't help the pang of jealousy I feel knowing she's here day in and day out with Brady. And, yeah, I'm a tad jealous that she stays here with Quinton overnight too, especially if she gets to see him shirtless.

"Hey, I was about to call you!" Kelsey says, nearly bouncing up and down with excitement. "Where have you been?"

"What's up?" I ask since I don't want to explain why I didn't come over yesterday. Quinton even called and texted me, but I ignored both. I was too busy throwing a pity party and couldn't be bothered. All I wanted was one day to cry into a pint of chocolate ice cream, watch sappy movies with Felix curled up in my lap, and mourn the loss of my sister, my marriage, and my chances of motherhood.

"Quinton left us tickets for today's game," Kelsey explains.

"Brady's off the light therapy, so Quinton wanted us to bring him to the stadium to meet everyone!"

"What?"

"Oh, and don't worry. Quinton says it's a family suite with seating indoors and out. So if it gets too chilly, we can bring Brady inside. He has the cutest Wildcats onesie to wear with the hat and diaper you made him. I put the diaper on the outside, so he looks like a tiny superhero. Wait until you see him!" she rambles excitedly.

"I'm not really a football person," I tell her as I shut the front door and follow her inside.

"Come on, Callie. It'll be fun. Quinton really wants you to come."

"He does?" I ask in shock. "Me? You mean you and Brady."

"No, he said and I quote, '*Even though she's gonna protest, I hope you can drag her along too.*'"

"Huh," I mutter, trying not to get excited about something so insignificant and ridiculous.

"So is that a yes?" she asks as we walk into the living room where Brady's sleeping in his pack and play. Thursday night, once Quinton knew Brady would be sticking around, he went and bought an actual crib after practice and set up the room across the hall from his master bedroom as Brady's nursery. Embarrassingly enough, Kelsey tells me that there's even a huge photo of Brady and me on the wall, along with some of the others we had made Friday.

Peeking over the edge of the pack and play to see Brady sprawled out in his cute little Wildcats outfit is too much. I have to pick him up and hold the cutie pie. Just being away from him for a day had me missing him. And if I refuse to go to the game today, Kelsey will take Brady, and I'll have to wait until tomorrow to spend time with him.

Before I can respond to tell her I'll go, the stacks of cardboard boxes sitting off to the side grab my attention.

"What's all that?" I ask Kelsey.

"Oh, fan mail. Quinton started working on it Friday night but

PERFECT SPIRAL

has barely made a dent in it. He's hoping to reply to all the kids before the end of the month."

"Wow," I mutter in surprise at yet another kindness from Quinton when it comes to children, first visiting the sick kids in the pediatric unit of the hospital and now responding personally to his fans. It's surprisingly...sweet. I can't help but wonder if becoming a father is the reason he's making such an effort. And, holy shit, he has a lot of fans. Maybe it's finally time for me to see him in his element, to figure out why so many people love him.

"Okay, fine. I'll go to the game," I reluctantly agree.

"Yay!" Kelsey cheers. "Oh, and I forgot to mention Quinton left each of us one of his jerseys. Well, they're not *his*, but the women's versions, you know? I'm so excited. We might get to be on television!"

"Settle down, girl. It's just a football game," I tease her, even if I'm getting somewhat excited too.

"Let's get changed, pack up Brady's bag, and then we'll be ready to leave."

THE STADIUM IS ALREADY PACKED when we get there, even though it's still forty-five minutes until kickoff. I have to admit that the family suite is impressive. There are rows and rows of free food and drinks at the buffet, and everyone's incredibly nice when they come over to meet Quinton's son for the first time.

Once the game starts, most of the group heads outside to the seats. Since the sun is shining down on the stadium, unobstructed by clouds and the temperature is seventy degrees, mild for October, Kelsey and I bundle Brady in a warm, fleece blanket and take him outside too.

The crowd below us and above us in the stands are shouting and cheering loudly for their team when the announcer starts introducing the players. When the booming voice gets to Quinton's name, he rushes out of the smoky, fire blazing tunnel to the applause of thousands of fans. It's the first time I actually realize just how famous the giant man is. A glance around the bleachers shows that everyone in this stadium loves him. Many of the fans are wearing his number eighteen jersey too.

And yeah, I feel sort of special sitting in the team's family section wearing a jersey provided by the man on the field himself. There may be dozens of other big, strong players down there with him, but Quinton is...different. His presence is impossible to overlook.

"This is so awesome!" Kelsey exclaims after the kickoff.

I'm not too familiar with football, but I do know which one is the quarterback position, and it's not Quinton.

"Wait. Why isn't Quinton playing?" Kelsey asks, voicing my same question.

"No clue," I mutter, glancing to the sideline where Quinton looks tense and frustrated, holding his helmet down by his side.

Everyone in the box with us is whispering, asking the same thing. The backup quarterback isn't terrible, but he rarely throws during the first quarter, handing off the ball to the running back on most plays.

Finally, in the second quarter, Quinton pulls on his helmet and jogs onto the field for the first time. The entire stadium erupts into deafening cheers.

After the huddle, Quinton stands tall and proud in his uniform, gold pants and a navy jersey over shoulder pads, looking powerful and confident as he shouts words I don't understand and his teammates move around to follow his orders. The ball snaps, and then Quinton's dropping back, looking down the field for a receiver. He throws the ball with the force of a bullet leaving a gun. It spirals in a perfect arch through the air and lands right in his teammate's hands.

Wow.

Quinton's so...commanding and sexy out there. I watch in awe as he continues to lead his team down the field and score a touchdown, the Wildcats taking the lead after neither team was able to score in the first quarter. The Wildcats' female kicker then adds six more points with two field goals before halftime.

During the break, Kelsey and I take turns holding Brady so that we can each grab a bite to eat ourselves before the game starts back up.

Kelsey's holding Brady when Quinton enters the game for the first time in the third quarter. I find myself holding my breath every time the ball is snapped until he throws it or hands it off to the running back, since there are several times when a defensive player breaks through the line and nearly takes him down.

And then, at the beginning of the fourth quarter, a Shark player spins around to avoid a block and plows into the front of Quinton. The ball barely leaves his hand before Quinton's slammed backward to the ground. He was sacked once in the first half, but he got up, brushed the grass off and kept going.

This time, though, Quinton doesn't move after the other man climbs off of him and celebrates his brutality.

Everyone in the crowd gasps in concern, and some of us get to our feet.

The medical staff runs out onto the field to check on Quinton as the jumbotron keeps replaying the vicious hit over and over again.

When Quinton finally sits up, the entire stadium blows out the breath they were holding and applauds in relief.

Thank God!

I'm not sure what happened to him, but it's a good sign that he's sitting up and talking. A few more minutes pass, and the men pull Quinton to his feet, helping him stagger off the field and back through the tunnel to the locker room.

"Oh my God, that was scary," Kelsey says, clutching at my upper arm with her free hand, Brady gripped in her other arm.

"Do you think he's okay?" I ask her.

"I don't know. I hope so," she answers.

"Should we try to go down there?" I ask.

"I don't think it's that easy, Callie. Security will never let us through," she tells me.

"Come on," a tall, older gentleman with whitish-blond hair says to us. "I can take you to the locker rooms."

"You can?" I ask him skeptically.

"Yeah, my daughter's Roxy Benson," he says proudly with a smile. "So I'm on the list to get through security."

"Okay, great. Thank you," I tell him as we follow him through the stadium toward an elevator.

We go down the many levels, and when the elevator doors open, again we're immediately greeted by stadium security guards dressed in all black.

"They're with me," the man says, showing the pass around his neck. "This is Quinton Dunn's son. These ladies are his guests from the family suite."

The two guards look at each other silently for a few seconds before one nods.

"Let's see your tickets, and we'll let you through this time, but Mr. Dunn needs to get them passes."

"Thanks," I tell him while showing him my and Kelsey's tickets, since her hands are still full with Brady.

After that checkpoint, we face two more that Roxy's father talks us through before we finally make it to the training room. Through the glass wall of windows, we can see Quinton sitting on a padded table while an army of men and women gather around him.

"Thank you, Mr. Benson," I tell Roxy's dad. "We'll wait for him here. I know you want to get back up there to watch your daughter."

"Good luck, ladies. Here's hoping the best for our QB," he says before starting back to the elevator.

Kelsey and I watch and wait as the attendants shine a light into Quinton's eyes, feel around his head and talk to him for several minutes. A few of the staff trickles out of the room; and when there's only one remaining, he shakes his head and says something to

Quinton that causes the giant man to pick up the helmet sitting next to him and throw it across the room where it slams into the wall.

I guess the news wasn't what Quinton wanted to hear.

"Do you think...you think we should come back later?" Kelsey asks. "He looks upset."

"Um, let me go in first and talk to him," I suggest, handing her Brady's diaper bag. I know Quinton wouldn't hurt us or anyone else, but if he's gonna cuss and yell in anger, I would rather it be at me instead of Kelsey and Brady, who might get upset.

Once the last doctor leaves Quinton alone, I ease into the room where Quinton's still sitting on the edge of the table, his head hanging sadly.

"Hey," I say with my approach.

Quinton's head whips around, and his eyes widen in surprise when he sees me. "What are you...how did you get down here?" he asks, holding a hand up to the back of his damp, sweaty head as if it still hurts.

"Oh, um, Roxy Benson's dad helped me, Kelsey and Brady get through security. Is that okay?" I ask since he didn't sound all that happy to see me

"Yeah, whatever. It's fine," he answers.

"Are you okay?" I ask, stepping closer to examine him myself.

"Fucking concussion protocol. I'm out the rest of the game," he mutters.

"You've got a concussion?" I ask, wringing my hands in concern.

"I only blacked out for a few seconds," he replies.

"Concussions are serious, Quinton," I tell him. "You can't risk getting another one so soon."

"Whatever," he grumbles. "I'm just so fucking frustrated and tired and...and horny."

Did he just say he's horny?

Wow, okay. Why does that cause a flutter down below?

"Sex is probably considered strenuous activity," I tell him, because I want to discourage him from engaging in casual sex with a stranger.

"What are you? A doctor now?" he snaps at me.

"No, I'm just the concerned aunt of your son," I tell him. "Remember him? Brady would probably like to grow up and get to know his father without any brain damage getting in the way."

"I hate how you're always right and shit," Quinton says, his speech slightly slurred before he jumps down from the table and immediately careens hard to the left. I reach out to grab his side, mostly just to hold him against the table since he easily has more than a hundred pounds on me. "Why did you yank the rug out from under me?" he looks down and asks.

"You're dizzy," I assure him since I'm not sure if he's joking or serious. "Sit here until I can find some trainers to help get you to the parking lot. I'll send Kelsey out with Brady to get him buckled in and come to the curb to pick us up."

"I'm fine," he says. "I can play."

"You're not fine, and you're not gonna play," I tell him, smacking my palms against his chest when he tries to move forward. It's about as effective as stopping Superman from going somewhere. "*Quinton!* Sit your ass down!" I order.

"Fine, I'll sit," he agrees while still standing with my hands pressed against the eighteen on his jersey.

"Good."

"If you'll flash me."

"What?" I exclaim. "Flash you? No way," I tell him with a shake of my head, removing my hands from him.

"Come on, Callie. Show me those titties. Just a quick peek," he slurs while reaching for the bottom of my jersey. Or his jersey that I'm wearing. Whatever. He's delusional if he thinks I'm gonna flash him in this fishbowl of a room with windows all around. Not that I would flash him in any other room either...

"I'm going to find the trainers," I tell him.

"They're back on the field with my team, where I should be," he declares, pushing me aside to walk past me.

Shit.

I grab his arm to stop him, but Quinton just drags me along as he staggers to the door. There's no way I can possibly restrain him on my own, and he definitely can't go back out into the stadium alone, or he might fall and bust his head again.

"Dammit, Quinton. Fine! Fine, I'll flash you. But you have to sit your ass down on that table and wait for the trainers to come back," I tell him, jerking on his arm and pointing a finger to the place where he can lay down in case he starts getting light headed.

"Okay," he agrees with a lazy grin before he stumbles back to the table and hops up on it, his legs so long they almost touch the ground. Almost. But his grass-stained cleats are about two inches from the floor, so they swing back and forth like an excited boy. "Let me see," he urges.

Oh, my God. Am I really gonna do this?

"Do you promise to sit there until the trainers come back?" I ask.

"Yep," he agrees.

Glancing around the glass windows, there's one security guard in sight along with Kelsey, who's looking at me wide-eyed in concern while bouncing Brady on her shoulder. My back will be to them both when I raise my shirt, so that's something at least.

"Fine," I sigh. "Here goes…"

"Wait," Quinton interrupts. "Let me do it."

"Do what?" I ask.

"Lift your shirt."

Ugh. This man-boy is such a pain in my ass. But he does have a concussion, and the odds are he won't even remember this in a few hours.

"Okay, but it has to be quick. Three seconds."

"Five," he counters.

"This is not a negotiation. Three or nothing."

"Agreed. But I count them," he replies.

With a resolute nod, I finally close the distance between us until I'm standing in the V of Quinton's spread thighs. I give a quick glance over my shoulder to check for witnesses, and it's still just one guard and Kelsey watching us. So, I do the only thing I can think of. I point at an imaginary person behind them before I say to him, "Go."

Quinton doesn't waste any time. His big fingers clench both sides of my jersey and jerk the material up past my breasts so that it's thankfully blocking my face, so I don't have to watch him staring at them.

"Mmm. Nice, Callie," Quinton mutters sending shivers down my arms. "Very nice. I like the navy blue lace. All it needs is a yellow bow, and it would be the team colors."

"That's three seconds," I warn him.

"Oh, I forgot to count. My bad," he replies. "One Mississippi."

"Quinton!" I warn, trying to take a step back, but he doesn't let go of the jersey.

"Two Mississippi."

"Three Mississippi," I huff and then jerk away from him, and he finally drops the jersey.

CHAPTER TWENTY

Quinton

Callie let me look at her tits.

I'm not sure why that amuses me so much, especially since I'm sitting in the fucking training room alone with her while my teammates are out on the field playing without me. I should be thinking about them, not how perfectly round and full Callie's tits were or how sexy the navy blue lace was, so sheer that I could see a hint of her pink nipples through it.

Like a juvenile boy with a Playboy magazine, my dick's hard from just looking at a pair of titties. Maybe I hit my head on the ground harder than I remembered.

"My head hurts," I tell Callie, rubbing my temple as a distraction from wondering how my team is doing and how Warren, my backup, is playing. Please let him hold this shit together.

"Sorry," she says with a frown. "I don't know if you can have headache medicine or not. Maybe I can get you some ice?"

"No. There's only one thing I need," I tell her seriously. "A soft place to lay my head. I know of just the spot, too. Why don't you hop up here so I can cozy up to your pillows?" I tease her, my grin breaking through despite trying to hide it.

"Oh grow up," Callie huffs.

"Something's growing, all right," I tell her, waggling my eyebrows.

"I'm gonna regret flashing you for the rest of my life, aren't I?" she asked. "Should've known better than to give in to the whims of the crippled."

"Hey! I'm not crippled, just concussed. And I've had worse."

"Concussions are dangerous, Quinton," Callie replies.

"I know," I agree with a nod. "If I had just hurt my ankle, you wouldn't have flashed me, would you?"

"We're never gonna talk about that again," Callie tells me through gritted teeth.

"Okay, fine. No more talking about it," I agree. "Doesn't mean I won't be thinking about them." Closing my eyes, I start fondling an imaginary pair of Callie's tits in the air in front of me before I bring my mouth down so I can flick my tongue over where one of her nipples would be.

"Jesus. He's worse than I thought," the voice I recognize as Lathan's says, causing my eyes to open and my hands to let go of the phantom boobs.

"Final score?" I ask anxiously, watching his face for the answer. I groan when he winces. "How bad?"

"The D was no joke. Warren got sacked. Twice," Lathan fills us in.

"But we were up by thirteen!" I exclaim.

"And he fumbled both times. The defense ran it back for a touchdown on the first one, and then our defense couldn't stop the Shark's offense when they recovered the second turnover at the twenty-yard line. Final score 14 to 13."

"Fuck!" I shout, wishing I had my worthless helmet to throw again.

"It wasn't your fault, man," Lathan says. "If you had been out there, you might have fumbled too."

"I don't fumble!" I yell in response. "One, I've only had one fumble in the last three years!"

"Watch and see. The Sharks defense is gonna be the best in the league this year," Lathan argues. "You just need to take it easy and be ready for next week's away game."

"If you or some of the other guys can help walk him out, I'll make sure he goes home and rests," Callie tells Lathan.

"I can walk on my own, woman!" I shout at her.

"No, he can't. He's dizzy and...and talking crazy. Don't believe anything he says," she whispers to Lathan.

"Don't listen to her! She's just regretting letting me see her boobs. Go ahead and show, Lathan, Callie. He's never seen a woman's breasts before."

"Knee him in the balls, Callie. Go ahead, he deserves it," Lathan mutters while glaring at me.

"Not in front of my son," I warn. "Wait. Where's my son?" I ask, looking through the glass to where Kelsey was just standing with Brady. Now there are tons of people crowded around, reporters, cameras and some fans.

When I glance back in question at Callie, she's looking at Lathan.

"Kelsey took Brady to get the car, remember?" Callie meets my eyes and asks softly. The hesitant look on her face is uncharacteristic of the usually feisty woman. "They came in to see you; then left about ten or fifteen minutes ago."

"Of course I remember," I tell her with a dismissive swipe of my hand through the air.

I don't remember.

"I must have been distracted, still thinking about your tits."

"What did Kelsey say she's making for dinner tonight?" Callie asks.

Fuck. Is that a trick question?

"Hamburgers?" I guess.

"No."

"Pork chops?"

"No."

"Okay, fine. I don't remember exactly what she said she was making."

"We asked you what you wanted, and you said you wanted takeout from the Burrito Barn."

"Oh," I mutter. "Right."

"Quinton, go home, take it easy and don't rush the doctors to release you to play," Lathan encourages.

"I'm sure the...forgetfulness and dizziness will pass in a few hours," I tell him.

"Check with Jon, the head of training, before you leave," Lathan tells Callie. "I'll go see if I can find him for you."

"Thanks, Lathan," Callie says, flashing him a smile.

A smile.

That's all it takes for me to be jealous of my best friend. How fucked up is it that I don't like Callie smiling at Lathan? Surely that's just the knot on my head fucking with me. Or maybe it's because I can see Callie with a nice guy like Lathan and it blows. After her husband cheated on her with her sister, it'll be impossible for Callie to trust another man, especially one with as big of a reputation as mine.

"I need to go shower and change," I say, climbing off the table.

This time the world doesn't tilt, so I think I'm good.

"Okay, but make it quick," she tells me through narrowed eyes.

"I'll keep an eye on him," Lathan assures her.

"What, are you gonna hold my dick for me while I shower?" I tease him. "I'm fine."

Callie

. . .

QUINTON IS NOT FINE. And the fact that he thinks he is concerns me even more.

He didn't remember the conversation we had with Kelsey. Sure, it was a short one, maybe two or three minutes, but it had just happened, and he didn't recall it.

"Hi, it's Callie, right?" An older man wearing a yellow Wildcats polo shirt comes up to me while I wait for Quinton to shower.

"Yes."

"Hi, I'm Jonathan Young, the head trainer. You'll be keeping an eye on Quinton tonight?" he asks.

I could decline and give the responsibility to Kelsey, but she may have her hands full with Brady while Quinton recovers.

"Yeah, I'll stay with him," I agree.

"Great. You'll need to wake him up every hour or two just to ask him a few basic questions, you know, what day is it, where he is, does he remember how he hit his head."

"Okay. I can do that," I tell him.

"If he doesn't wake up right away or if he can't answer the simple questions, you need to call an ambulance. And if you need anything or have any questions, give me a call," he says, pulling out a card from his wallet and offering it to me.

"Thank you, I will," I assure him. "Oh, and just a few minutes ago, Quinton and I were talking to his nanny, and then ten or so minutes later he didn't recall ever talking to her. Is that...normal after a concussion?"

He frowns in thought for several seconds. "Possibly, for the first few hours. But if he's still forgetting things tomorrow, you call me."

"Okay, thanks, Jonathan," I tell him, clutching his card between my fingers after he walks off.

I really hope Quinton didn't sustain any permanent brain damage, and I can't help but wonder how many other concussions he's had playing football. It's a dangerous sport, and I have a feeling based on the way he tried to get back on the field that he doesn't take the injuries seriously.

"Let's go," Quinton says when he reappears in the hallway, dressed in jeans and a plain blue tee with a Wildcats hat on and a pair of sunglasses.

"Nice disguise. The only ones that have ever turned out better were two kids underneath a long trench coat trying to look like an adult."

"Hard to come up with a disguise when you're six and a half feet tall," he counters before we start down the corridor. At least he doesn't look as off balance. In fact, he walks so fast that I nearly have to jog to keep up with his long legs.

"I'm staying with you tonight," I tell him, which brings him up short.

"You are?" he asks, looking down at me with an arched eyebrow.

"Yes. The trainer, Jonathan, said someone has to wake you up every few hours, and I didn't think it was fair to ask Kelsey to get up with Brady and with you, so...I'm staying," I inform him in a rush.

"Fine," he says, turning and picking up the pace again. "I'm starving. What's for dinner?"

Oh fuck.

"I'm joking," Quinton says, looking at me with his trademark grin. "I remember --- the Burrito Barn. Hope you like Mexican food."

"Sure, that's fine," I say, my breath rushing out in relief that he didn't forget again. Then I wince, wondering what else he remembers from earlier, which suddenly reminds me...

"Why didn't you play in the first quarter?" I ask him.

"Because I pissed off Coach," he mutters.

"What did you do?"

"I missed a team meeting Tuesday afternoon when we were in court. Then I walked out, missing practice Wednesday when Brady was in the hospital. If I had played, maybe we could've ran the score up early and won..."

"It's not your fault," I tell him. "And I'm proud of you for choosing Brady before you even knew he was yours."

Cutting his eyes over at me, he flashes me a small smile and says, "Thanks," effectively incinerating my panties yet again.

"Quinton. Quinton, wake up," I tell the sleeping, snoring giant, flipping on the bedside lamp before I start shaking his shoulder. I woke him at midnight, and now it's two a.m., and he's passed out on his stomach taking up a good portion of his humongous bed.

"Uhh," is his grumbled response, but he doesn't open his eyes.

"Quinton, I need you to wake up and talk to me for a second," I tell him with another shake.

"Flash me your tits again. Bet that will wake me up," he replies with a grin when he rolls to his side to face me.

"What's your name?" I ask him, ignoring the embarrassing reminder of what I did earlier.

"Well, that's an easy one since you just said it three times," he remarks.

Even though he's being a smartass, I'm glad he was alert enough to count the number of times I said his name.

"Where are you?"

"In my house, trying to sleep, but some harpy keeps waking me up and blinding me with a spotlight," he mutters around a yawn. "And I'm thirsty. Can you fetch me some water?"

"Fine," I grumble before heading down the hall to his kitchen and fixing him a glass. There's an empty bottle on the counter from where Kelsey just woke up with Brady around one. This whole not sleeping for more than an hour thing is seriously exhausting.

Cold glass of water in one hand and my cell phone with an alarm set for every two hours in the other, I return to Quinton's bedroom and find he's fallen asleep again.

"Quinton, here's your water," I tell him. His eyes blink open again before he sits up in the bed, letting the covers puddle around his waist and revealing his naked upper body.

Now I'm the one who needs the cold glass of water dumped over my head to cool my libido.

"Thanks," he mumbles, accepting the glass and downing it in one big gulp before placing it on the bedside table. Quinton lays his head back on the pillow but doesn't go back to sleep. Those sleepy blue eyes silently assess me as I stand there trying not to stare at his muscular arms or chest or shoulders...

"Thanks for waking me up even if I'm cranky," he eventually says.

"Why do you want to play such a brutal sport?" I ask him.

"Because I love it," he answers right away. "And I get paid a lot of money to do what I love."

"The money can't be worth the dangers," I say confidently.

"I get paid *a lot* of money," he says again. "Go ahead, Google it," he directs nodding to the phone in my hand. "It's public info. Why do you think women are so eager to get in my pants?"

I withhold my response that the money is only partially responsible for why women want in his pants. More than likely, it's because of his stunning good looks.

"Go ahead and look it up," Quinton urges while lifting his head to fluff his pillow. "I'll wait."

Curious only as an accountant who likes numbers, I give in and do the internet search. The first article from this past March says all I need to know in the headline, "Dunn signs seventy-five million dollar contract extension with the Wildcats, fifty-five million guaranteed over the next four years."

"Holy shit," I mutter, picturing all those digits for one man's salary. No, just four years of his salary, which doesn't include what he made the first few years of his career. "That's a heck of a lot of money to play a sport."

"The lifespan of a professional quarterback is short, but it's the most important position on the field," Quinton tells me, his eyes falling closed again. "They pay me well to take the hits."

"Yeah, but that's an outrageous amount of money," I tell him. "Especially when you have school teachers barely able to pay bills with their earnings and police officers risking their lives for a few measly dollars."

"I agree, but my career only lasts ten years, twelve if I'm lucky and don't get injured or too old and slow. I don't have any skills or a backup plan. What they pay me has to last me my entire life. It's enough for me to know that Brady will have everything he needs, that he can go to any college he wants, and I can pay for it."

"What if he wants to be a football player like his father?" I ask, and Quinton smiles in response.

"That would be great, but he's gonna finish his degree first. I didn't. I went into the draft my junior year, and that's the one thing I regret..." he trails off.

"You didn't finish college?" I ask.

"No. In case you haven't noticed, I'm not the brightest bulb in the box, and all I wanted to do was play football. Now I wish I would've finished, you know? Especially with Brady...I don't want him to be a dropout because I was."

"You can still finish your degree. You're only, what? Twenty-six or twenty-seven?" I ask.

"Twenty-five," he answers.

Damn, he's younger than I thought.

"So there's plenty of time for you to finish, especially if you only had one year to go."

"Doubtful," he mutters. "Without professors who pass me just for being on the school's football team, I'm shit out of luck."

"You're a smart guy, you could do it on your own even while you're playing football."

"How the hell could I do that?" he asks.

"Online. Lots of public and private universities have online programs. We could transfer your credits, and you could take classes during the spring and summer," I tell him, but he rolls his eyes before he closes them again. "I could help you."

Blinking his eyes open again, he stares silently at me. "You're gonna stick around until the spring and summer?"

"Of course," I reply right away. "Brady's my nephew. I'm not going anywhere."

"Oh, right," Quinton mutters, rolling over and putting his back to me, abruptly ending our conversation. "See you in two hours."

"See you then," I tell him, somewhat confused by the sudden, abrupt halt in our conversation before I give up, turning off his lamp and slipping out the room.

∽

Quinton

Between Callie waking me up every few hours and Brady getting up to eat, I didn't sleep much Sunday night. So, when I showed up to the stadium Monday morning, I was a little relieved that the team doctors said I wasn't cleared for practice.

After a long nap at home, I grabbed a shower and decided to get back to work on the fan mail. Placing one of the boxes next to my recliner, I have a pad of personalized stationary in my lap, along with a stack of envelopes, previously autographed postcards, and my favorite pen.

"So, do you want me to leave since you'll be home the rest of the day?" Callie asks when she walks into the living room, freshly showered, her hair still wet, wearing those damn pink and white striped satin pajamas that look like they would slide right off her body. She reminds me of a candy cane, one that my tongue is eager to lick from top to bottom.

"No, of course not," I tell her because I've gotten so used to having her around. "You can stay or go. Up to you."

"Catching up on fan mail?" she asks, gesturing to the pile around me.

"Yeah," I say on an exhale. "My manager had it stashed away for about six months, so now I'm *waaay* behind."

"Need any help?" she asks, taking a seat on the sofa, which I assume means she's gonna stay.

"Nah, I'll get through it, especially since I have free time until they clear me to practice again," I reply, withholding the real reason I don't want her to go through the stack.

I'm still looking for a letter or letters from Bianca. Since I don't know what they will say, I want to see them first before I consider letting Callie read them. And besides, these are my fans, so I should be the one to write them all back.

Hours later, after signing a few hundred more letters to fans, I finally find it, Bianca's letter. Dated March twenty-ninth, it reads,

Dear Quinton,

I'm not sure if you remember me. We met at Limelight several months ago, and well, I'm pregnant. And while I've been clean since I took a pregnancy test last month, I just don't think I can keep it up. That's why I've decided to have an abortion. I'm not even sure why I'm writing to let you know. You're probably relieved. I just wanted to tell someone, and I can't talk to my friends about it or my sister. She would hate me even more than she already does and would think it's someone else's baby.

Maybe I'm writing you because I'm hoping you'll talk me out of it. I guess you could call this my own personal Hail Mary pass, but everyone knows how those always turn out. Just in case, all of my contact information is below.

Bianca Williams

Holy shit.

She was seriously considering ending the pregnancy. Thank God she didn't even though I just found her letter. Honestly, I'm not sure what I would have done if I had received it months ago. I would've probably gone to see her and talk to her. Would she still be alive if so?

Maybe Callie's right. Maybe...maybe it is my fault that Bianca's dead. I knocked her up, left her to figure it all out on her own; and for some reason, she still decided to have Brady.

"Quinton, it's almost midnight. You going to bed anytime soon?" Callie asks, snapping my head up as I look around for the clock to verify the time. Fuck.

"Um, I'll probably stay up a little longer, until Brady's next feeding," I tell her, folding the letter up and placing it back in the envelope.

"You don't have to do all that in one day, you know," she says, nodding to the second box now at my feet. "And you need to get plenty of rest while you recover from the concussion."

"I know, just a little longer," I promise, touched that she's worried about me. In fact, I want to pull her on top of me and kiss the sad frown off of her beautiful face.

"Okay, well, good night," she replies.

"Good night, Callie."

Once she disappears down the hallway, I start digging through the rest of the boxes, hoping to find more letters from the same address as the local one from Bianca.

There's no more in the second box, but in the third, the more recent mail, I locate one. My heart is as frantic as a jackhammer in my chest as I carefully open it. It's almost spooky in a way, like reading mail sent from the grave. This one is dated August second, just weeks ago, and says,

Dear Quinton,

You're not an easy man to get in touch with. I've tried to get a phone number or home address for you with no luck, so I decided to write you again.

I couldn't go through with it. I couldn't have an abortion, not after I felt him move. I'm not sure, but I think it's a boy.

I'll find a way to contact you when he's born so you can see him, but I'm not cut out to be a mother. He's the only reason I've been sober and clean for eight months because I couldn't imagine hurting him. Once he's born, he deserves to have a mother and a father who loves him and can take care of him.

That's why I need your help.

If you don't want him, I'll understand, but I need you to take a test to prove the paternity. I don't want money or anything else from you. I just want proof for my sister. If you can do that for me, I know she would take him and raise him. All she wants is to be a mother. But I made a mistake, and only a test proving you're the father will convince her. Otherwise, she'll push him and me away again.

Please call me as soon as possible.

Bianca Williams

So BIANCA DIDN'T TAKE Brady to Callie because she didn't think Callie would believe he was mine and not John's. And when she finally tracked down my address, for whatever reason, she obviously decided not to stick around after she dropped off Brady and walked away. If I had seen her that night, could I have convinced her to stay? To not turn to drugs? Would she have come back for him if she hadn't overdosed?

If I show these letters to Callie, she'll likely blame me, or worse, herself for not believing her sister. But it doesn't feel right keeping them from her either.

After a few more minutes of deliberation, I take the letters down the hall and knock on her open bedroom door.

"Yeah?" Callie asks right away from inside the dark room, telling me she probably wasn't asleep yet. She reaches over to turn on the lamp beside the bed so she can sit up in bed and see me. "Everything okay?"

"I, um, I found these letters," I tell her while looking down at the paper, trying to figure out what to say to her. "They're from Bianca. Do you want to read them?"

"Bianca?" she asks. "She...she wrote you?"

"Yeah, apparently she tried to contact me months ago. I'm so sorry I didn't get them sooner," I tell Callie honestly.

"Should I read them?" she asks me, biting her bottom lip.

"That's completely up to you," I reply since I'm not sure if they will help or hurt her even more.

With a heavy exhale, she says, "Let me read them."

Climbing up on the empty side of the bed, I hand the two letters to her. Tears run down Callie's cheeks as she takes her time reading the first one, most likely because of how close Bianca came to ending the pregnancy. And on the second one, a pitiful sob escapes from her mouth before she slaps her hand over it.

Unable to witness any more of her heartbreak, I wrap my arms around her and hold her while she cries.

"I'm sorry," I say into her hair. "I should've read them sooner. Maybe I could've helped her."

"It's not...it's not your fault," she tells me through the sniffles.

"It's not yours either," I assure her. "They hurt you, and she didn't deserve your forgiveness until she had earned it, if she ever could have earned it back."

"Thanks, Quinton," Callie tells me, her damp face still pressed against my bare chest and her arms winding around my waist. "Will you...will you sleep with me tonight? I don't want to be alone."

"Yeah, sure," I tell her, surprised by her honesty and her request.

Without letting her go, I maneuver us both underneath the covers and lay my head down on the pillow. Callie's sweet, passion fruit scent fills my nose, and her pajamas are as soft and silky under my palms as I imagined. I bet her skin would feel even better and taste delicious.

Those are horrible, selfish thoughts for me to be having at this moment when she's so upset, but I'm a man, and a beautiful woman I want is practically lying on top of me.

And even though cuddling up to Callie without her naked is nearly torture, I like it. She's seeking comfort from me, and that means something, more than all the past hookups and flings.

CHAPTER TWENTY-ONE

Quinton

Tuesday morning was spent getting my head checked out and answering a billion questions for the team docs. That night, I had hoped that after sleeping in Callie's bed the night before that things would be different between us. But the woman went right back to her cool, aloof self, barely speaking a word to me. It was like Monday night never happened between us, that she didn't cling to me all night except for when she jumped up and offered to feed Brady. Either those few hours of intimacy didn't mean anything to her, or it did, and she's too scared to admit it. Both possibilities are frustrating and depressing as fuck.

On Wednesday morning, the docs finally clear me to start practicing again. I've felt fine and haven't had any more memory lapses or dizziness. In fact, I feel great running drills and plays on the practice field and off of it. Really good actually.

And so fucking horny.

Tonight's the night I'm gonna make Callie pony up on our bet; and thankfully, Kelsey is back at work this week and sleeping in her own house. She's agreed to come stay every weekend since I'm always so busy getting ready for games, but Callie's been watching Brady during the day, and even staying here at night.

After she slept here Sunday night to wake me up every two hours, I figured she would go back home Monday night. I'm happy she didn't since I ended up holding her. But I know that Brady is the real reason for her overnight stays.

Last night Callie slept alone in the guest room, and I found it hard to sleep without her. So, tonight I'm gonna try to seduce her to get her in my bed. I've been cleared by the doctors for all forms of "strenuous activity," and I haven't had sex in over a week. It's time to get back on the saddle. Callie's saddle preferably.

A few days ago I cranked up the heat in the house for Brady's sake, of course, and it's so warm I haven't worn a shirt around the house. I may not be the brightest crayon in the box, but I know Callie likes what she sees, so much so that I often catch her staring at me. It's the only time she's easily flustered, and I'm certain that she wants me more than just for comfort.

Tonight, I'm hopefully going to prove it. My methods may seem a little extreme, but Callie is a tough woman to crack. She's the only woman to sleep in a bed with me all night and not fuck me, and my balls still ache from the tease.

"Oh, Callie! Do you know what today is?" I call out to her from the sofa in the living room. She was cleaning the kitchen after she fixed an amazing dinner, but she should be nearly finished. And I just fed Brady his last bottle of the night and changed him, so he should be good for a few hours.

"What? The first time you've gone twelve hours without looking in a mirror?" she asks with a smirk when she joins me in the living room.

"Ha-ha, but no," I reply. "Today is one week since we made that bet. You know, the one about me not fucking anyone for a week? Or did you think I would forget after the concussion and all?"

"Well, congratulations. I'm not sure how you were able to survive such a painful feat. Would you like an award?" Callie asks dryly, her hands braced on the hips of her silky pink and white striped pajamas.

"I would like my *reward*," I answer. "Remember our terms?"

"Oh, right. A kiss," she says with an eye roll. "Let's just get it over with."

"Let's," I agree. "Come here."

With a heavy sigh, she starts to move closer to me. Since I refuse to sit up on the sofa, she braces a hand on the back of it to lean down towards me.

"I didn't say *where* I was gonna kiss you," I tell her when I press my finger to her parted lips. Her eyes widen in surprise right before I use my lightning quick reflexes to tug her pajama pants and panties down her legs. Then, I bury my face in her pussy, kissing her mound while grasping her thighs in each of my hands.

"What the hell are you...*oh God*," she moans, clutching my shoulders at the first long stroke of my tongue through her slit. She tastes sweet and salty, and I crave more.

When Callie doesn't tell me to stop or punch me in the back of my head as I half expected, I nudge her legs further apart to give me more room to delve my tongue into her tight, wet heat.

Her thighs tremble when she releases another low moan that sounds sort of like my name, so I pick her up off the floor, tug her bottoms off and pull her down on top of me, lining her up so that her pussy is right above my face. And then, I explore every inch of her with my tongue, teasing her clit with just the tip, thrusting inside her opening. I'm so absorbed in my task that it takes me a minute to realize when Callie starts bearing down, grinding herself on my face rather than trying to get away.

Fucking hell, she likes it.

Soon she's bucking and rolling her hips above me like a champion bull rider. I'm not gonna let her get off after just eight seconds, though. My palms slide up to cup her clenching ass cheeks and squeeze them while I eat her out.

"*Uh! Uhhh God!*" she shouts above me before her body shakes, tits bouncing beautifully under her pajama top as her juices flood my tongue almost faster than I can lap them up.

When Callie doesn't make any sort of move to get off this ride, I up the ante. While I'm sucking on her clit in a way that has her pulling my hair out and screaming my name, I slip two fingers inside of her pussy with one hand and use the other to press my fingertips to the puckered hole in the crease of her amazing ass.

"Yes!" becomes her new chant until I coax another orgasm from her. Watching her head thrown back, eyes closed, lips parted above me, I could do this all night. My only regret is that her shirt is still on.

After Callie slumps forward limply, catching herself on the armrest above my head, I relent and remove my tongue and fingers from her body. Tugging her down until her head is on my chest, I run my fingers over her hair, unable to help the smile on my face as I wait for her to recover. I even brace myself, worried that once the pleasurable high clears she'll go back to being angry at me for catching her off guard and tongue fucking her. Sure, it will hurt if so, but I know it's all just a defense mechanism because of all her trust issues that asshole husband of her caused.

Soon to be ex-husband.

"Mmm," Callie moans as she relaxes and cuddles against me even more. I'm pretty sure I even feel her damp lips on my chest before I'm distracted by her wandering hand. One heading right for the bulge of my sleep pants. Her palm strokes my length through the soft cotton material, causing me to hiss in a breath through my clenched teeth. When she grips me tentatively in her fist, it's nice, but it could be better.

I cover her small hand with my own and show her how I like to be squeezed and jerked. My lungs suck in another deep breath when her palm slips underneath my pants and boxers to grip my flesh tightly.

"God, Callie," I groan.

"It won't break, will it?" she asks softly, running her tongue over my collarbone while she jerks me off. Her words sound familiar. So does the way her hand feels on me...

Wait a second.

"That day in the hospital," I start to ask, and then her thumb swirls over the head of my dick just like I do when I masturbate. "Did you..."

"Yes," she answers. "But you started it. I just...finished it."

Holy fuck. All this time I thought I had some juvenile wet dream in public when, in fact, Callie had jerked me off.

"You're so big and thick," she whispers while her lithe and mostly naked body wiggles on top of me, doubling the size of my already enormous ego and cock. "How do you run around with this baseball bat between your legs?"

I bark out a laugh at her unexpected compliment to my cock.

"I'm not usually this hard on the football field," I tell her. "Feel free to get an up close and personal look at it, though."

That's all the motivation Callie needed to start moving her mouth down my chest, licking over my abs and around my belly button before she unleashes the beast from my pants.

"Wow," she mutters in awe as she continues to stroke it. "It'll take two hands and the suppression of my gag reflex to handle all of this."

"I'm sure you can handle it just fine," I tell her.

"Mmm," she replies, looking up to hold my eyes while her tongue takes its first lick from base to tip.

"Holy shit," I groan, grabbing the sofa cushions in my fists to keep from reaching down and shoving her mouth on me.

"I want to taste you a little, but then I want to feel you inside me," she says before swirling her tongue over the head of my dick, over and over again until my eyes roll back in my head.

"Who the hell are you, woman?" I ask through gritted teeth to try and hold off my release. This is so unlike the Callie I know. She doesn't answer my question, and I don't complain since her mouth is suddenly full of my cock.

I've gotten used to the Callie who barely tolerates me because

I'm the father of her nephew. The one who acts like it's punishment to be under the same roof as me. I thought she might want me, but it would be like pulling teeth to get her to admit it. Who knew she could be this damn sexy and forward?

Callie works hard to take all of my length but can only handle about three-quarters of my dick before she gags and pulls back. She gets an A for an enthusiastic effort.

"That's enough," I tell her, reaching to pull her up my body to kiss her lips. While I'm savoring her sweet fruity taste, she starts lowering her soaking wet pussy down on my cock.

"Fuck," I pull my mouth from hers to cry out at the unbelievable sensation. Her tight heat surrounds me like a too small glove that I'm dying to stretch. I've had a lot of sex, and I don't ever remember it feeling this fucking good.

Oh shit.

"Condom!" I shout as Callie lifts up and slams her pussy down on my shaft so hard I see stars. "I need a...need a...need you to do that again," I urge her. Just a little longer and I'll insist she climb off me so that we can take this to the bedroom where I have a drawer full of condoms.

My hands squeeze Callie's hips to hold her down on me or to pick her up and slam her again, I'm not sure which until I look up and see the shirt still covering her tits. I push it up and over her head while the champion bull rider makes another appearance, bouncing so good on my cock.

"Condom?" I say again. It's more of a question than a statement this time while filling my hands with her full, bare breasts for the first time. God, I've dreamed about these babies ever since she flashed me at the stadium. Fuck! I'm getting distracted again. "We need...we need to stop for a sec," I tell her. I sure as fuck don't want to stop. I want to cum so bad my dick is already leaking.

"So close," Callie moans, bracing her palms flat on my chest to work her hips faster.

"No, no, no," I tell her through panting breaths when I feel her walls constrict around my cock. "If you come, I'll come. No more...no more babies."

Callie falls forward, pressing her tits to my chest, and the new angle of filling her pussy to the hilt is so incredible I forgot what I was saying.

"I want a baby," she whispers while kissing my neck and grinding on my dick, so wet and hot. "More than anything."

"*Yesss, baby, yes*," I groan, grabbing her ass to move her faster.

Wait a second.

What the fuck did she say?

"Callie, stop!" I find the strength of all the Norse gods in the universe to say while pulling her mouth from where she's sucking hickeys on my neck so I can look at her face. "I can't just...just knock you up. That's insane!"

Dropping her forehead on my chest, her breath hitches as she says, "I know. You're right. If my husband couldn't do it in seven years, there's no way you could either."

That same competitive blood that flows through my veins and made me a professional quarterback starts to sizzle. It refuses to ever allow me to admit defeat.

"I didn't say I *couldn't* knock you up. I said I *wouldn't*," I clarify. My proud cock still buried deep inside of her twitches in absolute agreement.

Lifting her head, Callie's sad, stormy gray eyes lock with mine before she says the words that I know I'll regret but forever be powerless against.

"Prove it."

Blood roars in my ears, my heart hammers in my chest, and both of my lungs seize up as I try to find the strength to walk away. Whether it's my competitiveness or my compulsion to give Callie not just what she wants, but what I know she needs, I flip us over, putting her on her back. And then, I fuck her. Harder and deeper than anyone before. Not that I can think of anyone but the woman underneath me at this moment. The way her nails claw my back as I pound inside of her, how her heels dig into my ass urging me on, the sound of her whimpering moans that grow louder with every thrust until her legs stiffen and her pussy clamps down on my cock, preventing my retreat. She milks every drop of my explosive release from me. Those nails of hers hold me to her even closer, a silent plea that her body accepts all that I give her and not disappoint her again.

And just like that, my euphoria disappears into thin air thanks to the burden of regret. Not regret that I'll knock her up, oddly enough, but with the worry of how to deal with the regret if I don't.

CHAPTER TWENTY-TWO

Callie

"Oh, God, Quinton," I sigh in contentment from underneath him while combing my fingers through his dark hair and kissing the sweat slicked skin of his smooth chest that's above my mouth. Never before has sex been so... satisfying. Or maybe it's just the satisfaction of knowing this incredible man relented and agreed to try and give me what I've always wanted. More likely, it's the optimism that comes from being certain that if anyone can do this for me, it's Quinton.

The longer he remains quiet and unmoving on top of me, though, the more I begin to worry that he regrets his in-the-heat-of-the-moment decision and will refuse to do it again. It wasn't really fair for me to ask this major thing of him, knowing how tough it would be for him to stop as far as we had already gone without a condom.

"You okay?" I ask him, unable to take his silence any longer.

Finally lifting his head, he says, "Give me a few minutes, and we'll go again." The look of sheer determination on his face makes me smile even wider.

I kiss his lips in relief before I respond.

"Thanks for the offer, but, um, fertility wise it's best to only have sex once a day to give you time to increase your sperm count."

Lifting a dark eyebrow, Quinton says, "So no sex again until *tomorrow*? That's no fun."

"Hey, I didn't make the rules," I tell him with a laugh since I wouldn't mind another round right away. "And really, every other day is probably better, but since I'm likely ovulating now, we can try once a day for the next few days. I'll take a test tomorrow to narrow it down."

"So, what? You want me to just be your on-call sex stud from now on?" Quinton asks with his crooked smile. "I'm a little offended."

"Yeah, right," I mutter with a slap to his chest. "You've been trying to get in my panties since day one. Now pull out so I can lift my hips for half an hour to try and keep some of your studly swimmers up in there."

"You talking about wanting to keep my cum in your pussy shouldn't sound hot, should it?" he asks before crawling off of me to stand next to the sofa and pull his pajama pants back up over his swing-batter-batter cock.

"Oh, I think it's hot," I tell him as I shift my legs around so that they're resting on the top of the sofa and then tilt my head to look back at Quinton again. "And I've never come during sex before, so kudos for that since it's supposed to help draw the sperm in."

"You've never gotten off during sex?" he asks, and I shake my head. "Another challenge I accept. I'll make damn sure you come every single time I'm inside you," he says before strolling his cocky ass down the hall.

My ovaries do a little celebratory happy dance, suddenly liking the giant football player a little more.

He's gonna try to give me a baby!

While I love Brady to death, I know I'm only his aunt, nothing more to him. And I want to experience childbirth for myself, feel my baby growing and kicking in my belly. I reach down and rub a hand over my flat stomach, hoping to have a bump there soon.

And in the meantime, having sex over and over again with Quinton is no hardship. In fact, it may be difficult for me to resist him all but once a day when I already yearn to have him inside me, fucking me with that sexy determination of a true competitor. I've come to realize just how much Quinton loves to win, how he works hard to make himself an even better athlete. I'm certain that he has that same drive in everything he does. So now that he's agreed, he'll fuck me like his life depends on it until I get pregnant. All I have to do is lie back and hold on tight while he goes to work.

After I watch the clock for thirty minutes, I finally get up and shower, ridiculously sad to wash away any remnants of Quinton's stud missiles. Then, instead of sleeping in the guest room, I crawl into his bed where he's already laid down despite the fact that it's only a quarter past ten. You've gotta sleep when you can in a house with a baby.

I slide across the soft cotton sheets until I'm curled up to the front of his big, warm body, practically purring with happiness since he's my new best friend, my champion baby maker. "I'll get up with Brady tonight," I tell him when he throws out an arm over me. He humphs in what I assume is agreement. "Thanks for doing this, Quinton," I whisper in the darkness.

"Don't thank me yet," he mumbles.

How can he possibly doubt himself in this?

"Can I make a request?" I ask him. He humphs again in response. "Could you try not to, you know, sleep with anyone else while we're doing this? I need you to bring me your strongest stud missiles."

His sigh feathers through the front of my hair. "You get all my stud missiles," he concedes.

"Thanks," I reply with a smile on my face. "And, um, no masturbation."

"Then I guess you better pack your bags for all my upcoming away games," he says.

"I can do that," I agree with a smile. "And maybe I'll let Kelsey stay home some of them with Brady. You know, so we can catch up on our sleep and fuck as long as we want without any distractions or interruptions."

"You better stop talking," he mumbles, rocking his hips forward against my pelvis so that I can feel he's ready to go again.

My stomach muscles clench with desire, so I reach down to cup his bulge, causing him to growl and thrust into my palm.

"How long has it been since before, you know, you came earlier?" I ask him.

"The night at the hospital when *you* jerked me off," he replies.

"Oh, right," I mutter while I keep stroking him. "Well, in that case, we should probably relieve you of a little more sperm to make room for a fresh batch."

That's all it takes to get Quinton to roll on top of me, stripping me out of my clothes at record-breaking speed to get inside of me again.

Quinton

LAST NIGHT WITH CALLIE WAS...BEYOND incredible. Both times. And this morning when I woke up, I couldn't wait to be with her again, but she quickly put on the brakes and said we had to wait until tomorrow since it was close to midnight before I came inside of her the second time.

Now, I'm running drills on the practice field, counting down the hours until tomorrow morning when Callie said we can have sex again. She's got me panting for her, like a dog begging its master for a bone. One hell of a big bone.

And I'm starting to think that last night was so damn good because it was the first time in my life that I was *trying* to get a woman pregnant. The urge to give her what she wants was so intense I thought I would explode, and I did, coming inside her so hard I nearly blacked out the second time I flooded her with my stud missiles, leaving an enormous wet spot on the bed. We laughed about who was gonna sleep in it since we were both too tired to get up and change the sheets. Callie ended up sleeping halfway on top of me all night except for when she got up to feed Brady around two. And I liked it, all of it, the affectionate way she now looks at me and touches me after sex, like I'm her own personal hero, capable of doing anything, including finally give her a baby. My baby. I guess it will be our baby? How the fuck will that work? Will Callie raise the baby at her house? When will I ever get to see them?

"Holy shit. What was I thinking?" I freeze in mid-throw, the football in my hand falling limply to the ground at my feet.

Last night I wasn't able to think clearly about the implications. Callie was hot and wet, and I was horny. I couldn't think of anything but coming inside her. Now...now I'm wondering if I've made a huge mistake, fucking up some unborn kid's life by not being able to give them a normal family if Callie decides she doesn't want me around.

"Dude, why didn't you throw me the ball? I was open!" Nixon yells at me, and when I look up, all the guys on the scrimmage offense and defense are gawking at me.

"I fucked her without a rubber," I mutter. "That was stupid, right?" I ask no one in particular.

"Sort of too late to worry about it now since the baby's already been born," Lathan comments with a slap to my shoulder pads.

"No, I mean, last night."

"What the fuck, Quinn? How bad was your concussion?" Nixon asks, patting the top of my helmet.

"I did it on purpose," I admit. "Callie wants a baby."

"Can we get a trainer over here? Quinton's obviously got severe brain damage," Cameron shouts over to the sidelines, but I wave the trainers off.

"What were you thinking?" Lathan asks.

"I dunno," I admit. "But I wanna do it again."

The whistle blows loud and long before Coach Griffin shouts at us, "What are you women chit-chatting about? Get your asses back on the line and run the damn play!"

"Drinks after practice," Lathan shouts as he moves down the line and gets into position.

"Quinton's buying first round," Nixon calls out.

During the season my teammates and I try to steer clear of alcohol unless there's a really good reason for a drink. If this isn't a good enough reason, then I don't know what the fuck is.

CHAPTER TWENTY-THREE

Callie

"What are you smiling about?" Kelsey asks, making me jump when she suddenly appears in front of me in the baby store.

I wanted to get Brady out of the house, so I decided to do some shopping with him. He's sleeping in his carrier while I stroll him around the store, and yeah, I'm imagining one day shopping for my own baby.

When we got here, I waved at Kelsey, who was running the register, but didn't go over to say hi since she looked swamped.

"Hey, Kelsey," I say when I recover. "You scared me! I was just trying to pick out a baby monitor. Any suggestions?"

"Sure," she says cheerfully. "I would go with this video one so you can see what cutie Brady is up to." She hands me a box and then comes around the buggy to give Brady a kiss on his head. "You still haven't answered my question. What are you so happy about?"

"I'm just happy, spending the day with my beautiful nephew," I answer.

It's not like I'm gonna admit that I'm happy because I took an ovulation test this morning and it showed that I should be ovulating in the next twenty-four to thirty-six hours. I texted Quinton as soon as I found out, and he asked if midnight counts as tomorrow. I just responded that it definitely did, and he texted back that he would set the alarm on his phone.

"There it is again, another smile!" Kelsey exclaims. "You slept with him, didn't you?"

My jaw drops at how quickly she figured out our secret. Well, I have been spending the night at Quinton's house, and he's gorgeous, so it wouldn't take Sherlock to figure out this mystery.

"Maybe," I reply, putting the baby monitor into the cart.

"You have! Oh my God, you're so lucky," she whispers. "So, how did it happen?"

Heat spreads over my face at the reminder of how things quickly progressed last night. I had no idea what Quinton intended to do when he said he was going to kiss me, but there was never a second that I thought about stopping him.

"It...it started with just a kiss," I tell Kelsey, which isn't a lie.

"Wow," she gasps dreamily. "Do you think you will, you know, again?"

"Oh yeah," I answer with a bigger smile.

Quinton

"I THINK you need to wrap it up until you undergo more mental evaluations," Nixon offers helpfully as the four of us put down our first round of beer at a table in no other than *Limelight*, the scene of the original crime. Although, now I'm glad to have Brady in my life.

"Agreed. You haven't been a father but what, like a week, and you're already thinking about a second kid?" Lathan asks.

"See, that's what I would've said too if someone had asked me that a few weeks ago," I reply. "But that was before I had Brady and before I met Callie."

"That's my point!" Lathan exclaims. "You just met this woman, and yet she's somehow convinced you to knock her up. I'm sorry, Quinn, but this has get-rich-quick scheme written all over it."

"What? You think I'm capable of being conned into getting pussy whipped?" I ask. "Hell no. I can spot a gold digger from a mile away, and that's not Callie."

"So this chick just wants a kid from you; that's it? No money or strings attached?" Cameron asks, his forehead scrunched in confusion.

"Yes," I answer after I force a sip of beer down my throat.

Hearing the truth so bluntly just makes it sound like Callie's using me too, like all the other women before her. I try to tell myself that since she doesn't want anything material from me that it's okay, but maybe I'm just fooling myself.

"Look, I get that it sounds crazy, but think about it this way…all we've ever wanted is to play professional football and win the Super Bowl, right? What if we hadn't made it here to the Wildcats, but someone came along and told us they had the ability to give us what we wanted. Not just that, but that they were our *only* shot of making our dreams come true. That's what I am to Callie," I explain.

Three confused sets of eyes stare back at me, blinking silently for several long moments.

"But it's not like Quinton Dunn is the only man in the world who can knock this woman up," Nixon eventually remarks. "There are plenty of other single men, ones who aren't famous or rich that could just as easily get the job done."

"Yes," I agree through clenched teeth, not liking the idea of Callie with any of those other men. "And most of those men would run the other way at the idea of knocking a woman up and having to pay child support."

"Exactly! So why aren't *you* running the other way?" Lathan asks with an arched eyebrow.

"I have plenty of money, so I don't give a shit about child support," I explain.

"So it's sort of like you're having sex with her now, and later on you're gonna be paying her for it," Cameron says, making me want to punch him for even implying that Callie's a prostitute.

"I think you're forgetting one important thing here, Quinn," Lathan says. "You're not giving her a car or...or a puppy. This is a kid's *life* we're talking about. How will it feel when he or she is old enough to realize that daddy was just a sperm donor it never actually sees?"

"It won't be like that," I tell him. "I'll see the baby all the time. Callie is Brady's aunt, so it's not like she's gonna up and disappear."

"The thing is, bro, she could do just that, and there's nothing you or the kid could do to stop her," Nixon explains.

Callie wouldn't do that to me, would she?

No.

No way. She loves Brady and will always want to be a part of his life.

Regardless of what the guys say and the doubts they try to fill my head with, I still want to do this with Callie. If I'm able to get her pregnant, everything else will works its way out.

I hope.

CHAPTER TWENTY-FOUR

Quinton

I wake up to my phone alarm at a little after midnight, my dick already hard as a rock. Time to wake up Callie.

Tonight she went back to the guest bedroom to sleep since she didn't want there to be any temptation.

After I push my boxer briefs off, I grab the new video baby monitor Callie bought earlier today and tiptoe down the hall naked, so I don't wake Brady. Slipping into the guest bedroom, I climb underneath the covers with Callie. Warmth radiates from her, along with her familiar, sweet, fruity scent that makes my mouth water. Her back is to me, so I press my dick against her ass while sweeping her hair over her shoulder to make room for my lips on her neck. It doesn't take long to wake her.

Callie moans and then arches her back, pushing her ass against my cock even harder. Knowing she's more awake, I ease my hand underneath her pajama top to squeeze her breast and tease her nipple.

When I can't take anymore, I pull her pajama bottoms and

panties down her legs and line my already dripping dick up to plunge inside her from behind.

"No," she whispers, making me freeze.

Suddenly, I feel like a gigantic asshole for sneaking into her bed and accosting her in the middle of the night. After she sent me an excited text message earlier that she was ovulating and if midnight counted, I thought she would welcome the invasion of my stud missiles.

A moment later she follows up her objection with, "Missionary. Better chances."

Thank fuck.

I roll her to her back and climb on top of her, taking off her pajama top while our mouths find each other in the darkness. Our kiss quickly grows hot and desperate. Worried I'm moving faster than she's ready for and knowing all too well how big my cock is, I scoot down Callie's sexy body and use my tongue to get her good and wet between her legs. The sheets and comforter over my head muffle the noises she's making, but I know she likes it based on the way her fingers tangle in my hair, pushing my head down while simultaneously lifting her hips. As soon as her thighs quiver and she shouts her release, I'm moving up into position and thrusting inside her.

Fucking hell, it's amazing to feel her tight, wet heat without the barrier of a condom. It's just her and me; our bodies pounding together. My need for her is so intense, I can't seem to get deep enough or take her hard enough. I want more.

Her repetitive moans of *"Yes! Yes! Yes!"* ease my concerns that I'm being too rough with her petite body that's so much smaller than mine.

I slow my strokes when it becomes obvious that I won't last much longer. Thankfully, Callie shouts, "So close" before she starts coming on my cock, taking me with her to the finish line. I bury myself as deep as I can get when I unload inside her, urging my boys to get to swimming upstream.

By the time our bodies have stopped shaking, and the sweat on my skin starts to cool, Callie's body goes completely limp, her thighs releasing me from their grip, and I realize she's fast asleep.

Well, I'll take that as a compliment.

Slinking off to my own bed now seems like a shitty thing to do, so I roll over onto the pillow next to Callie. Just as my eyes begin to close, I remember the thing she did the other night, lifting her legs or whatever on the sofa after we had sex, so I reluctantly part with the two pillows under my head and wedge them underneath her hips. There.

My work here is done.

For now.

I fall asleep with my head flat on the mattress, content and happy trying to calculate out how many hours before I can be with Callie again.

Callie

I STARTLE AWAKE to the sounds of a baby crying.

Not a dream, but Brady.

When I try to roll out of bed, I realize I'm naked, and my lower body is propped up on top of pillows.

"I'm awake, I'll get him," Quinton says softly, sounding much more alert than I am, and then the mattress shifts when he leaves.

Did we...

The dampness between my legs is an obvious sign that we did.

I was sound asleep when Quinton climbed in my bed and had his way with me after he went down on me. Now I remember. God, it had been good too, those two mind-blowing orgasms.

Did he put the pillows underneath me?

I don't remember doing it, and reaching over, I feel around the other side of the bed and notice they were his pillows. Quinton could've gone back to his bed, but he stayed here in the guest one with me.

"Shhh, buddy. I've got your titty bottle right here."

I smile to myself hearing Quinton talking to his son over the baby monitor he left on the nightstand.

If I hadn't been so tired and confused, I would've gotten up with Brady to feed and change him before Quinton even realized he was awake. He would happily get up each time with his son, but I work from home during the day and can take a nap. Quinton doesn't have that luxury.

Feeling unsure about how long it's been since we had sex and I passed out, I keep my legs raised just in case while Brady eats. When I hear Quinton putting him down, I get up and use the restroom, redressing in my discarded pajamas before I intercept Quinton in the hallway.

"Let's sleep in your bed," I tell him, grabbing his arm to pull him that way.

"Why? Yours too messy now?" he whispers, following behind me.

"Yes."

"I like the mess," he says as we climb in each side of the bed. "Fuck condoms."

Once we're both settled in, Quinton now in just a pair of boxers and me in my pajamas, he throws an arm over my waist and says, "I have to leave tomorrow afternoon to fly up to Baltimore for Sunday's game. Are you coming too?"

"If you don't mind," I reply since I'll likely be ovulating over the weekend and don't want to miss three days without sex.

"You should. My parents can't make it, so I would really like for you to come. I can't get you on the team's plane, but I'll buy you a ticket tomorrow," he says.

"I can pay for it..." I start to say, but Quinton silences me with his lips.

"Did you forget how much they pay me?" he asks.

"Right," I reply on a sigh. "Millions."

"You can stay in my room with me Sunday night but not Saturday. Coach's rules."

"Yeah," I say with less enthusiasm since I can't help but wonder if that's the truth or if he wants to leave his options open. I tell myself that it's just my chances of getting pregnant I'm worried about, not Quinton having sex with other women that bothers me.

"Believe me, Callie. I want you in my room; and if I wouldn't be risking getting benched, I would sneak you in."

CHAPTER TWENTY-FIVE

Callie

Sunday morning in Baltimore I wake up around nine after a fitful sleep without Quinton and go down to eat breakfast in the hotel restaurant.

After just two days, I didn't realize how much I missed having Quinton in the bed next to me all night. John moved out months ago, and I was perfectly fine sleeping alone. Guess I missed the cuddling more than I thought.

Last night my flight was delayed, so I texted Quinton that I was here and would see him in the morning since I knew he needed sleep and we couldn't cohabitate per the coach's rules the night before a game.

While I'm sitting at a table that faces the lobby, sipping orange juice and checking emails on my phone, I see Quinton get off the elevator with a few guys who must be teammates based on their sheer size. I consider going over to say hi, but I know they're in a hurry to get on the bus waiting out front and get to the stadium for warmups. Tonight, when we get back to the hotel, he can warm me up.

A few fans recognize the men and come up to them; several of them female. Watching as they practically try to molest Quinton, my stomach hollows out, and I realize...I'm jealous. Which is ridiculous. He's not mine; I'm just...borrowing him and his powerful, virile body for a few weeks while I try to get pregnant.

After that, I'll either get pregnant or I won't. And he'll only be the father of my nephew, who I see occasionally. I tell myself that the sadness I feel at that thought is just for Brady, who I'll miss being around. But I can't help but wonder what happens afterward?

If I get pregnant, do I just move back into my house and raise our daughter or son there, away from their father? It's not like I can live at Quinton's permanently. He's a handsome, famous football star who is young and enjoys the life of a playboy millionaire. If not for his hard cock, I wouldn't believe he's physically attracted to someone as plain, old and ordinary as me. Quinton may have flirted with me and tried to sleep with me initially, but I get the feeling it's more of a compulsion of his, sleeping with every single woman he comes into contact with, just because he can.

The fact is, Quinton and I have an expiration date. Even if we have a child together, that won't change anything. He's only doing this as a favor and because, once I presented him with the challenge, the competitor in him refused to back down. So while Quinton might stay away from other women temporarily, I'm not foolish enough to think that he's capable of settling down with just one woman, especially not me.

If John, a man of average intelligence and average looks can't stay faithful to me, there's no way Quinton or any other man, for that matter, ever could either. And I don't need a man to be happy. I'm a smart, strong woman with a great life other than mourning my drug addicted sister and the giant gaping hole in my heart that can only be filled by becoming a mother.

I have no doubt that even as a single mother I could raise a child with so much love they'll never miss having a permanent father figure. Sure, I think Quinton is a great dad to Brady and would be the same with a child we conceived. I'm just not crazy enough to think he could ever love one woman for the rest of his life.

CHAPTER TWENTY-SIX

Quinton

Since I started the game against the Baltimore Badgers, our team surged ahead with two touchdowns, fourteen points in the first quarter. From there, the momentum helped our defense roll over the other team.

Our offensive line held strong, and I didn't get sacked a single time, so my noggin remained fully intact.

Now I'm showered and sitting on the bus, anxious for the rest of the guys to get their asses on here so we can head back to the hotel where Callie is waiting for me. I left her a key to my suite at the front desk last night, sort of hoping she would ignore my warning that women aren't allowed in players' rooms the night before an away game. She didn't, though, and I missed having her curled up next to me. It was also strange to only hear the sound of chatter in the hallways and a few slamming doors during the night rather than Brady's cries. Not being under the same roof as him for the first time has me worrying incessantly.

This morning before we left for the stadium and then as soon as I got back to the locker room after we won, I texted Kelsey to ask how my little guy's doing. She assured me he's great and even sent a few pics of him sleeping soundly in the swing I had her pick out for him Friday before I left.

Now that I know my son's okay, I can concentrate on other things, like fucking Callie as soon as I get to the room. The woman better be there and ready for me, because I can't wait much longer. I haven't been inside of her since the middle of the night Friday, nearly two days ago.

Back at the hotel, I take the elevator up and slip the key card into the slot, jerking down on the door handle as soon as I get the green light. The entry way and living room are both dark, causing my shoulders to sag in disappointment that Callie's not here yet.

Just as I start to reach for the light switch to flip it on, I hear her say, "In here" and a relieved smile spreads across my face.

"Hey," I call out as I quickly cross the room, searching for her. The whole place is dark except for the suite's bedroom where there's a flicker of soft candlelight. Callie stands up from the edge of the bed, revealing the sexiest lingerie I've ever seen --- a navy blue lace teddy with a small yellow bow in the center and bright yellow thong panties underneath, the Wildcats team colors.

"Damn, woman," I say when she's in front of me, wrapping her arms around my neck. I grab her ass and jerk her up my body so that she can wrap her legs around my waist.

"Congrats on the win," she says against my lips. I didn't see her before the game or during, but I liked knowing she was there, in the stands watching.

"You're quite the prize," I tell her, walking us toward the bed and then falling backward on it so that she stays on top of me. "How are we gonna celebrate?" I ask, barely refraining from jerking the thin straps down her shoulders to get her naked.

"Well," she says, holding herself above me with her blonde hair falling forward. "First I thought I would suck your dick until it's nice and hard..."

"I have no objections to that," I quickly assure her.

"Afterwards I'm gonna ride you until I come," she tells me, grinding her pussy over the growing bulge behind my jean zipper. "And then, I want you to roll us over and pound your cock in me until you come deep inside, giving me everything you've got."

I groan and grab her hips to push her down on my dick that's already leaking because I'm so turned on. When she unzips my pants, I gladly let her do everything she offered.

It's even better than I imagined.

Callie

Sunday night was…hot.

I went back and forth on whether or not to wear the revealing outfit for Quinton since I knew there was no way I could compete with the gorgeous, young models and celebrities he's used to fucking. But he agreed to only sleep with me for now, and he must be attracted to me to make that sort of offer, so I put on the blue and yellow lingerie and waited for him.

He liked it more than I expected.

Monday morning came too soon, and we both had to get up and get ready to catch our flights. We did have enough time for a quick buffet breakfast in the lobby, though.

That's where the guys with cameras found us. First, there were just two, and then they began multiplying and asking Quinton questions. *Was I his latest one-night stand? Am I his girlfriend? His baby's mama?* And my favorite, *What's our age difference?*

By the time my flight touched down, my face was all over the sleazy, tabloid internet sites. And I wish I had never read the comments people made. They were so harsh and…cruel, saying

Quinton can do better, that I'm too old for him and I'm just a gold digger. Although, I have to admit that most of them were right, which could be why it hurt to read them. It was a brutal reminder that Quinton and I are not really together. Bets were even being taken saying that I wouldn't last with the famous quarterback through the Wildcats' game next week.

Between the criticism and facing the fact that my fertile window is over, I was in a shit mood Tuesday. I was asleep when Quinton got home Monday night, and he left with barely a word Tuesday morning since he said he was running late.

The separation gave me plenty of time to remind myself that Quinton's part of our deal is finished for now, which means he likely *will* be fucking some other woman before the next football game. That stupid thought shouldn't make me as angry or sad as it does, and I hate myself for caring who he screws. I guess I hate him a little for making me care about him.

"So, I guess I'm gonna head home," I tell Quinton Tuesday night after we put Brady down. Last night I stayed over, but we didn't fuck, even if I was sort of hoping he would try and wake me up with his cock when he got home and take me fast and furiously before falling asleep.

But he didn't. He barely touched me, reminding me that the past week was only about him fulfilling his role. Now it's time for the two-week wait to see if he managed to do the impossible.

"What? You're not staying tonight?" Quinton asks, following me to the living room where I pick up my crochet mess and pack it all up into my canvas tote.

"I'm no longer fertile, so..." I answer with a shrug before turning around to face him. "I'll be back in the morning to watch Brady before you have to leave for practice."

"I want you to stay," he says, effectively opening the butterfly cages in my stomach.

"Why?" I ask, certain I must have misinterpreted his reasoning. "To get up with Brady during the night?"

"No, of course not," he responds with a frown.

"Then if I'm not ovulating and you don't need help with him, there's no reason for me to stay here. I have a perfectly nice house just down the road. And my cat misses me."

"You could bring Felix over here, and you know, some people have sex just because it's fun and feels good," he remarks.

"I guess I'm not one of those people," I say, not because I don't want to sleep with him but because I need to start putting distance between us. As a woman, I stupidly confused sex with having feelings.

"So what now? I'm supposed to just wait around and be celibate for however many weeks until you decide you want to fuck me again?" Quinton asks, raising his voice at me for the first time since, well, since the day we met and argued over who was gonna keep Brady.

"That was our deal," I remind him. "But if you want to…be with other women until I know if I'm pregnant or not, I can't stop you."

"I'm not gonna cheat on you, Callie!" Quinton exclaims. "You can act like you wouldn't care if I went out and fucked a different woman every night, but you would, and I know that."

"It wouldn't be cheating on me. We're not together," I remind him and myself.

"No, I guess we're not. I'm just the guy with the cock you need to get knocked up. Do you think I would do this for anyone else?"

I shake my head since I know he wouldn't. "No. And you're sort of insane for doing it with me," I tell him honestly.

"I like you. I like knowing you're gonna be here when I get home every day. And yeah, I like the sex too. It's no chore for me to tongue fuck you to get you ready for my cock or to come inside you. I almost get off on going down on you, that shit's so good, hearing you scream—"

"Quinton," I warn him, lowering my eyes in embarrassment as my face starts to burn.

"Stay," he says. "If you don't want to fuck me, fine. Sleep in the guest bedroom and have breakfast with me in the morning before I leave. Or," he starts and reaches for my hips to bring me flush against his hard body, causing a gasp to slip from my parted lips at how good it feels to have him be aggressive with me. "Stay and sleep in my bed for no other reason than because you just want me to make you feel good."

My mouth dried up like a desert during Quinton's short speech, all the moisture in my body apparently being relocated for what it decided was a far more important function. The needy place between my legs hasn't forgotten how long or thick Quinton is since the last time we were together, and it wants to be well prepared to take him.

"So, what's it gonna be, Callie?" Quinton asks, rubbing his thumb against my hip.

"I'll stay," I concede, my heart already racing with anticipation.

"Where?" he inquires while easing his knuckles underneath the hem of my shirt and brushing them over the skin of my lower stomach. The shiver of desire that runs through me is my response, so I reach for Quinton's zipper and pull it down. A moment later his pants and boxers are lowered, freeing his proud, battering ram of a cock. If I weren't so desperate to feel him inside me, I would sink to my knees and suck him off until he comes.

Our mouths crash together, and then my jeans and tee are quickly discarded by Quinton before he lifts me in his arms, impaling me on his shaft while his massive palms on my ass bounce me up and down his dick. He's so strong that he fucks me right there standing up in the middle of the room. And it's just as good as all the other times when I was hoping he would get me pregnant, intense and almost painful because of his size. But he hits that spot deep inside me so good the pain turns to pleasure.

"*Oh God, I'm coming!*" I say, squeezing two handfuls of his hair to try to warn him before the ecstasy spikes through my core and my entire body trembles in his arms.

"Fuck yes," Quinton groans, and his cock pulses inside me with his release. "I need you again," he says before he even starts to soften.

The next few hours, Quinton takes me again and again, showing me what I've been missing with only allowing him to orgasm once a day. His stamina and endurance are incredible; and before he finally lets me fall asleep, I remember thinking to myself that he may be worth all those millions the team pays him after all.

CHAPTER TWENTY-SEVEN

Quinton

Over the next two weeks, after I convinced Callie to bring Felix over and stay with me even though the time to knock her up had come and gone, the two of us got into a comfortable routine with Brady. In fact, where football used to be the one thing I woke up and looked forward to more than anything, I was starting to really love just being home at nights with the two of them.

Callie and I give Brady a bath together a few nights a week, and I know she could do it during the day but waits until I'm home to spend time with him. She fixes dinner for us during the day and heats it up at night whenever I get home without complaint, even if it's sometimes late. We text each other during the day whenever I got the chance, and I can't deny that the nights alone with Callie are pretty fun too.

We don't have sex every night, but we never go two in a row without. Some would even say I'm pussy whipped because I'm willing to do anything to make Callie happy so that she'll keep sleeping in my bed. The problem is, there's only one thing she really wants; and for the time being, it's out of my control. Both of us are trying to function with the growing anxiety. For Callie, it's while she waits to see if she's pregnant; and for me, it's because I'm having a shitty season on the field.

The Wildcats lost their Monday night game, which means we're 2-2. If we lose two more games, then our chance of making it to the playoffs in January will be doomed. I blame myself for the two losses, the first one where I got a concussion, and the second I was just...off.

So for our next game, I'm determined to do whatever it takes to win. My mind will be clear, and I will live and breathe football. Or so I told myself.

But then, when I'm getting ready to leave for the stadium Sunday, I come out of the shower to find Callie still in bed, highly unusual for her since she's a morning person. At first I think she's just sleeping in since Kelsey is over today helping with Brady, but then I hear her sniffles.

"Callie?" I ask, crawling up on the bed behind her. "Hey, you okay?" I ask when I find her face buried in a pillow. She doesn't respond, and I'm not sure what the hell to do, so I rub her back through her pajama top. "What's wrong, baby?" I try asking again.

"I'm not...I'm not pregnant," she says through the sobs.

Fuck.

I don't know what to say to that news. *I'm sorry for disappointing you?*

A crater opens up in my chest, hating that I let her down, that I couldn't give her a baby. There are millions of dollars in my bank account, and this is the one thing money can't buy.

Or can it?

"Callie, I'm really sorry, but it's only been one month. We'll keep trying and...and I'll take you to the best fertility doctors in the world. We'll do whatever it takes, okay? Whatever it takes for you to be a mother," I assure her, but she doesn't respond.

"Come here," I say, rolling Callie over and pulling her to my chest. She cries against me, soaking through the cotton of my shirt, and I ache for her, even though I have no idea how she's feeling, how much it hurts after how long she's been trying...

I hate that I have to leave her, especially when she's so upset, but Coach will bench me again if I'm late for warmups, and there's nothing else I can do for her today.

"I've got to go, but Kelsey will be here, and I'll be back as soon as I can," I tell Callie, kissing the top of her head before I slide out from under her.

"Good luck and be careful," she looks up with red-rimmed watery eyes to tell me.

"I will," I promise before I make my feet leave her.

Kelsey's in the living room, curled up on the sofa with Felix, who has made himself at home, watching television. "You mind staying here to look out for Callie today?" I ask her since they had all planned on coming to the stadium to meet my parents and watch the game. Of course I want them there, but I know Callie needs to sit this one out.

"Sure," Kelsey says with a nod. "Is she sick?"

"No, she's just...upset," I tell her. "Take care of my boy, and I'll see you all later." With a scratch to Felix's sleeping head and a quick kiss goodbye to Brady, I head out the door.

On the drive over to the stadium, I try to get my mind focused on football, but all I can think about is seeing Callie look so devastated and not being able to do anything about it.

But I told her the truth; I will do whatever it takes to get her pregnant.

Callie

My pity party comes to an end around noon because it's more important for me to get a shower and watch Quinton's game on television than continue to mope alone in his bed.

"Hey, you okay?" Kelsey asks when I join her and Brady in the living room.

"Yeah, he'll make me better," I tell her, stealing Brady from her arms to cuddle him for a little while. "Sorry I didn't want to go to the game today. We'll make it to the next one," I promise Kelsey since I know she likes to go to the stadium.

"It's okay. I'm more comfortable here anyway," she says.

"Yeah, it's not so bad. At least we can see what's going on down on the field a little easier."

"Are you avoiding the tabloids?" Kelsey asks randomly, rubbing Felix, the traitor, who has taken up with her. Surprisingly, he even likes Quinton and hasn't scratched him once, maybe because he knows he has to be a good boy around the baby.

"Ah, yeah, for my own mental health, I'm staying off the internet. Why? Did they find a new way to make me look like shit?" I ask.

"They found out your name and that you're still technically married," she informs me with a cringe. "Sorry, Callie."

"Those bastards. The divorce will be finalized in days!"

"There's an interview with your husband --- I mean ex-husband in one article," she adds.

"Awesome," I mutter sarcastically. "What did that idiot say?"

"Oh, that late one night Quinton threw him out of his house and told him to stay away from you," she replies with a smile.

"That is actually true, but that was before Quinton and I started...seeing each other," I finish rather than say fucking each other.

"I think it's sweet that Quinton was standing up to that jerk for you," she tells me. "He really likes you, you know."

"Who? Quinton?" I ask. "No, it's not like that between us. We're just...sleeping together. Casually."

"Uh-huh," she mutters. "Whatever you say."

But for the next week, we won't be sleeping together while I'm on my period. I know we technically could, but the cramps are just too painful to consider it.

Will Quinton look for sex somewhere else in the meantime?

Unlike John when we were married, Quinton's sex drive is a force to be reckoned with. He wants sex often, usually once a day, if not more. And while I enjoy every second, I'm just not sure if I alone am enough for him.

CHAPTER TWENTY-EIGHT

Callie

When I see the team's bus pull up out front of the hotel in Cincinnati, I head over with the crowd that's gathering to look for Quinton before his coach's mandated isolation tonight.

Players start to filter in, causing the group of mostly young men and a lot of women to start screaming and flashes to go off as they snap pictures.

And then there's Quinton.

He swaggers in looking edible in his three-piece gray suit, and the place goes crazy. The team's security guys try to press the crowd back, but Quinton smiles as he signs hats and shirts and takes selfies with fans. I see at least three women slip their phone numbers into his pockets, copping a feel of his ass or dick before removing their hands.

Sluts.

When I got to the hotel, I needed to shower and to change after the flight. So instead of my casual jeans and tee, I put on a form-fitting black strapless dress that ends a little above my knees with a pair of sky-high heels.

Now I'm officially a free woman since the divorce was finalized last week, which is empowering, and I guess I just wanted to look nice for Quinton since we haven't had sex in a week, and I've missed it. I've missed him wanting me and can't stand the thought of him finding what he needs with someone else.

This past week Quinton was a perfect gentleman. Even though we were sleeping in the same bed, he never made a single move on me. The rest of our routine stayed the same --- breakfast before he would leave for practice, texting through the day, dinner and a bath for Brady at night before we put him to bed and the two of us snuggling on the couch to watch corny reality shows together.

By last night when Quinton didn't try and feel me up, I was starting to think he doesn't want to have sex with me anymore. But he hasn't kicked me out of his house or bed, and he invited me to travel to Cincinnati to watch his game. So here's hoping that explosive heat between us hasn't died down yet and that it just needs rekindling after a week off.

Unable to wait any longer to find out, I stroll over to the crowd and march right up to him even though he's talking to another woman.

"Do you have plans tonight?" I hear the slutty brunette ask him while rubbing a hand over his chest.

"I do, sorry," he says with a small smile that I hope he's just using to ease the sting of rejection because he's a nice guy even if he is a world-renowned player.

Quinton looks around the room; and when he sees me, his head does a double take before his eyes lock with mine and he flashes me his trademark smile. "And here she is," he tells the woman before removing her hand from his chest and closing the space between us.

"Hey," I say with an amused grin.

Quinton's sparkling blue eyes take me in slowly from head to toe before meeting mine again. "You look...wow," he says before he leans down and kisses me, right there in front of the crowd. In fact, I hear a collective gasp from the women who were probably all hoping to end up in his bed tonight.

"I want you, but I can't let you in my room," he says against my ear when he pulls his lips away.

"I can have you in mine," I tell him, grabbing his tie to lead him to the elevator bank.

"I've missed you," he says, wrapping his arms around my waist and kissing my neck as we ride the elevator up to the eighth floor along with other hotel guests.

"I've missed you too," I tell him.

We start kissing as soon as the room door shuts, and then my dress is quickly removed, along with my black thong. Spinning me around so that I'm facing the foot of the mattress, Quinton growls, "Put your hands on the bed."

"What?" I ask him over my shoulder. "But missionary is better –" I start, but my words are cut off when he presses a palm in the center of my upper back, forcing me to bend forward and down.

"This month we're doing it my way. How I want it, when I want it, and as many times as I want it," he leans over me to tell me as he fills his hands with my breasts and grinds his still covered dick against my ass. "Deal?" he asks while slipping a hand between my legs and working two fingers inside me.

Trying to think at this moment is rather difficult, but I consider his request and say to hell with it. The other way clearly hasn't worked to get pregnant, so let's try something new.

"Deal," I tell him as my knees begin to go weak. I bring them up on the bed too but stay on my hands and knees in front of Quinton.

While Quinton keeps fucking me with his fingers, I hear his zipper go down. Then his fingers are gone, and he's plunging inside me without warning, making me cry out at the sudden fullness. His big hands gripping my hips hold me in place as he stands at the foot of the bed and slams into me over and over again, causing the headboard to slam violently against the wall.

"God, that's good," he groans from behind me. "I jerked off in the shower...every night last week...thinking about you...you in the blue and yellow...*fuck!*"

"Why...why did you do that?" I ask him, looking over my shoulder to watch him take me hard and fast. "I would've...I would've sucked you off if you'd asked."

"Fuck, Callie. Now you tell me?" he replies with a chuckle before he grabs my face to turn it so he can kiss me as he keeps up his punishing thrusts. After that, our muffled moans are almost as loud as the wet slaps of our bodies and the rhythmic thumping of the headboard against the wall.

Slipping a hand underneath me, Quinton strums my clit with his fingertips to send me over the edge, screaming; then he quickly follows.

He doesn't pull out before he flips me over, lifting my legs to his shoulders and starts fucking me again.

My orgasm never stops, it just spikes again and again until I'm nothing but a panting, writhing mess in the hotel sheets.

Quinton collapses next to me, still dressed with only his pants undone. That's no good. I want to snuggle against him, feel his warm, smooth skin against mine. I reach for the buttons on his vest and start undoing those first.

"I have to go, Callie," he says, sounding truly remorseful. It still sucks that he's leaving, but I try to keep the disappointment off my face.

"Well, thanks for the sperm donation," I tell him since that's the reason we're doing this. He likes to fuck me, and I want him to get me pregnant.

"Fuck, woman. Don't be like that," he grumbles as he sits up and buttons his vest and zips up his pants again. "I wish I could stay with you all night. Without the sex."

"But the sex *is* pretty good," I remark.

"It is," he agrees, leaning down to kiss my lips. "The best I've ever had."

That nonsense only makes me snort as I try to push him away with my palms on his chest. It's about as successful as pushing over a brick building. He doesn't move an inch. "I'm sure that's what you tell all the girls."

"You know," he starts, reaching up to rub his scruffy chin thoughtfully. "I've been with a lot of women, and I mean *a helluva lot* of women, but I don't actually remember a single one before you."

My breath catches in surprise at hearing him say something so sad yet...sweet. But I refuse to allow myself to think for even a second that he won't forget about me once he moves on to the next woman and the one after that... He only remembers me now because I'm the present.

"None of them had faces or names worth remembering if they even told me what it was," he says. "But they knew mine. *All* they knew was my face and my name, so it didn't matter if I was a sleazy asshole or not. They had one goal in mind --- to try and get a piece of me."

"I'm sorry," I say since I'm not sure how else to respond. And yeah, I feel a little guilty because of how, in my own way, I'm using him too.

"With you, Callie, I know you don't give a shit about my money or fame, but no matter how hard I try, I'm still not sure if you really see me as more than a means to an end."

"I see you," I tell him, blinking back the tears. "I see what a great father you are to Brady and how much you love what you do, how everyone looks up to you and how strong and determined you are. Those are the reasons I asked this monumental favor from you. If I just wanted a baby, I could've gone to a sperm bank. But I wanted your baby and you to be in its life."

"So, I'm not just a sperm donor?" he asks, and I shake my head. "Then what am I, Callie?"

"I-I dunno," I reply. "I guess we're friends."

"Friends?" Quinton huffs. "We're a helluva lot more than friends."

"Dating?"

"You sleep in my bed every night, and we've never been on a date," he replies. "Which is sort of fucked up because we're doing this all in reverse, so I'll try to work on that. Now try again."

"We're exclusive?" I offer.

"Yeah, for nearly four weeks now. That's about three weeks longer than any other relationship I've ever had," he informs me.

"*Boyfriend* just sounds ridiculous when referring to a man as giant as you," I tell him with another snort.

"I agree," Quinton says with a smile. "But you're getting warmer. And you better not say fuck buddies or future baby daddy because that shit won't fly either."

Nodding, I try to think of another term to explain what Quinton is becoming to me and what I hope I am to him.

"Significant other?" I ask hesitantly.

"Significant other," he repeats, trying it out. "I like it. Tomorrow I'll have my manager announce it to the press," he says before getting to his feet to leave.

"No, Quinton. That's not really necessary," I tell him. When I start to stand up, he pushes me by my shoulders back down on the bed and walks around the mattress to grab two pillows. Bringing them over, Quinton lifts my hips and slips the pillows underneath.

"I think it is necessary," he replies, stealing a quick kiss. "Especially if we're gonna announce we're expecting sometime soon."

"Right," I agree, unable to help my smile at his confidence and the fact that he remembered I needed to lift my hips after sex.

"I'll call you later," he says, pulling out a key card from his pocket. "And here's the key to my room for tomorrow night, twelfth floor, room twelve-ten. Call my room if you need anything."

"Okay," I agree, taking the offered card from his hand and knowing it's also a symbolic gesture. He's giving me access to his room at all hours of the day, even if I'm not allowed in, to prove to me that he doesn't have anything, or anyone, to hide from me. "Good luck tomorrow," I tell him.

"Thanks. Can't wait to see you after we win, baby," he says with a wink before he walks out the door.

Quinton

We didn't win Sunday.

It wasn't even a close game.

The Cincinnati Cougars tore us up in a thirty-five to six loss.

The bus is silent on the way back to the hotel as we all think about how shitty we played individually and as a team. The offensive line didn't hold, so I was sacked three times in the first quarter. Thanks to the pressure the defense put on me, I didn't throw worth a shit, completing only sixteen out of thirty-six passes with one interception. Davis, our running back, fumbled the ball twice. Kohen is the only one who did anything right, taking over his starting position again by kicking two field goals.

In a post-game interview I was required to attend, one of the reporters asked me if I was playing badly because of all the drama in my personal life. With a great deal of restraint, I didn't tell the guy to go fuck himself. Instead, I told him that football players are just like everyone else in the world. We have lives, families, and drama but that we put that aside when we step out on the field.

Sometimes shit doesn't go our way, and we lose.

I fucking hate losing.

Dragging my ass up to my room, the only thing I'm looking forward to is seeing Callie. And unlike most nights after we lose and I feel the urge to bury myself in some random woman to forget the game, tonight I know Callie can offer me more than that. She's not just a temporary solution.

I slide my key card through the door and push it open. Inside the room, I toss my duffle bag down and then fall over face down on the bed next to her.

"You okay?" she asks, combing her fingers soothingly through my hair that's still damp from my shower.

I nod in response because I know she means physically, because she worries about me getting another concussion.

"Do you want anything to eat?"

"No, thanks," I mutter into the linens.

"Anything I can do for you?" she asks.

"Just be here," I tell her, reaching over to grab her and pull her to me like a life-size teddy bear.

"Done," she says, pressing a kiss to my cheek.

We lay there in silence for half an hour or so before I finally roll to my back, tired of dwelling on the loss and ready to start thinking about next week's game and how to win.

Sensing that I'm ready to leave the pity party, Callie says, "I have something that might cheer you up."

"Oh really?" I ask, rolling to my side toward her. Just because I wasn't in the mood earlier doesn't mean I'm not now.

"Yeah, Kelsey sent me a photo," she says before leaning over me to get her phone off the nightstand, which presses her breasts into my face. Nuzzling my face in her shirt, I'm definitely getting more interested in sex.

Callie laughs and pushes me playfully away. "Let me show you this, and then we can get naked."

"Deal," I agree.

She taps on her phone and then turns the screen around, showing me a photo of Brady in his game day Wildcats attire, his blue eyes open...with a smile on his chubby little face.

"He's smiling?" I ask, taking the phone from her hand to look closer.

"He's smiling," she replies with a giggle. "Notice anything else?"

"Well, he's decked out in his team duds, of course," I reply with my own grin.

"No, about his smile," she says. "It's crooked."

"Hey now!" I exclaim indignantly. "So is mine..." I trail off as the realization hits me. "Brady has my smile."

"Yeah, he does. It's adorable," she says, followed with a laugh.

I stare in wonder at the photo, and yeah, I can already see it, his resemblance to me even though he's only a few weeks old. And the thought makes me feel proud, not just because I think I'm a handsome motherfucker, but because there's someone in the world who is well and truly mine.

My happiness at this newfound awareness is short-lived, because I know it's what Callie's missing and wants more than anything. It's a shame that an asshole like me gets to experience something so amazing by an unexpected surprise from Bianca while she's tried for years to have it.

"Does Brady remind you of your sister?" I ask her when the thought hits me. Callie rarely mentions her, and I assume it's because of how bad Bianca hurt her.

"A little," she answers on a sigh.

"What was she like?"

"Bianca was...she was always getting into trouble, even when we were little. Actually, it's hard for me to remember the good parts of our childhood because the most recent years overshadow them. All I can think about is our mother's lies and drug addiction, Bianca following in her footsteps, stealing from me every chance she got and then the affair. The bad parts are all there's been for the past few years."

"I'm sorry," I tell her, brushing a strand of her blond hair behind her ear.

"She wasn't a good person, but I never thought she would hurt me as badly as she did," she admits, tears swimming in her eyes. "I feel guilty because I'm not sure if I could've loved Brady if he had been her and John's."

"Hey, that's perfectly reasonable given the circumstances," I assure her. "You loved them, and they hurt you. Of course you wouldn't want to see the proof of their affair thrown in your face, especially when he's the one thing you've always wanted."

"I'm so glad you're his father," Callie says, reaching up to rub her hand over the side of my face. "You're a better man than John will ever be, and Brady's lucky to have you."

"I couldn't do this without you," I tell her honestly. "Brady may never know his biological mother, but that's probably for the best. He'll grow up thinking of you as his mother and knowing she couldn't have loved him more."

Even though Callie loves Brady, she probably won't ever let herself think of him as her son. She wants her own children, and she deserves to be a real mother. I'll do my best to make it happen for her.

And there's no time like the present to try and put a baby inside of her.

Rolling over on top of Callie, I cover her lips with mine and kiss her slowly, unhurried, different from most of the times we're together when it feels like a race to get inside of her. Actually, that was pretty much how it went with every hookup I can remember. Urgent and needy. But Callie's different. I'm not in a hurry to get us off so that I can make my escape. Neither of us have to go anywhere until tomorrow morning, so there's no reason to rush. Even after that, I know Callie will stick around, and I want her to.

"I'm glad you're here," I tell her. "And I want us to go out, like a real date."

"A date?" she repeats with a stunning smile. I want to see that smile on my son's or daughter's face too someday.

"Yeah, a date," I reply. "There's this team Halloween party next Friday night if you want to go with me."

"Do I have to wear a costume?" she asks.

"Yes. And I get to pick it."

"Fine, but I get to pick yours," she responds, her gray eyes shining with mischievousness.

"Okay. Are you gonna tell me what it is in advance?"

"No. It'll be a surprise."

"I'm gonna look ridiculous, aren't I?" I ask, knowing she will go out of her way to put me in something outrageous.

"Oh yeah," she answers. "And I'm guessing I'm gonna look like a slut, right?"

"Oh yeah. I'm picking the sluttiest outfit I can find."

"This will be Brady's first Halloween," she reminds me. "We'll have to get him a costume."

"It is, isn't it? What do you think he should be?" I ask.

"I could crochet him a brown hat and sack with the white lines to make him look like a football," she offers.

"That would be perfect!" I tell her.

"Then, we could get some photos of you in your uniform holding him."

"How is it that you always guess what I want before I even know what I want?" I ask her as I kiss her again.

"Just lucky I guess," she answers and then squirms underneath me. "Now, based on the battering ram between your legs, I'm guessing you want us to both get undressed."

"Right again," I tell her, rubbing my nose against hers.

CHAPTER TWENTY-NINE

Callie

Things with Quinton the past few weeks have been good. Really good, and I don't just mean in bed. He's been incredibly sweet, holding my hand while we watch late night television, and especially when he's snuggling with Brady. I'm pretty sure I'm falling in love with both of them.

While things between Quinton and me may have started as just a friendly favor, now I'm starting to think it's much more than that. By owning my body he's starting to gradually conquer my heart. And I'm starting to think that maybe I'm actually beginning to win over the notorious bachelor.

Quinton has publically called me his significant other in the media, which he's never done with a woman before. I met his parents when they came to the Monday night home game, and afterward, at dinner, I blushed the whole time while Quinton gushed about me. They were nice, and it was great to see that he was raised in a loving home with both parents instead of a broken, dysfunctional home like mine and Bianca's with our drug addicted mother.

Trusting Quinton will never be easy given his reputation and my past, but I'm trying to overcome that as best I can.

For example, tonight's the team's Halloween party at a fancy hotel ballroom, and I'm trusting Quinton not to dress me in lingerie. Well, at least not until we get home later.

On the other hand, getting to see him in the costume I picked may be worth the public humiliation of dressing like a slut in front of all his teammates.

"Oh, Callie!" Quinton calls as soon as he walks through the front door of his house.

"Ugh, let's get this over with," I say when I get up from the sofa to meet him. Underneath the white plastic clothing bag, he's holding what I'll be forced to wear for the next few hours. The lopsided grin on Quinton's face says he can't wait.

"I knew you wouldn't want a costume too...revealing," he starts and reaches out to grab me, running his massive palm down the curve of my side. "Even though you would look sexy in anything."

"Whatever," I mutter, certain that I'm nowhere near as attractive as most of the women he's been with.

"So I picked one that's basically a dress," he tells me.

"How short of a dress?" I ask while trying to raise the plastic bag to see it.

"Uh-uh," Quinton says, jerking the concealed costume up and away from me thanks to his gigantic height. "I haven't gotten my welcome home kiss yet."

"It must be bad if you think that after I see the dress all you'll get is a slap across your face instead of a kiss," I remark.

"Shut up and kiss me, woman," he orders, his palm squeezing my side.

"Fine, but just a kiss. I only have an hour to get ready," I warn him since most of our greeting kisses result in us getting naked and fucking on various places in the entry way or living room.

"Just a kiss," he agrees as he leans down.

"On my lips only," I clarify based on previous experience.

"Just a kiss on the lips. Jeez," Quinton mutters before covering my lips with his and shoving his tongue into my mouth. That's all it takes for me to start trying to climb him. My arms wrap around Quinton's neck, but I instruct my feet to stay on the floor instead of wrapping around his waist, lining up certain body parts...

Okay, fine, I didn't say I wasn't the main instigator of our naked greetings, but we really don't have time tonight.

Pressing my palms against Quinton's chest, I force myself to stop kissing him and take a step back.

"Let's see it," I tell him, hoping he can't tell how embarrassingly much I want him from just a kiss.

"Fine," he huffs. "But I could've made it a quickie."

"Yeah, right," I mutter sarcastically. "The only time you've been quick was when Brady started crying; and then when you got back, we went at it for another hour."

"Is that a complaint, because I'm certain you weren't complaining after those three orgasms, or was it four I gave you?" he asks with a grin.

"Quit stalling and show me the costume," I tell him before I take him up on his non-quickie quickie.

"Okay, okay," he finally agrees. "I'll just save it up for later when I get to fuck you as a fairy."

"A fairy?" I ask.

"Yep," he says as he lifts the plastic bag, revealing a forest green spaghetti strap piece of satin that could pass as a shirt. A poofy, dark purple tutu billows the skirt out from underneath, matching the purple flower on the sash around the waist.

"That's...small," I say.

"There are wings too," he informs me, turning it around.

"Right, I'm sure they will distract from my ass that will be hanging out," I reply.

"You don't like it," Quinton says, his shoulders slumping in disappointment.

"It's cute and sexy," I admit. "But about twenty years too young for someone my age to wear."

"What's with you and your age?" he asks. "You look hot, better than most women in their twenties. You should dress more like you did in Cincinnati."

"I dunno," I grumble, glancing down at my jeans and tee. "When I dress that way, I just feel like I'm trying too hard to be young and trendy but epically failing."

"You're not," Quinton tells me. "And who cares what anyone else thinks? You're not fake or plastic, and that's what turns me on. You're naturally beautiful, and I can't wait to see you in this costume."

"Well, when you say things like that," I tell him with a playful shove to his rock hard, unmoving chest. "Besides, it'll be worth it to see you in your costume."

"I'm gonna be humiliated, aren't I?" he asks.

"Yep. Which is quite a feat, making the big, handsome Quinton Dunn look silly, but I'm pretty sure I can accomplish it."

"It can't be worse than the ladybug costume Kohen had to wear, so let's see it," he says, right before the doorbell rings and interrupts the surprise.

"Oh, good! That's Kelsey," I tell him since she's coming to stay with Brady tonight. "Let her in, please. Your costume is in your room. Go change, and I'll get ready in the guest bedroom before the big reveal," I say as I take the bag with my costume and start down the hall, smiling to myself.

Quinton

"Ho, ho, ho, green giant," Lathan says to me with his phone in front of him, snapping photos of me once he recovers from his long fit of laughter. "I can't wait to post these all over social media."

"Great," I mutter, running my fingers through my green hair before I realize that, by lifting my arm, I'm nearly flashing the room my boxer briefs thanks to the short, leafy green dress. That's right, I'm wearing a fucking dress because Callie thought it would be funny to dress me up as the Jolly Green Giant. Although smock sounds much more masculine for this one shoulder garment.

"So, what are you, a burglar?" I ask Lathan as I examine his black face mask revealing only his eyes and a tunic with dragons on it.

"I'm a ninja!" he replies indignantly, pulling out his sword.

"At least I have the excuse of being forced into this costume. What's yours?" I ask him with a snort.

"Hey, anything is better than a dress," he counters, sheathing the sword again.

"It's a smock, and Callie picked this one because I'm big and giant," I tell him, trying to preserve what's left of my masculinity.

"She picked it to make you look like an idiot," he says, followed by a chuckle. "And it worked."

"Yeah, but have you seen *her* outfit?" I ask him. Turning around, I point across the ballroom to where I left Callie standing with Roxy while I wait in the long line for drinks at the bar.

"Damn," Lathan mutters. "She looks so much better than you in a green dress."

"It's a smock...oh, forget it," I mutter in defeat as I watch my woman laughing, so beautiful and fuckable in that sexy dress that nearly reveals her ass, her petite legs looking long and lean thanks to the gold heels.

I quickly look away and turn back around in line to avoid getting a hard on that would definitely be noticeable in the dress. Smock. Whatever.

"So have you really only been with her for the past, what, five or six weeks?" Lathan asks quietly, so no one else will overhear.

"Yes," I admit honestly. "And I don't miss the anonymous hookups at all."

"Really?" he asks. "I find that hard to believe."

"What Callie and I have is better."

"Better for now, but what happens when you get her pregnant?" Lathan asks. "Do you really think she'll stick around after she gets what she wants?"

"I do. And if not, then I'm not doing something right," I admit.

The truth is, I'm scared. Terrified even, that Callie doesn't feel the same way about me. I'm in love with her, and I'm not sure what it will take for her to want us to be together for the long haul. Lately, I've started thinking about crazy shit like marriage, something I never thought I wanted before. Maybe I'm hoping that if I get Callie pregnant, she'll be so happy that she'll realize that she actually cares about me too.

On the flip side, I worry I'll keep letting her down every month until she gives up on me. On us.

CHAPTER THIRTY

Callie

"So is this the infamous ladybug costume that Kohen had to wear?" I ask Roxy while I wait for Quinton to return with our drinks.

"It is!" she replies with a grin. "Oh my God, that was so funny. Almost as funny as Quinton as the Jolly Green Giant."

"Yeah, I figured a little humility would do the arrogant ass some good," I tease while glancing over at him in line. "But it doesn't seem to have much of an effect on his allure," I add when two girls dressed as slutty Wonder Woman and an even sluttier Harley Quinn walk up to him and Lathan. The women are young and very...fit.

"Oh, you don't have anything to worry about," Roxy tells me. "See how those Lady Cats are touching him and batting their fake eyelashes?"

"Unfortunately," I grumble.

"Quinton hates that shit. In fact, he told me that for the past few months he's tried to use the corniest pick-up lines he can think of to run women off, and failed every time."

"Aww, how sad," I mutter sarcastically.

"Yeah, he was waiting for you," she says with a smile.

"Me?" I ask. "Quinton never wanted someone like me."

"Oh yes he did," Roxy replies. "He wanted someone who could see past the famous name and the big pay day. Someone who still thought he was an asshole and told him so because he was tired of being used. Then you came along and not only turned him down but punched him."

"So he just wanted a challenge?" I ask, the thought making me feel a little sick.

"Yes, the challenge of convincing a woman who couldn't stand him to love him anyways, for who he is when he's not on the field," she clarifies in a way that sounds...sweet.

"He's a good guy, and an even better father," I admit. "I was wrong when we first met."

"That's all he wanted from you," Roxy says. "Now he's just worried about what you want from him."

"He, um, he told you about that?" I ask, somewhat embarrassed that Quinton told his friends that we were sleeping together because I want a baby.

"Yeah, and we all thought he was crazy to agree to it, not because of money or anything, but because he has the most to lose if he gives it to you."

Is that what Quinton thinks? That if I get pregnant I'll up and leave, taking the baby with me?

"I would never do that to him," I tell Roxy.

"Good," she says. "Now I won't have to kick your ass."

That makes me laugh, her being protective over a giant man like Quinton.

"And if I were you, I would march on over there and tell those bitches to keep their hands off your man."

She's right. Why should I just stand here and watch while they paw all over him?

"Nice meeting you, Roxy," I say to her before I cross the room. When I reach Quinton and the women, I grab Quinton's hand and start pulling him out of line. "Forget the drinks, giant. It's time for you to fuck this fairy," I tell him loud enough for the slutty superheroes to hear.

Chuckling behind me as I lead him out of the ballroom and through the glass doors that leads to the pool and beach, Quinton asks, "Are you jealous, baby? Because you shouldn't be."

Now that we're outside in the cool fall darkness without witnesses, I turn to Quinton and ask him, "Why? Have you already slept with them?"

"Yes," he says, which is definitely not the answer I was expecting. Before I can walk away, Quinton wraps his arms around my waist and pulls me against him, trapping me, warming me and blocking the windy chill from the ocean. "But I don't remember either one of them."

"Like I believe that," I mutter with my face turned away toward the sounds of the waves crashing on the other side of the deck.

"I couldn't even tell you their names," he says.

"Like that makes it better?" I huff.

"All I remember is you," he says, bending down to kiss my neck and spreading a different type of cold chills down my arms. "Our first time on the sofa. The second time in our bed. The third in the guest room. The fourth when you wore the blue and yellow lingerie in Baltimore. Should I keep going? Because I remember all thirty-six times."

"Thirty-six?" I repeat.

"Yeah, thirty-six," he says as his lips continue to move over my neck, making my knees go weak. "I couldn't forget them if I tried."

"Hold on. Did you say *our* bed?" I ask when my brain catches up. With Quinton's mouth on me, it makes it hard to think.

"Come on, Callie. You've been staying over for weeks now. Why don't you just move in? Make it official?"

"I-I can't. It's too soon."

Quinton pulls his lips away and straightens to his full gigantic height. "You just want to have an exit strategy, right?" he asks. "So you can up and leave Brady and me whenever you want? Well, that's bullshit. I know you have trust issues, but do you really think I would be trying to make a baby with you if I wanted anyone else? Or ask you to live with me and travel with me if I was gonna cheat on you?"

"No, but –" I start.

"No buts. I'm not him. I would never hurt you like he did."

"Right, because you've already slept with Bianca."

Once the words leave my mouth, I know they're a low blow to my sister, who is gone, and Quinton. But I don't get the chance to apologize for them.

"I didn't sleep with her," he tells me. "I fucked her, once, when I was drunk in a bar. It was stupid and careless, but I don't regret it. Now I have you and Brady. He needs you to be his mother, and I need you to love me enough that you'll stick around even when things get tough."

"I could never recover from you cheating on me," I tell him, tears burning my eyes.

"That's only one of the reasons I would never hurt you that way," he says taking my face in his hands. "I'm in love with you, Callie, and I don't want anyone else."

"I...I love you too," I admit to him, even though it's so scary to step out on that cliff and chance getting thrown off of it again.

Before my doubts and fears can come creeping in, Quinton's kissing them away, as if he knows our words aren't enough. Now, he's determined to show me how much he loves me. His hands move down my back and lift when they get to my bottom, hoisting me up his body so that my center is aligned with the proof of his need for me.

Without breaking our kiss, Quinton moves us to the dark corner of the deck where he sits me on the wooden rail. I reach underneath his tunic and jerk his boxers down just enough to free his cock, then my arms are back around his neck, urging him to keep his mouth on mine. Thanks to the short skirt of my dress, Quinton's fingers easily seek and find my pussy covered only by the narrow fabric of my purple thong. Yanking the material to the side, his fingertips start to play me like a familiar instrument, knowing exactly how to touch me, to make me crazy with need for him. Quinton swallows my moans as he prepares me for his thick cock, making me orgasm in record-breaking time.

"Thirty-seven," he whispers against my lips right before he withdraws his fingers and thrusts his cock into me.

My head falls back when I cry out at the sudden fullness of his invasion. And when he grips my hips and starts to move, I wrap my legs around his waist to try to keep him from retreating. Quinton's mouth devours my neck and moves lower to my cleavage while he slams his powerful hips desperately into me. I should be worried about someone seeing us like this, but I'm not. This is what I need, right here, right now.

Grabbing a handful of Quinton's green Mohawk, I give a sharp tug on it so that when he lifts his face, I'm able to kiss his lips, tasting him, mating our tongues in the same erotic rhythm of our lower bodies.

Like the waves crashing behind us, the pleasurable pressure builds again until it crests and breaks from deep inside me. At the same moment, Quinton slams into me one last time, groaning through his own release.

"Better every time," he whispers against my lips as he keeps kissing me.

"The dress is convenient," I tease him. "Yours and mine."

Chuckling, he says, "One of the few benefits."

"You should be proud," I tell him, combing my fingers through his hair. "Not many men could wear this costume with green hair and still look hot."

"It's a curse," he says as he slips out of me and pulls his boxer briefs back up. "At least you can see what's underneath. Literally and figuratively."

"True," I admit. "And yet, I still love you."

"Then I'm a lucky man," he says placing a kiss on my temple.

"Oh, that reminds me," I tell him when I remember the email that came in earlier today. "You know how you told me a few weeks ago that you would like to finish your degree?"

"Yeahhh," he says slowly like he's not sure what direction this is headed.

"Well I heard back from the University of North Carolina at Wilmington, and they've accepted you into one of their online programs for the spring semester. They were able to get your transcript from Ohio, and you're only thirty credits away from a business degree!"

"Seriously?" Quinton asks. "You got me into school here?"

"Ah, yeah. But I mean, you don't have to go if you don't want to..."

"I do, I want to," he interrupts. "It's just...I'm not sure if I can do it on my own."

"Of course you can," I assure him, combing my fingers through his green hair. "And I told you, I'll be here to help you out."

"Thank you," he says, kissing my cheek. "For the acceptance and for agreeing to stick around."

"It's nothing," I tell him.

"It's everything. *You* are everything," he replies, kissing my lips. "Now, should we go back to the party?" he asks when he pulls away.

I consider facing all those people again, the women who have been with Quinton and want him again so badly you can practically see them salivating. I think I would rather deal with my annoying ex-husband or the tabloids than go back in there.

"Can we just go home?" I ask as he picks me up from the rail and places my feet back on the deck's wooden planks.

"Yeah, sure," Quinton agrees when he takes my hand to lead me back inside, heading toward the parking lot. "We could put on a movie and pop some popcorn if you want."

"That sounds like the best date ever," I tell him, giving his hand a squeeze of appreciation.

Everything almost seems too good, too perfect to be true. Which makes me start to wonder if it really is.

CHAPTER THIRTY-ONE

Callie

The next Friday, I wake up with my nose so stuffy I can't breathe, but even worse are the horrible stomach cramps. Forget the stupid cold, I just know that another month has sadly come and gone. I feel so shitty and depressed that I never want to leave this bed again. But Quinton's leaving soon for another away game. We haven't had sex since last Friday night at the Halloween party because of long practices during the bye week and my snotty, very unsexy head cold. If I don't go with him this weekend, will he give in to temptation?

"Morning," Quinton says, pressing a kiss to my neck, his prominent morning wood attempting to bury itself in my ass if it's not taken care of soon.

And while I want him, and I always want him, this morning I just can't do it. Especially when his palm slips around and rubs over my bloated, aching stomach with all the doubts running through my head.

Removing his hand from my belly and placing it on my hip, I ask him, "Shouldn't you be getting ready?"

The team leaves around one today to fly to the west coast for Sunday's game, traveling a day earlier than usual to give all the players some time to adjust to the jet lag.

"We've got time for this before I have to go," he assures me before he starts tugging down my pajama bottoms.

"I'm not in the mood this morning, Quinton," I say sternly and jerk them back up.

"What's wrong?" he asks, rubbing his palm up and down my arm. "Is your cold getting worse? Maybe you should go to the doctor since you've been sick for almost a week."

"It's not the cold," I tell him, sniffling through the tears. "I just...I don't want to have sex with you every freaking day."

His hand freezes on my arm, and I instantly regret my words.

"Right, well, I'm sorry you've had to endure all the orgasms I've given you even when it's not the 'right time' of the month to get knocked up," he snaps. "All you have to do is tell me so, and I'll leave you alone."

"Yeah, and then you'll just go and get off with one of your many adoring fans instead," I remark.

Quinton scoffs from behind me. "I can't believe you said that. Is that really what you think I'll do even after I told you I love you? That if you don't fuck me, I'll find someone who will?" he asks. "Is that...is that the only reason you fuck me if you're not ovulating?"

I shrug because, while that's not entirely true, it is partially why I don't ever turn him down even if I'm not really in the mood. All Quinton has to do is kiss me for about ten seconds, and that quickly changes; but still, I also worry that he'll wander if his sex drive doesn't get its needs met.

"I'm not gonna cheat on you, Callie, whether we go weeks or, hell, even months without sex," he tells me.

"You say that now, but wait until it's been a few weeks like this one when I'm sick, and some slutty younger woman throws herself at you like they always do," I tell him. "You'll give in."

"No, I would never do that to you," he argues. "Before we met, yeah, I would've. That was when I was still single and didn't have anyone to come home to. When I didn't know what it felt like to actually need someone else in my life. But I need to know that you want to be with me because you love me and need me too, as much as I need you. Not just because you're trying to get pregnant."

"I do love you, but how could I ever trust someone like *you* when a regular man couldn't stay faithful to me?" I ask him.

"I don't know," he answers on a sigh. "I guess it's gonna take some time for me to prove it to you."

"That's the problem," I argue. "You won't be able to prove you *didn't* do something."

"So you're telling me that no matter what I do or say, you're gonna always assume the worst of me?" he asks.

"Probably."

"Then I'll just take you with me everywhere I go," he says before climbing out of bed. I hear dressers opening and closing as he moves around the room. "Let's move your flight up so you can leave today too."

"No," I reply, unmoving from the pillow.

"Then get some rest and go to the doctor so you can come tomorrow."

"No, I'm not coming this weekend."

"What? Why not?" Quinton asks, coming around the bed to stand in front of me, naked, with his fists on his hips, his cock swinging long and proud. If we weren't arguing, I would point out his resemblance to the Jolly Green Giant. Instead, I tell him the truth.

"Because I don't feel like leaving the house. I'm sick and my stomach's cramping. My stupid period is about to start," I admit, more tears overflowing from my eyes.

"Fuck, Callie," Quinton mutters, scrubbing a hand over his face.

"That's what this argument is all about? You're upset because I failed you again?"

"You didn't fail me. I'm the one who can't get pregnant! Brady is proof that you're not the one with a problem."

"It's only been two months. We'll try again –"

"Don't," I interrupt him with a shake of my head. "Just go, okay?"

"I want you to come with me," he says. "Please? It might be good for you to come out to California and get your mind off everything."

"I can't keep following you around just to make sure you don't cheat!" I yell at him since there's not a single ounce of motivation left inside me to get out of this bed today.

Quinton curses under his breath before he walks into the bathroom and slams the door shut behind him.

∽

Quinton

The flight to California passed in a blur of me alternating between brooding and being grumpy, snapping at other players for annoying me. I'm frustrated with seeing Callie so heartbroken and not being able to do shit about it.

"My card doesn't work," I tell the young, bleach blonde hotel clerk at the front desk. The team usually has someone hand out all the keys and room assignments when we get off the plane so that there's no waiting around when we get to the hotel. Today, of all days, when I just want to hide out in my room, my key card is broken.

"I'm so sorry. Let me get that fixed right away for you," the clerk replies with a smile that only makes me frown harder. After I give her my room number and name, she swipes another card for me.

"Thanks for joining us this weekend, Mr. Dunn. Is there anything else I can do for you?" she asks.

"No, thanks," I assure her.

"Well, complimentary dining is included for your stay, along with the spa services if you need a massage in the privacy of your own room. We really appreciate your team staying with us here at the Pavilion. And as the daytime manager, I promise that we'll take care of any and all of your needs while you're here."

That's an invitation for sex if I've ever heard it.

And yeah, while in the past I would work off my frustration with a nameless, faceless woman, now, the thought of being with anyone who isn't Callie is impossible. Even if she distrusts me, currently hates me, and hasn't bothered to answer any of my texts from before our flight left hours ago.

Without even replying to the clerk, I grab my new key cards and walk toward the elevator bank, ready to get to my room and sack out. I try calling Callie once I'm settled in, but she doesn't answer. Not wanting to call the house phone since it's getting late and Brady's probably asleep, I send her a text with the hotel's phone number and my room number in case there's no service on my cell and hope to hear from her tomorrow after she's calmed down.

CHAPTER THIRTY-TWO

Callie

"Hey, I brought you another box of tissues," Kelsey says when she knocks on the bedroom door Saturday morning.

"Thanks," I tell her.

"Maybe you should go to the doctor today. Your nose sounds even stuffier than it did yesterday."

"Ugh. My face is so swollen that my head feels like it's about to explode," I tell her, rolling over in bed to accept the box of tissues. Kelsey picks up the empty one on the side table to trash it for me.

"Call the doctor. It's Saturday, so I don't know about yours, but most offices close around noon."

"Fine," I agree, reaching for my phone and ignoring Quinton's texts and missed calls to try and get an appointment. They set me up for noon, the last one of the day.

"There, happy?" I ask Kelsey once it's done.

"I'll text Quinton and let him know since he's been asking about you," she replies, taking a seat on the edge of the bed. "Why are you ignoring him?"

"We sort of had a fight, and I told him I didn't feel like going to the game."

"I'm sure he understands. You've been sick for days."

"The argument was about more than the game," I tell her, reaching for a handful of tissues to blow my nose. Some of the previous boxes of tissues I've been through were for my tears, not just the cold.

"Well, maybe some time apart will cool things down," she offers.

"Maybe," I agree, thinking I was a pretty big bitch to Quinton yesterday morning. The only way I can trust him is to give him time to prove he can be faithful to me. And the fact that he wants me to go with him on all the away games is a pretty good sign that he doesn't want to cheat on me. If he did, he would insist I stay home instead of buying my plane tickets himself.

A few hours later and I'm death warmed over, sitting on the edge of the exam table in Dr. Sutton's office.

"Hi, Callie," my family doctor says when she walks in with her electronic tablet.

"Hi," I croak.

"Bad cold that's getting worse?" she asks.

"Yeah. It started about three days ago and doesn't seem to want to go away," I tell her as she puts on her gloves and comes over to shine the light in my eyes, ears and down my throat. "Does it hurt here?" she asks, pressing on the swollen skin underneath my eyes.

"Yes," I tell her with a cringe.

"Have you been upset? Crying? Because some of this is from what is definitely a sinus infection, but your eyes look a little bloodshot."

"It's nothing serious," I admit. "My...significant other and I have been trying to get pregnant, but it looks like this month is a failure too."

"But the nurse put down that your last period was five and a half weeks ago. Are your cycles normally that long?"

"Oh, no. I'm usually right around twenty-eight days if not shorter because of the endometriosis. I've been having bad cramps for a few days, so I'm sure I'm about to start," I tell her.

"Before I prescribe any antibiotics for this sinus infection, I want you to go over to the hospital and have lab work done," she tells me while turning back around to type on the tablet.

"Lab work?" I ask, and she pauses to look up at me.

"A pregnancy test," she answers. "I don't want to get your hopes up, but cramping is common the first few weeks as the ligaments begin to stretch. Before you take any prescription or over-the-counter cold medicine, I think we should be certain."

"Okay," I agree, already certain that the results will be negative.

"Usually we could do the test here, but we're a skeleton crew on Saturdays," the doctor tells me as she types. "Okay, you should be all set. Head over to the laboratory at the hospital, and they'll take care of you. Once I have your results, I'll call and let you know what I can prescribe to get rid of the infection."

"Thanks," I tell her, climbing off the table and following the doctor into the hallway.

"Good luck, Callie. I know you've been trying for years," Dr. Sutton says before we part ways.

On the short two-minute drive to the hospital, I consider calling Quinton to tell him I'm taking a test or responding to one of his many texts, but I decide to wait. Most likely it will turn up negative, and I don't know how long I'll have to wait for the results. There's no reason to have him worrying about it when he needs to be thinking about winning tomorrow.

"Hi, I'm Callie Clarke. Dr. Sutton scheduled me for a pregnancy blood test," I tell the lady at the laboratory window.

"The office forwarded us your insurance information, so have a seat, and someone will be right with you," she tells me.

The waiting room is nearly empty except for one other man, so I don't have to wait long before I'm called back. A vial of blood is drawn painlessly by a tall, thin brunette who distracts me the entire time by making small talk about our cats.

"Do you want to wait for the results?" she asks while placing a bandage over the small puncture mark.

"Sure. How long will it take?"

"About fifteen to twenty minutes. I'll see you out front as soon as it's ready," she tells me, so I go plop down in the same navy blue waiting room chair and pull my phone out just to give me something to do to pass the time. I reread Quinton's messages telling me the plane was about to leave and then when they arrived in San Francisco last night. He sent me the number for the hotel and his room number in case he didn't have cell reception. And today he's told me he misses me and hopes I'm feeling better.

I'll respond to his messages in a few minutes to let him know I went to the doctor and have a sinus infection, just as soon as I have the results and know there's nothing else he needs to know.

"Miss Clarke," the same technician says when she opens the door to the lab holding a small, white plastic bag. Seeing the mostly empty room, she comes over as I stow my phone away in my purse and get to my feet. "Congratulations," she whispers, offering me the bag. "Here are some samples of prenatal vitamins for you to try until you can see your obstetrician. You should call Monday and set up an appointment. Oh, and use gloves when changing your cat's litter pan."

"I'm sorry, what?" I ask, taking the bag from her hand and looking inside at the rows of boxes before glancing up at her again.

"Your test was positive. You're pregnant," she clarifies.

"Are...are you sure?" I ask in shock.

"Yes, ma'am. We'll forward the results to your doctor," she tells me. "Are you okay?"

I stumble backward until I'm sitting again, the bag of vitamins falling to the floor. Certainly, I must be dreaming.

"Are you sure?" I ask her again, tears filling my eyes and overflowing down my cheeks.

"Our tests are very sensitive and detect pregnancy before most pharmacy tests, so you're likely only a few weeks along," she says, taking the seat next to me and offering me tissues from the table beside her. "I would print you the results, but they're just numbers. Maybe you would feel more confident about the results if you go buy a test to take at home and see the results for yourself?"

"Yeah, okay," I answer with a nod while mopping up my face. "It's just that, I had given up, you know?" And then I lose it, bawling into my hands like a baby. *A baby.* There's one inside me right now!

I sob like a crazy person in the lobby for several long minutes before I finally pull myself together. More tests. I need more tests to see for myself, a handful of them at least.

"Thank you," I say to the kind lady who sat with me during my breakdown.

"Are you able to drive yourself, or should we call someone for you?" she asks when I get to my feet.

"I'm fine, really. Just...shocked and happy," I assure her. "Deliriously happy."

As soon as I get in the car, I drive to the closest pharmacy and grab three different pregnancy tests before heading home. Not my home, but Quinton's. Lately, it feels more like home than mine ever did with him and Brady. Even Kelsey. Maybe it is time for me to officially move in.

I slip through the front door and go straight to the bathroom where my shaking hands rip open each test, and I carefully follow the directions.

After I'm finished, I line the sticks up on the sink counter and watch the colors change on two, and an hourglass blinking at me on the third. The marks on the color sticks are hard to read, but there's no mistaking the "Pregnant" that pops up on the digital one.

"Ahhh! I'm pregnant!" I scream, then slap a hand over my

mouth. But that doesn't keep the words from spilling out again. "I'm pregnant."

Reaching down, I press my palm over what I thought was just my bloated lower belly, but it's actually a baby.

"Kelsey!" I yell for her as I go over to open the en suite bathroom door in Quinton's room. "Kelsey!" I shout again when she doesn't come fast enough.

"What, what, what? Are you okay?" she asks when she comes through the door.

"I'm pregnant!"

"You are?" she exclaims, her jaw falling open in surprise. "Congratulations!"

Kelsey sweeps me in a hug as I start crying again.

"So you and Quinton..." she asks as she pulls back with a smile on her face.

"We've been trying," I admit. "He was crazy enough to give in when I asked. Now we're having a baby!"

"Oh my God. This is so great. Brady's gonna have a little brother or sister, barely a year younger than him. I bet they'll be such good friends! You have to call Quinton and tell him!"

"No," I tell her with a shake of my head. "I can't tell him he's gonna be a father again over the phone."

"Then go! Go to California and see his game like you were supposed to!"

Go and tell Quinton in person, this weekend?

Yes, that's what I want to do, because I can't wait until Monday night when the team finally returns.

"Shit! What time is it?" I ask, glancing around the room for a clock. "My plane left an hour ago!"

"Maybe there's another one tonight or in the morning. With the three-hour time difference, you could probably still make it to the game pretty easily," Kelsey says.

"Yeah, I'll get packed, and then I'll look for flights," I tell her.

CHAPTER THIRTY-THREE

Quinton

Around ten o'clock Saturday night there's a knock on my hotel room door. Of course I wasn't asleep. How could I be when I've not heard a word from Callie since I left the house Friday morning?

Kelsey has been texting, letting me know she did go to the doctor and has a sinus infection, so I'm hoping she's just tired and resting, not avoiding me.

Getting out of bed, I walk over to answer the door, not caring that I'm only wearing sweats without a shirt. It's gotta be one of the other guys, Lathan or Nixon, just bored and wanting to hang out.

I open up without giving it another thought and immediately wish I hadn't.

"Hi," the blonde woman I vaguely recognize from the front desk says with a smile. Instead of her stiff dress shirt uniform, she's wearing a red dress that isn't much bigger than Brady's clothes. And there's no avoiding her big, fake tits since so much of them are hanging out the top of her sleeveless dress that I can see her areolas.

"Hi. Can I help you?" I ask and force my eyes back up above her neck, even if it's pretty obvious why she's standing outside my door.

"Are you up for some company?" she asks, licking her lips while her gaze zeros in on the front of my sweats, not the least bit subtle.

Thinking quick because I don't want to be a complete asshole to her, I say, "Ah, sorry, sweetheart, but no ladies allowed in our rooms the night before an away game."

"Aww," she replies with a pout. "What about if I find us an empty room?"

"Can't tonight," I lie since that wouldn't technically be against the rules.

"Are you sure I can't change your mind?" she asks, reaching for the waistband of my sweats.

"Maybe some other time," I tell her, just to get her to leave. I quickly remove her wrist before she tries to tug down my pants and finds my half-hard cock.

What can I say? I'm a man, and she's a pretty woman, standing here nearly topless offering to fuck me. Of course my dick is interested, but not my head or my heart. There's no way in a million years I would ever cheat on Callie with some slutty hotel chick, or anyone else for that matter, regardless of how my lower body chooses to react. I would rather jerk off tonight to the memories of being with the woman I'm in love with than have the real thing with a nameless jersey chaser.

"Okay, handsome. Good luck tomorrow," she says with a wink before she saunters down the hall, swaying her ass with purpose.

Back inside my room, I lay down and pull my dick out to start stroking it to the memory of Callie in the hotel room back in Baltimore wearing the sexy navy blue and yellow lingerie.

I wish she were here so I could see it on her again tomorrow. Hell, I just wish she would talk to me.

I understand why she doesn't trust me, but that doesn't mean I'm not frustrated by it. If there were something I could do to prove to her I don't want anyone else, I would. The problem is, there's not. And what happens to us if she keeps pushing me away like she did this weekend because of it?

Callie

NOTHING CAN GET me down today, not my flight getting delayed an hour back home because of a thunderstorm, or the fact that when I finally arrived at the stadium in San Francisco half an hour after kickoff, they had already sold out of tickets.

So, I came back to his hotel, thinking I could head up to Quinton's room and watch the game there while I wait for him.

"Hi, I need to get a key for room eight-nineteen," I tell the young clerk at the desk when it's finally my turn.

"Name?" she asks with a smile, her polished fingernails poised over the keyboard.

"Well, the room is actually in Quinton Dunn's name, not mine," I tell her, and she just stares at me like I'm a martian speaking in a language she's never heard. "I'm his significant other. You've probably seen the photos of us together in all the tabloids. My name's Callie Clarke."

"Sorry, but I'm afraid Mr. Dunn doesn't have you down as a guest so I can't give you a key to his room," she says. "I'm sure you can understand that we're not allowed to just give out keys to anyone who asks for one to a famous quarterback's room or any other guest, for that matter."

"I'm not just anyone to Quinton. I'm...I'm important to him," I say, nearly spilling the news that I'm carrying his baby before I catch myself. This bitch is trying to drag me down, and it won't work. Nothing can kill my buzz today.

"Fine," I say with a sigh. "Do you have a restaurant with a television so I can grab something to eat and watch the game while I wait for him?"

"Sure, right through those doors," she says, pointing to the double doors on my left.

"Great, thanks," I tell her, wheeling my luggage in that direction. Of course the place is crowded with everyone eating while watching the game. There's a thirty-minute wait before I'm given a booth, and I'm finally able to relax a little. The game is already in the fourth quarter, and the Wildcats are up by nine. Thank goodness.

I sip my water while I watch and wait for my burger and fries, giving in to my craving for greasy food. It's still hard to believe that I'm pregnant and having cravings. The cramps have been coming and going, so I hope the doctor was right that they're normal and nothing to worry about. Tomorrow, when we get back home, I'll call and make an appointment with my obstetrician. Because I'm over thirty-five, I know that my pregnancy will be treated as high risk.

The hotel food is delicious; and after the Wildcats win, I decide to splurge on a piece of chocolate cake since it will probably be another hour or so before the team gets showers and the bus returns to the hotel.

Once I'm finished, I pay my tab and then wheel my suitcase back out into the lobby to wait for the players to arrive, ready to surprise Quinton with my presence and the news. While I'm waiting, I get a text from Quinton asking how I'm feeling and telling me they won. I want to reply back, but I've waited this long to surprise him, so I put my phone away to avoid the temptation of spoiling it. My knee bounces impatiently, and my heart begins to race knowing he'll be here any minute.

Sure enough, the buses pull up out front, and the lobby is soon packed with people and players. Since the Wildcats are the visitors who just beat the home team, not everyone is a fan of theirs. Some shout obscenities, and then there's pushing and shoving. Security guards show up to help the players get through, including Quinton. I yell his name, but he doesn't hear me before he gets on the elevator with a group of his teammates and disappears upstairs.

Well, that was disappointing, but at least I know his room number.

It takes several minutes to squeeze onto an elevator, and then I'm on my way to the eighth floor, smiling to myself, wondering how Quinton will react to the news. Weeks ago, when we first started this arrangement, I wasn't entirely sure if he would be looking forward to being a father again so soon, especially since Brady was such an unexpected surprise in his life. Now, I'm almost certain he'll be excited.

Taking a deep breath outside of his room, I finally raise my knuckles to knock.

When the door swings opens, I'm certain I must have the wrong room.

Instead of Quinton, there's a big breasted blonde standing in front of me. And I'm not one to usually notice the size of another woman's breasts, but it's impossible not to on this woman since she's naked except for a pair of skimpy pink panties and heels, holding what could pass as a dress in her hands.

"Callie?" Quinton's voice asks, and then I see him, standing in the middle of the room, looking at me over the naked woman's shoulder. "Callie, what are you doing here?" he asks as he starts toward me. "You need to get the fuck out," he looks down and says to the girl when he's right beside her.

"I was, just as soon as I get dressed again," she tells him with a smile before she slips the dress over her head and pulls it leisurely down her hips, not the least bit hurried. It's the equivalent of watching two high-speed trains colliding on the track in exaggerated slow motion. When there's impact, everything erupts into flames. It's a perfect representation of the catastrophic state of my life. I survived the first collision but never prepared myself to go through this moment of epic heartbreak yet again.

With the handle of my luggage still in my clenched fist, I turn around and rush back to the elevators.

"Callie, wait!" Quinton yells from behind me as I hit the button to call the elevator over and over again. "It's not what it looks like," he has the audacity to say, making a sobbing laugh bubble up out of my mouth since it's so fucking cliché and absurd.

"Callie, please give me a chance to explain," he says, spinning me around to face him. I can't bear to look at his face, so I keep my eyes on the center of his Wildcats tee. "I just got back, and when I walked into my room, she was in there, waiting for me. She must have gotten a key to my room."

Unable to speak, I shake my head in disbelief since I tried to get a freaking key to his room and the hotel refused me.

Thankfully, the elevator door dings behind me, my escape from this nightmare, and it gives me the courage to tell Quinton, "I'm taking you to court for custody of Brady."

"What?" he staggers back and asks, his eyes wide in shock. "No, Callie. Please don't say that..."

The elevator doors shut, and I can't hold back the tears any longer. I'm angry at him, but mostly I'm angry at myself for trusting him. That was the stupidest thing I've ever done, and I should have known better.

CHAPTER THIRTY-FOUR

Quinton

"No, no, no. This cannot be happening," I mutter to myself as I run down the stairway as fast as I can to get to the first floor and stop Callie from leaving.

I came up to my room when we got back to the hotel to try and call her, only to find the hotel bitch naked in my bed. As soon as I saw her, I yelled at her to get dressed and leave. Then she had to take her sweet ass time, climbing off the bed and bending over in front of me to put her panties on. That's about the time Callie knocked, showing up at the worst possible time. Of course she thought I fucked the girl; and no matter what I say, she'll probably never believe the truth because that's exactly what it looked like.

Pushing open the stairway door to the lobby, I run through it, looking through the crowd of people trying to find Callie and coming up empty. Outside, there are a million cars coming and going, but she's nowhere to be found.

"Fuck!" I shout in frustration wanting to slam my fists through the concrete.

Knowing yelling and freaking out won't do any good, I pull out my phone and try to call her. She wouldn't talk to me before, though, so I seriously doubt she'll answer now. It goes to her voicemail, so I lay it all out for her in the recording, from the moment I first checked in and saw the girl, to her coming to my room last night, and the fact that I turned her down, and then her waiting for me in my room this afternoon. I beg Callie to believe me.

∽

THE NEXT NIGHT when I get home, Kelsey's car is in the driveway but not Callie's.

"Hey," I say to Kelsey when I come dragging through the door. My first stop is to check on Brady, who is sleeping in her arms. She hands him over to me, and I sit down on the sofa cradling him to me.

"Have you seen Callie?" I ask.

"She came by to get Felix and her things in the middle of the night," she informs me. "What the heck happened, Quinton? Did you react badly to the news?"

I shake my head, wishing I could forget the look on Callie's face when she saw the naked slut in my room.

Wait a second...

"What news?" I ask Kelsey in confusion.

Her mouth forms a big O before she looks away. "Nothing."

"What news, Kelsey?" I ask again, but I already know.

Goddamn it.

"She's pregnant, isn't she?" I ask, getting to my feet. "Kelsey?" I beg when I lower Brady back into her arms. "Is she? Please tell me. Is that why...is that why she came to California?" I ask, my voice cracking with emotion.

"Yes," she answers softly, nearly bringing me to my knees.

God, Callie must have been so fucking excited; and even though she was sick, she flew out to tell me the news in person that I'm gonna be a father again. Then she walked into that shit in my room...

"I've got to go try and see her," I tell Kelsey, wiping the moisture from my face.

"Sure, I'll be here," she says. "Good luck. I don't know what you did, but it must have been epic if she didn't tell you. She was so happy."

"It was," I agree before jogging out to my car and speeding over to Callie's house.

The lights are all off, but her car is in the driveway.

Banging on the front door with my fist, I call her name and beg her to answer. In fact, the knock and beg routine goes on until the blue lights show up at the curb and two officers shining flashlights approach me.

"Sir, the lady who lives here has reported a disturbance. You need to leave," one of them says.

"She's having my baby, and I just want to see her and tell her I'm sorry," I explain as I rest my forehead on the wooden fixture.

"Come on, big man. Time to go," an officer says, grabbing my elbow to pull me away. "You're Quinton Dunn!" he exclaims when he sees my face.

"Yep," I agree, not resisting as he guides me back to my car. "Could I use your phone to call her? She won't answer my calls."

"Sorry, sir. Sometimes you have to give them some room to breathe."

"But I can't breathe without her," I tell him.

"Now that's about the saddest thing I've ever heard," the cop says. "Go home and try again tomorrow. You're Quinton Dunn; she has to forgive you!"

With a nod, I reluctantly get into my car. The police officers stand in the front yard and watch until I leave.

On the drive home, I send up a prayer, promising that I would give anything to talk to Callie, to beg her to believe me.

And then, I want to take it back when Kelsey wakes me up at four a.m.

Callie's on the way to the hospital because she thinks she's having a miscarriage.

CHAPTER THIRTY-FIVE

Callie

I didn't think it was possible to be more heartbroken than the night I caught my husband screwing my sister in our house, or Sunday afternoon when I found Quinton with another woman. But I was absolutely wrong.

Early Tuesday morning when I woke up and saw the spotting, I fell into a darkness so bleak I'm not sure I'll ever find my way out.

Kelsey called late last night and told me that she was sorry for letting the news slip with Quinton. She assumed he already knew. I couldn't be upset with her for telling him. And on the way to the hospital, I called Kelsey and told her to let Quinton know what's happening.

And while he has a right to know what's going on as the father, the angry, devastated woman I am, I also want him to blame himself for being the reason I'm losing our son or daughter. I want him to hate himself for what he did, for upsetting me, so that maybe a little of the guilt I'm drowning in can be lifted. It's probably all my fault for traveling while I was sick and then getting so worked up over being hurt again.

Curled up in the fetal position in the emergency room bed, I sob into the pillow until it's soaking wet with my tears.

"I'm so sorry, Callie," Quinton says when he comes into the curtained off room.

Feeling his hand on my hair, I don't pull away or yell at him. I'm too weak, emotionally and physically. So, I let him hold me and comfort me, even though I hate him.

"Miss Clarke? Sorry to bother you, but I need to draw some blood," a nurse says sometime later. Quinton lets me go, and I roll to my back and pull my arms out from the sheets to give her access. When Quinton offers me a handful of tissues, I accept them and dry my face with my left hand while the nurse draws a few vials of blood from my right.

"Have they told you anything?" Quinton asks softly once the nurse leaves.

"Only that they won't know for sure until they do some tests and an ultrasound."

"So there's still a chance?" he asks, and I nod, trying to remain optimistic; but between the cramps and bleeding, I know there's not much hope.

"Callie, I don't want to upset you even more, but that woman you saw in my room Sunday *worked* at the hotel. That's how she had a key to my room and was inside before I got there. Here's the business card for the operations manager who I met with, and he fired her that same day. You can call him and talk to him. And if you want to see them, I have the videos from Saturday night in the hallway when I turned her down, and she left without ever coming in my room, and Sunday when she went into the room fifteen minutes before me," he says, sliding a card under my hand. "I know it looked bad, but I promise you, I never touched her and wouldn't have touched her even if you hadn't been there."

"How can I possibly believe that, Quinton?" I ask him, my voice wavering.

"Because it's the truth, the only truth there is," he says. "And because I love you, so much that there is nothing and no one who could ever make me do something to hurt you. It's killing me to see you upset now. You don't trust me, I get that, but believe this --- I will do whatever it takes to change your mind."

"Maybe you should just leave," I tell him as more tears fill my eyes. "I don't want to think about this right now."

"Please, Callie. Just give me the benefit of the doubt. Watch the video. And then if you want me to leave, I will, even though I don't want to leave you here alone."

Glancing around the sterile, curtained room, waiting and worrying that the life inside me is slowly slipping away, it's hard to concentrate on anything else. But if what Quinton is telling me is really true, maybe we could move past this, because I truly do need him, whether I want to admit it or not.

"Fine," I agree, swiping away the tears from underneath my eyes.

Quickly pulling out his phone, Quinton gets the video started and then offers the device to me.

"This is Saturday," he says, and I watch as the scantily clad blonde woman in a red dress walks off the elevator and strolls up to a room where she knocks. From the angle, it's hard to see much of Quinton except for the occasional glimpse of his profile. He remains inside the room, with the woman in the hallway, her body language making it clear what she wants, especially when she reaches for Quinton's pants, but he removes her hand before she turns and walks back to the elevators.

The video skips, and then the same blonde appears in the hallway, this time in a bright pink dress. She doesn't knock on the door, but instead, slips a key card into the reader and walks right in. The video fast-forwards until Quinton appears at the room and goes inside, right before I step off the elevator. Since there's no fast forward, I'm assuming it was only a few minutes.

Obviously, he didn't have time to sleep with her, not that I figured that he had when I was there. I assumed he was getting ready to when I knocked.

And did he actually send her away Saturday, or could there be other video that shows she came back later and he let her inside?

"You still don't believe me," Quinton mutters when he takes his phone from my hand.

"I...I don't know," I admit.

Taking my hand in his, he says, "Please don't do this to me, Callie. I love you, and I need you to trust me, because I don't want to lose you."

Before I can respond, the nurse returns to the room with another woman in green scrubs pushing a wheelchair. "They're ready to take you over to radiology for your transvaginal ultrasound," she says.

"Okay," I agree, my stomach turning flips with nervousness. And I realize that I don't want to let go of Quinton's hand just yet. "Can he come too?" I ask them.

"Yeah, of course," the nurse agrees before helping me to the wheelchair even though I'm fine to walk. The bleeding and cramps aren't that severe; it's the emotional pain that's crippling me.

"Thank you," Quinton says to me once we're out of the ER and starting down the hallway. The aide pushes me in the wheelchair, and he walks beside us.

Several people we pass recognize Quinton, and he says hello back to be nice, but I can hear the tenseness in his voice. He's probably just as worried as I am; and no matter what happens between us, this is his baby too.

I'm taken to an exam table in the radiology department, and from there, another woman in scrubs comes in and sits down at the equipment next to me.

"Hi, I'm Denise, and I'll be conducting the transvaginal ultrasound. Have you ever had one of these performed before?" she asks.

"Yes," I tell her. "I have endometriosis."

"Okay, well, that's good in a way, because some people freak out the first time even though I assure them it's completely painless."

Once she prepares the wand with a latex cover and lubricates it, she inserts it with Quinton observing silently.

"So you've been having some cramps and bleeding?" she asks.

"Yes," I reply, and then hold my breath while watching the screen as she begins moving it around.

"Let's see what we can find. Here's the gestational sac," she tells us, pointing to the black circle on the screen. "But it's just too early to see anything else. You're only about four weeks out from the date of conception, right?"

"Yes, so that's normal?" I ask, thinking there should be more to see.

"It is," she says.

"Okay, thanks," I reply, disappointed that there's not an actual baby on the screen.

Back in the ER, Quinton and I sit in silence, waiting for the doctor to provide us with more news. He paces around the small space, and the constant movement only makes me even more nervous.

"Could you please sit down?" I eventually ask him.

"Sorry," he says, flopping back down in the plastic chair beside the bed. "I just want them to tell us what's going on."

"I know," I reply.

"How's your cold?" he asks, probably just to have something to talk about.

"Better, finally," I answer, which is followed by more silence.

There are no televisions back here, and I'm not sure where my phone is. Quinton doesn't have his out and in his hands either. So we have nothing to do but remain silent, making the time go by even slower, or talk to each other. Giving in because I want to have something else to think about as a distraction, I finally tell him, "I, um, I finished Brady's outfit for Wednesday if you want to take him out."

"Thanks," Quinton looks over at me and replies with a small

smile. "Guess he's too young for trick or treating...but since it's his first Halloween, he should at least dress up for photos."

"Yeah," I agree. "Bianca always loved Halloween. Even when she was a teenager she liked to dress up for school."

"Oh, really?" he asks.

"Yeah. I would try to talk her into staying home with me, but she would find some party to go to and get drunk. Later that night, I would usually end up having to go pick her up and drag her home."

"I'm sorry, Callie," Quinton says, reaching for my hand again, and I don't try to pull away. "It sounds like you spent a lot of time taking care of her."

"She was stubborn and wouldn't listen to me, always repeating the same mistakes, hurting herself over and over again."

"That was her fault, not yours. You couldn't make her change if she didn't want to."

"No, I couldn't," I admit. "So maybe it's hard for me to believe that anyone can change."

"I'm not her. Or your ex-husband," Quinton says. "And I haven't claimed that I've changed, because I haven't. The difference is that before, I didn't love the women I was with. That's why I couldn't commit to any of them. Even if I had, it never would have lasted. But this, us, we have something special, and I would never do anything to ruin it."

"All it takes is one moment of weakness," I tell him, the words and tears burning my throat.

"Nothing I say or do will prove to you that you're it for me. Not saying I love you, or getting married, or having a baby together. It's up to you to decide if I'm worth taking the chance on," Quinton says softly. "You have to trust me; and if you don't, well, then this will never work. But if there's anything for certain that you know about me it's that I'm *not* weak. There won't be any moments of weakness either."

"Why would you want me when you could have anyone else?" I ask since that's the part I've never understood.

"Because you are the only woman that I've ever needed in my life, so I would give anything to keep you. You don't make it easy on me, and never will. That's what I love about you. I'll always have to work at it to feel like I deserve you. But if I'm able to win you over, I'll know I've actually earned it."

"That sounds like a lot of work," I admit.

"It is worth it. *You* are worth it," he replies, lifting my knuckles to his lips so he can kiss them. "I like a challenge, so why would I ever take the easy way?"

"You didn't want her, in San Francisco?" I ask him.

"No. I wanted you there with me, because win or lose, you're the only person I want to be with. That's why I begged you to come," he assures me. "In fact, I want a do-over. You should've been the one to tell me the news, not Kelsey by accident. You still haven't actually."

"Quinton," I start, wetting my dry lips to say the words that I hope won't be contradicted anytime soon. "I'm pregnant. We're gonna have a baby. But I've had some cramps and spotting..."

"Oh, sweetheart. I'm so fucking happy to hear that. And everything is gonna be fine, you'll see," he says, dropping my hand to wrap me in his arms.

"I hope so," I say against his chest, breathing in his comforting woodsy scent in. "God, I really hope so."

"It will be," Quinton replies, kissing the top of my head and then my cheek. "This is my kid we're talking about, and I bet she's also strong and determined like her mother."

"She?" I pull back from his chest to ask him. "It could be a boy."

"I guess we'll have to wait and see," he says with a crooked grin before his lips brush mine.

Even though it's only been a few days, it feels like a lifetime since the last time we kissed. I've missed it. I've missed Quinton.

Trusting him is scary, but the alternative is even more frightening. I don't want to lose him or what we have that's so good, better than anything I've ever imagined.

Our kiss deepens, our tongues becoming reacquainted, right before someone clears their throat and interrupts.

"Miss Clarke? Hi, I'm Dr. Trevor. I've got some good news," the man in a white lab coat says. "Your HCG levels are up significantly from the lab work you had on Saturday, which is a great sign. The ultrasound confirms that the pregnancy is not ectopic. So we're gonna send you home to rest, but I'm sure your OB/GYN will want to schedule you for more labs on Thursday and a follow-up ultrasound in a few weeks."

"That's great, thank you," I tell him with a smile.

"The cramping and spotting this early in the pregnancy is pretty normal. Just notify your doctor if it becomes heavy or unbearable. Let me get your paperwork, and you'll be ready to go," he says before leaving.

"See, everything is gonna be fine," Quinton says, pulling me to him for another kiss. "Come home with me so I can take care of you?"

"Yeah," I agree. "Let's go home."

EPILOGUE

Quinton

Eight months later...

"Come on, baby. You can do this," I tell Callie, pushing the sweaty hair back from her face.

"I hate you," she growls. "You're never touching me again!"

If she weren't in so much pain, I would probably laugh since me touching her is not only how she got knocked up, but it's also what the doctors say was the catalyst that helped put her in labor last night. As it is, Callie's now ten centimeters dilated and has been pushing for almost an hour. She refused all pain medicine until about fifteen minutes ago, when she offered her life savings and mine to the doctor if she would hook her up.

It would have been money well spent too, but the doctor told her it's too late for pain medicine and that she needs to keep pushing or they'll have to do a fucking C-section.

"Here comes another contraction," the doctor warns Callie, and I help her into a sitting position again. "Get ready to push in three, two, one..."

"*Ahhh!*" Callie screams with effort, her entire face tomato red and pinched with pain.

"There's the head! Just one more big push, Callie. You've got it," the doctor says as Callie grits her teeth and gets it done.

"I love you, baby. You're doing so great," I tell her, covering her hand that's squeezing the bed rail with mine.

"It's a girl!" the doctor exclaims before the sounds of a crying baby fill the air and Callie falls weakly back against the pillow.

"A girl? We...we have a girl?" she looks at me and asks, crying because of the pain or the joy; I'm not sure which anymore.

"A healthy girl," the nurse says, handing over the baby wrapped in a blanket to Callie.

"Aww, she's beautiful! Hello my sweet girl," Callie says to our daughter as she gazes lovingly down at her in wonder.

"I knew it. A gorgeous girl, just like her mother," I tell her, placing a kiss on Callie's forehead. "You did it, baby. I know it wasn't easy, and I'm so proud of you."

"It wasn't so bad," Callie replies with a smile, having apparently already forgotten the six previous hours of labor and hour of pushing she just endured. "Now I'm just tired."

"All you have to do now is rest and enjoy meeting our daughter," I tell her. "I love you. Both of you."

"I love you too," Callie looks up and says. "Thank you for giving me something so amazing. I can't wait for Brady to meet her."

"He's gonna love her too," I reply, imagining our rambunctious almost one-year-old seeing his new sister.

"You want to hold her?" she asks me.

"Of course I do," I say, and Callie hands her over. I take her and cradle her in my arms like a pro. "Happy birthday, sweetheart. You almost share one with your big brother."

"Congratulations, Mr. and Mrs. Dunn. Let the nurse know if you need anything," the doctor says to us before she leaves the room.

"Thank you," Callie and I both tell her.

"So what should we name her?" Callie asks me. Over the past few months, we've thought about some names; but since we decided to let the gender be a surprise, we hadn't picked one out yet.

"How about Peyton?" I suggest.

"Seriously? Another quarterback?" Callie replies with a grin, and I shrug. "Fine, Peyton's not so bad for a girl."

"What do you think, Peyton?" I ask the blinking baby in my arms. "I'll teach you and your brother how to hold a football and throw a perfect spiral. Maybe you'll be the first professional female quarterback in the league."

"That's a lot of pressure to put on a girl minutes after she's born," Callie teases.

"I just want her to do whatever makes her happy," I assure her.

"She's lucky to have you, and so am I," she says when I place our daughter back in my wife's arms.

"So does that mean you've rescinded your statement about never letting me touch you again?" I ask her with a grin.

"I would never say something so crazy about my husband who I love more than anything," Callie replies sweetly.

"Right. I must have been mistaken," I tell her, followed by a chuckle. "So how long are we gonna wait before we start trying to make another baby?" I ask, causing Callie to scoff.

"You know it'll be at least six weeks," she reminds me.

"So, six weeks and a day?" I ask, leaning over the bedrail to kiss her.

"That sounds about right," Callie agrees, smiling against my lips.

The End

ALSO BY LANE HART

Delay of Game is now available!

My mom is dying. The cancer is eating away at her body a little more each day, and the worst part is I know she's so tired of fighting. She's starting to surrender to the sickness.

That's why I stupidly blurted out at Thanksgiving that I had met a woman and was engaged. The truth is, there's no woman in my life and never has been. I just wanted to give my mother something to live for, a few celebrations, an extravagant wedding, the possibility of grandchildren...

Now I just need to find a nice girl to pretend to be my fiancée and walk down the aisle with me in a matter of weeks.

Actually, that may be a piece of cake compared to trying to stay away from the one person who has managed to ignite something deep inside of me for the first time in my life. Something I can't ignore or forget no matter how hard I try.

This is a sweet and sexy standalone M/M romance.

ABOUT THE AUTHOR

New York Times bestselling author Lane Hart lives in North Carolina with her husband, author D.B. West, and their two children. She enjoys spending the summers on the beach and watching football in the fall.

Connect with Lane:

Author Store: https://www.authorlanehart.com/
Tiktok: https://www.tiktok.com/@hartandwestbooks
Facebook: http://www.facebook.com/lanehartbooks
Instagram: https://www.instagram.com/authorlanehart/
Website: http://www.lanehartbooks.com
Email: lane.hart@hotmail.com

Find all of Lane's books on her Amazon author page!

Sign up for Lane and DB's newsletter to get updates on new releases and freebies!

ABOUT THE AUTHOR

Join Lane's Facebook group to read books before they're released, help choose covers, character names, and titles of books! https://www.facebook.com/groups/bookboyfriendswanted/

Made in United States
North Haven, CT
23 September 2025

80043283R10157